FAST JUSTICE

DEA FAST SERIES

KAYLEA CROSS

FAST JUSTICE

Copyright © 2018
by Kaylea Cross

* * * * *

Cover Art & Print Formatting by
Sweet 'N Spicy Designs
Developmental edits: Deborah Nemeth
Line Edits: Joan Nichols
Digital Formatting: LK Campbell

* * * * *

ISBN: 978-1986383950

Dedication

For the amazing Katie Reus, my bestie and sister from another mother. Because you've always got my back, and because you get me.

Love you. xo

Author's Note

Dear readers,

Here we are at book 6 of my **DEA FAST Series**, and I hope you've been enjoying the ride so far. Buckle up for this one, because it's got lots of twists and turns, and I hate one of the villains so much I wanted to crawl through my laptop screen and kill him myself several times.

Up next is Hamilton and Victoria's story, and I can't WAIT. So much angst and action. Gah.

Happy reading!

Kaylea Cross

Chapter One

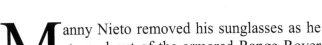

Manny Nieto removed his sunglasses as he stepped out of the armored Range Rover parked out front of the humble house on the outskirts of town, and tucked them into the pocket of his designer shirt. His head of security was waiting for him on the front porch, having already ensured the area was safe and without prying eyes.

"Well?" Manny asked in Spanish as he walked up the front steps. The July heat in this area of Mexico was dry, but still oppressive. He wanted to finish this business and get back into his air-conditioned vehicle as soon as possible. "Anything?"

"No." David stepped back and opened the door for him.

Impatient for answers, Manny walked inside. The sounds of muffled sobbing came from somewhere in the back. He made a face. "How long has he been in there?"

"About an hour."

"Let's make this quick. I've got another meeting to get to."

David led him down the short hallway and turned left down another. The sobbing got louder as they approached a closed door at the end on the right. Broken, pitiful sobbing of a man who knew he wasn't going to live much longer.

At Manny's nod, David knocked once on the door and opened it. Another security member stood inside, guarding the door. Yet another was positioned at the back of the room, near the far wall, a three-foot-long, thin metal rod in his hands.

The male prisoner dangled from chains attached to a hook in the ceiling. He hung by his wrists, his toes dangling a few inches off the floor. With his arms stretched out overhead like that and his full weight hanging from them, the strain on his shoulder joints would be unbearable.

The twenty-something, dark-haired man was naked, head bowed as he hung there, chin resting on his heaving, glistening chest. Slowly his head came up. He looked at Manny through eyes nearly swollen shut, his limp body jerking with the residual force of his muffled sobs. Blood ran from his nose, trickling over his mouth and chin, dripping onto his chest. His sweat-slicked torso was covered in welts, bluish-purple bruises already forming across his ribs and stomach.

Standing just inside the doorway, Manny folded his arms and regarded the prisoner for a long moment. "You know who I am?"

Glazed with pain, those beaten eyes gazed back at him with fear and pleading. But more importantly, recognition.

Manny intended to make this quick. He needed answers, and he needed them fast. "You were one of Ruiz's *sicarios*, no?" The former *Veneno* lieutenant Manny had replaced recently. Right after Ruiz was captured by U.S. federal agents in a highly secretive sting back in May.

The man tried to shake his head. "I...no," he slurred through battered lips. "I was...new. Only worked...for him...a month."

Manny glanced at the man who had been beating him. "This true?"

"He seems to believe it," the guy said with a shrug, tapping the rod against his thigh. "Hasn't changed his story."

Manny turned his attention back to the prisoner. The man was in a lot of pain, kept moving restlessly in a futile effort to relieve the pressure on his shoulder joints. Likely he had a few cracked ribs as well. There was no reason he would keep lying under that kind of torture.

"Ruiz is gone for good. He's either going to die in prison, or by lethal injection one day. Either way, he's already dead as far as we're concerned." We meaning Manny, the other *Veneno* lieutenants, and *El Escorpion* himself—the shadowy and reclusive head of the cartel. "Anyone who worked for him belongs to me now. And I expect my people to transfer their loyalty to me also." He hardened his tone. "Not to run to the Americans and try to cut a deal."

"They came to me," the prisoner rasped out. "I didn't...tell them anything." He wheezed the last word, shuddered.

Whether he had talked or not was irrelevant now. Manny had taken steps to change procedures within his part of the organization, and brought his own people on board since becoming the new lieutenant. They were almost done cleaning out the dregs of Ruiz's old operation. A necessary purge, since most of them had proven to be mindless animals.

But that wasn't why this man was being questioned. Manny had come here for another purpose. One he wanted answers to immediately. Beneath the cold, detached exterior and terrifying reputation he guarded so well, he was a desperate, frantic man.

The moment he showed any sign of weakness, he was as good as dead.

A cold, hard fury burned deep in his chest as he faced the prisoner. None of the others had given him anything of use. *Someone* had to know.

"Where is my daughter, Jesus?" he demanded in a deceptively calm voice. "Oceane. Where is she?" She and her mother had been attacked by gunmen at their house outside of Veracruz a few days ago. They had apparently survived and had gone into hiding, but Manny didn't know where. Perhaps even to the United States. He needed to find them. Wanted them both back on Mexican soil and back under his control and protection immediately, before it was too late.

The man's bleary eyes focused on him, his expression freezing with fear. "I don't know."

"Don't you." He said it quietly, each word filled with menace.

"No. I swear it." Another sob ripped out of him.

Manny kept staring at him but spoke to the man holding the rod. "What else did he say?"

4

"Not much. He says he never heard about her. Not even rumors. He said the first he heard of her and her mother disappearing was when we brought him here."

Manny shoved back the sudden rise in fury that erupted in his gut. "You don't know anything about this, hm?"

Jesus shook his head. "No, I swear."

He let out a humorless laugh. "I find it so hard to believe that Ruiz ordered the attack from inside a supposedly secure U.S. prison, yet every single one of his men we've questioned knows nothing about it." He paused a beat, tilted his head. "Don't you find that hard to believe, Jesus?"

A pained groan came from the prisoner. "I don't...I don't know anything. Please," he begged. "I haven't done...anything to you...or your family." He dragged in a shallow breath, his face contorting with pain. "I will be loyal."

No, he wouldn't. Not after this. And Manny was too pragmatic a businessman to be swayed by a man's pleas. Under torture, men would say anything. So the fact that this one hadn't made up some story to try and save himself proved he was either stupid, or innocent.

Manny didn't tolerate stupid. Innocence was of no use to him either, except when it came to his daughter. He still loved her mother, Anya, in his own way. Not in the intensely passionate way he had when they'd begun their relationship twenty-five years ago. Yet enough that he still harbored a certain fondness and loyalty toward her. He'd kept tabs on her this whole time in between his visits, made sure she was financially comfortable and had adequate protection.

But Oceane. She was his future. He would do whatever it took to find her and bring her back to begin the work of learning how to run the empire he'd built at such risk to himself. An empire he and her mother had gone to great lengths to keep her mostly ignorant of throughout her life. That illusion was no doubt shattered now, and it put everything in jeopardy.

Manny shifted his stance, his anger transforming into disappointment. He'd hoped this prisoner might be the one to give them a solid lead to follow. "Do you have anything at all of use to tell me about my daughter's whereabouts, or who carried out the attack?" he asked.

Jesus blinked, his swollen, bruised eyelids flickering. "No. I told you, I know nothing."

Then you're of no further use to me. Sighing, Manny looked at the man holding the rod, gave a nod of consent, and turned to go.

"No, wait," Jesus begged, his voice catching with tears. "Wait!"

Manny ignored him, unwilling to give him a second more of his time. On his way to the door, his gaze snagged on the tray of instruments laid out on a small table next to another wall. Some delicate medical and dental ones for intricate means of extracting information. Larger, cruder ones, to carry out more heavy-handed punishment...and death.

Manny walked out the door as Jesus's frantic pleas followed him into the hall. He never stayed to watch his men work on a prisoner. Some men got off on that kind of violence. The brutal show of force and power against a helpless victim. Ruiz had been one of them. Manny didn't enjoy it, and didn't partake in the physical side of the business. Never had, never would.

Torture and death were necessary means in his world, he wasn't naïve enough to believe otherwise, and it had helped him secure his position within the cartel. But at his core, he was a businessman. He preferred working in boardrooms and making deals over a meal at an expensive restaurant.

It was why *El Escorpion* had given his blessing and allowed Manny to take Ruiz's place so quickly. The elusive head of the organization had been weary of Ruiz and his ways, to the point that rumors had been circulating that *El Escorpion* himself had aided in Ruiz's capture, giving the Americans critical intel on Ruiz's secret location.

Sickening, bloodcurdling screams echoed off the walls as he reached the front door with David. Manny was far better at compartmentalizing things now than he had been at first, didn't even flinch now, although he wished his men would just put a bullet in Jesus's brain and end it already.

Except he'd learned an important lesson about power over the years, something he'd studied in his business dealings. The people he employed were tools, and he couldn't run this without them. His lawyers were like surgeons, wielding their legal scalpels in delicate matters. Whereas his *sicarios* were instruments of extreme violence, who craved the power of acting on their sadistic needs to dole out suffering and death.

From a human resources point of view, keeping his people happy in their jobs meant they were more likely to be loyal. Sometimes it was best to let them have what they wanted.

As for the people responsible for the attack on his daughter and mistress, and those involved with keeping them hidden…

Once he found them, his *sicarios* would get plenty more opportunity to hone their gruesome skills.

****

Rowan Stewart mentally reviewed everything she needed to accomplish today as she exited the freeway and turned toward her office in the heart of D.C. She and her boss were still compiling evidence in a big case they were working on—the biggest one of her career thus far. Every night this week she'd been up until one going over her notes to make sure she was prepared for the upcoming witness interviews today, and she would likely be working late tonight as well.

Sleep deprivation and long hours came with the territory.

She yawned and reached out to turn up the music a bit louder. At this point she was well accustomed to burning the proverbial candle at both ends. Not her favorite thing, but it was one of the price tags that came with the title of Assistant U.S. Attorney, a position she'd worked her ass off for. And if she wanted to become U.S. Attorney one day, then she had to keep working just as hard to make it happen. If she ever earned that, she wanted it to be on her own merit, not because of who she knew or who her father was.

Pushing out a deep breath as she reached the end of the lineup of cars waiting at the next light, she forced aside everything she had to do today and let her mind wander, dying for the cup of coffee waiting for her once she made it to the office. Traffic was insane as usual at this time of the morning, but since it was early July, at least it was bright and sunny out.

When she finally made it into the left-hand turn lane at the light, a call came in on her car's hands-free device. Finding her father's name on the dash console, she suppressed a groan and answered anyway as she edged into the intersection, waiting for a gap in traffic to turn. It wasn't like she was going anywhere in this traffic, so she had time to talk. "Hey, Dad."

"Hey, sweetie. You on your way to the office?"

He sounded bright and chipper, had probably been up since she had, even though he didn't need to anymore. Once a workaholic, always a workaholic. Rowan shook her head. When she retired, she wasn't getting up until at least eight every day. "I'm about ten minutes out." If she ever made this damn turn.

"Good. So many criminals to put away, so little time."

He used that line so often that all she could do was manage a grunt of acknowledgment. "What's up?" *Please don't add anything more to my plate today.*

"Got some paperwork here for signing authority on my accounts, power of attorney and whatnot. I'm just in the process of reorganizing my estate and will, and it's pretty complicated. I'll walk you through everything when you get here. I need to have it in by eight tomorrow morning. Can you swing by to-night?"

She huffed out an irritated breath, hoped he didn't hear it over the car's speakers. She couldn't say no, she was the eldest, and paperwork like that was important. Things like this had always been her responsibility. It was her role in the family. "Not sure. I'm in meetings all day, so I don't know when I'll be done."

"Okay, so you can stop on your way home then. It'll just take a few minutes to sign everything. I'll leave it all on my desk."

"Fine." Her parents lived ten minutes from her, and it was on her way home. "I'll text you once I'm done at work. Could be late, though."

"All right. Working on a big case, huh?" The interest in his voice was impossible to miss. He was still a legend in legal circles around here, even though he'd "retired" a few years ago. He missed it every day, as though he'd lost part of his identity when he'd stopped working.

"Pretty big, yeah." Her office had three key witnesses ready to testify against Carlos Ruiz, but the former *Veneno* lieutenant had agreed to a deal and given them damning evidence against other key cartel members. His arrest and incarceration had created an epic power struggle within the remaining players. Everyone involved with the case was still trying to figure out what the hell was really going on within the organization.

"Makes me miss the good old days," he said. "How's traffic?"

She was a bit surprised that he seemed to want to

prolong the call. Usually he was brusque, got business taken care of and ended the conversation as soon as possible. "A mess."

A car coming the opposite way entered the intersection after the light turned amber and got stuck behind the lineup of cars, preventing her from making the damn turn.

"Hang on a sec." Rowan shot the driver a dirty look and zipped out to maneuver around its rear bumper, needing to get the hell out of the intersection before the other cars began moving with the green light.

"You can give me some hints about the case when I see you tonight."

Safely on the other side of the intersection, she slowed down for the stopped traffic ahead of her at the next light and tapped her thumbs on the steering wheel impatiently. *Come on, people,* move. "Won't be able to give you much to go on—"

She broke off on a gasp as a car suddenly came out of nowhere and veered in front of her, almost T-boning her. She barely managed to wrench the steering wheel sharply to the right in time to avoid the crash. Two cars beside her in the left lane weren't so lucky. They collided, narrowly missing her.

"Rowan?"

She couldn't answer him, too busy stomping on the brakes to avoid hitting the truck in front of her. A split second later, a car slammed into her from behind.

She grunted as the impact jerked her forward against the shoulder strap of her seatbelt, her head snapping back into the headrest. With her foot jammed on the brake she somehow managed to miss the truck, then a second vehicle hit the right side of hers with a crunch of metal, snapping her head to the side and knocking her left shoulder against the door.

"Shit," she gasped out, heart hammering as her vehicle jerked to a halt.

"Rowan? Are you all right?" her father asked sharply.

Dammit. She put the car into park and shut off the engine. "I gotta go," she blurted, and ended the call. Her heart was still beating fast, a mix of anger and shock coursing through her, quickly followed by annoyance. She had to be at the first meeting in just over twenty minutes. She didn't freaking have time for this mess.

Her hand shook a little as she unlocked her door and reached for the handle. Before she could summon the strength to push on it, someone ripped it open for her.

Startled, she blinked up into the handsome, familiar face staring back at her. *Malcolm?* DEA Special Agent Malcolm Freeman, the man she'd walked away from but couldn't forget.

He leaned down to peer at her, hands on either side of the doorframe, his expression full of concern. "Are you okay?"

"Yes," she answered automatically. She didn't think she was hurt, just shaken up. What on earth was he doing here?

He ran that melted chocolate gaze over her for a moment, assessing her for injury, then reached in to wrap his powerful arms around her and pull her to his chest in a quick hug. "You sure? That second guy hit you pretty hard."

Automatically she flattened her palms on his back, drank in his warmth and strength. Seemed like a lifetime ago since she'd had his arms around her, and right now they felt like heaven. Safe. Secure. That innate protectiveness of his was one of the things she'd loved most about him. "I'm not hurt," she managed. At least not seriously. She was breathing fast though, kind of choppy.

All too soon he released her and leaned back to study her eyes. "Cops are on the way."

She half-swiveled in her seat to look out the passenger window, put a hand to the side of her neck as a twinge of pain shot through it. If traffic had been bad before, now it was a tangled mess. "What about the other drivers?"

"They're okay. The second guy took off. I let him go because I wanted to make sure you were all right, but I got the plate number."

She gingerly turned back around to face him. God, he looked more incredible than ever. Black hair cropped close to his head, wearing dress pants and a sapphire blue button down shirt that set off his deep brown skin and stretched across his muscled chest and shoulders. "Where the heck did you come from, anyway?" It was surreal that he'd just appeared out of nowhere at a time like this.

"I was five cars behind you at the light."

"Going into work?"

"No. Meeting with your boss."

Oh. She hadn't realized they would be interviewing him today with the others. "Shit, I'm going to be so late," she groaned, anxiety forming a tight ball in the pit of her stomach.

"Don't worry about that." He took her arm, his grip gentle but sure. "Can you stand?"

"Yeah." Her legs were a little weak as she got out of the car, her high heels wobbling slightly on the pavement. Malcolm steadied her, and she had to keep from reaching for him when he withdrew his hand, leaving her feeling strangely bereft.

Letting out a deep breath, Rowan took a moment to get her bearings. Two people—presumably the drivers from one of the collisions—were in a heated argument next to their vehicles. Traffic all around them was a snarled nightmare. It would take forever for emergency crews to reach them and clean up the mess.

She walked around to look at her back bumper, then the damage on the passenger side. The front door was caved in and the safety glass in the window was cracked into a thousand pieces. "It's still driva-ble, right?" she asked Malcolm.

"Yeah, but you've got zero visibility out the pas-senger window."

Damn. The cops would have to document every-thing before she could leave. She'd also have to talk to the other drivers involved and fill out insurance paperwork. At least she didn't need to have her car towed. Once she got to the office she could have her assistant arrange to have it taken to a body shop and get a rental.

"Your insurance and registration in the glove box?" Malcolm asked her.

"Yes, but I can get—"

He ducked inside the open driver's side door and

leaned across the seat to grab it for her, more muscles flexing along his spine and shoulders beneath the shirt. Although she'd felt the hard planes and contours of his body against hers and under her hands in the few weeks they'd dated, she'd never gotten the chance to see him shirtless. She'd certainly fantasized about it plenty, though, and had a clear mental picture of what he'd look like.

As he climbed back out, he stilled, staring at something. Following his gaze to her key, still in the ignition, she realized he was looking at the keychain. The one he'd bought for her on their third date when she'd finally braved one of the big roller coasters at Busch Gardens. It had the coaster's name on it. She'd kept it all this time because...

"Here," he said, straightening and handing the papers over.

"Thanks," she murmured, feeling slightly awkward as she took the papers from him. The wail of a siren came from down the street. She sighed, feeling calmer, more irritated now than anything else. "I'd better call my boss."

Malcolm nodded, his alert gaze taking in the chaos around them as she dialed her boss and filled him in on what was going on. When she ended the call, Malcolm focused on her again. "You'll be okay?"

"Fine," she answered with a half-smile, reaching up to rub the back of her neck. She hadn't hit her head or anything. Her neck was going to be stiff and sore for a while though.

His gaze caught on something behind her, and he beckoned to someone. Rowan turned to see three firefighters heading their way, carrying medical kits.

"Oh, no," she protested, not wanting to delay her arrival at the office any longer than strictly necessary. "I'm fine, really. I don't need to be checked over."

"Won't hurt to make sure," he said.

The firefighters insisted on assessing her, and then the cops arrived. Malcolm spoke to one officer while Rowan talked to another. Once she was done, Malcolm came up to her, glanced at his watch. "My meeting's at seven-thirty, so…"

"Right, you should get going," she told him, then put on a smile. "At least one of us should be on time this morning."

He met her gaze, hesitated. As if he was reluctant to leave her yet. It made her miss him, and she didn't want to.

"Really. I'm fine. Val's a stickler for punctuality. You'd better get going. Plead my case for me with him, will you?"

One side of his mouth lifted, turning him from gorgeous to heart-stoppingly sexy. And an unexpected wave of sadness filled her. "Will do. See you there, maybe."

"Hope so." Her heart sank when he turned and walked away, the overwhelming sense of loneliness taking her off guard. He didn't owe her anything. She'd been the one to slam the brakes on and put an abrupt end to their relationship just over a year ago. Yet he'd come rushing to her aid today anyway, to make sure she was okay. Why did that make her throat ache?

"Malcolm," she called out before she could stop

herself.

He turned back to face her, raised his eyebrows.

"Thank you."

With a nod, he spun around and headed for his vehicle, parked along the curb across the far side of the intersection.

The empty sensation inside her expanded. Rowan sighed, berating herself. She had no cause to feel abandoned. She'd let him go a year ago. He wasn't hers.

But watching him walk away right now, she couldn't deny that a part of her wished he still was.

Chapter Two

R owan finally arrived at work almost three
hours late. She tossed her briefcase onto the
counter that ran along the back wall of her
office, and turned to confront the current state of her
desk. Her beautiful, antique mahogany desk that
dated back to before the Civil War. A present from
her parents when she'd passed the bar exam, and she
loved it so much she'd moved it here so she could
use it every day, instead of keeping it in her home
office.

At the moment, every inch of it was piled high
with folders and legal boxes for her to go through,
and there were more stacked on the floor beside it.
She had to be done with all of it by Friday night, and
all of it had to wait until she was done interviewing
the next batch of witnesses for the Ruiz case.

She rolled her head back and forth to ease the stiffness in her neck. A dull headache pounded in her

temples and the base of her skull. The medics had deemed her well enough to skip the hospital and go to work, but warned her she would be sore for a few days. If she was this sore already, she dreaded what tomorrow morning would feel like.

At a sharp knock on her door, she looked up to find her boss, Val, standing there in a charcoal-gray business suit. He was in his early fifties, his thick, light brown hair graying around the temples. "Heard you just got in. You okay?" he asked, running a concerned eye over her.

"Yeah, I'm good. Are you finished with the first set of interviews?"

"No, just took a quick break because Commander Taggart had to take an important call. You ready now, or do you need a few minutes?"

"I'm ready." She grabbed her laptop, files, and purse and trailed after him down the hall to the conference room. Their first step was to gather evidence and interview witnesses pertaining to the case, including victims. The defendant's counsel had also hinted that they might be open to considering a plea arrangement, so she and her boss were also working on a possible offer.

Supervisory Special Agent Taggart, commander of FAST Bravo, stood at the far end of the hallway speaking on his cell phone to someone. He gave her a nod of acknowledgment, then looked away as he continued his conversation.

In the waiting area outside the conference room, two more members of FAST Bravo waited, including the team leader. They nodded at her, smiled politely and she did the same, their presence making her heart speed up. If they were still here, then was Malcolm as well?

The moment Val opened the conference room door, Rowan got her answer, her eyes immediately connecting with Malcolm's. He was seated on the far side of the long table, his big frame taking up the entire chair.

"Hi," she said, taking her seat across from him and setting her things down, trying to ignore the way her heart fluttered. This was the second business meeting she'd had with him over the past couple of weeks, and it felt every bit as strange and stilted as the first time. "Sorry to keep you waiting."

"Not a problem," he answered. "You get everything sorted out?"

"Yes." Her boss didn't know she and Malcolm had dated a year ago, and she didn't want him to. Their past relationship didn't affect this case whatsoever. At least here in her work environment she had other things to focus on besides the magnetic man across the table, and the undeniable pull he still exerted on her. Work had always helped her center herself, push all her personal problems into the background.

"Go ahead and pick up where you left off. I'll catch up as we go." Not wanting to take up any more of Malcolm's time than necessary, she opened her file, then glanced at the papers in front of Val to orient herself.

"We were just going over Agent Freeman's recollection of the night FAST Bravo rescued Victoria Gomez," her boss said, pointing to a section on the page so she could read over it.

Rowan nodded and continued skimming the report. Miss Gomez was a former investigative reporter who had been kidnapped and brutalized by Carlos Ruiz's men for several weeks. The woman had been subjected to horrific things that made Rowan's skin crawl, and she had a huge amount of respect for Miss Gomez's strength.

The cartel had intended to punish her for exposing Ruiz and his network in an article published in the New York Times. She'd been working on a book about her findings when Ruiz had targeted her. His men had slaughtered her family in front of her, abducted her, used her in horrific ways with the intention of selling her into sexual slavery in Asia when they'd had their fill.

Thankfully Malcolm and his teammates had gotten there first. Now Miss Gomez was the government's star witness against Ruiz. Rowan and Val had already interviewed her several times. Miss Gomez had volunteered to enter the WITSEC program, for her own protection, and was currently at their orientation center somewhere here in D.C. After she testified and the trial was over, Miss Gomez would begin a new life under a new name somewhere else, and hopefully find a sense of peace and security.

"Okay," Rowan said as she finished skimming the notes, delaying the moment when she had to look up at Malcolm again. "Please continue." The more members who corroborated the details of her rescue, the stronger the testimony would be.

"Special Agent Freeman wasn't in the forest when Miss Gomez was discovered," Val told her. "Tell us your recollection of what happened after she was found," he said to Malcolm.

"I was still at the house we'd raided, about seventy or so yards from where she was found in the woods. My team leader and a couple other guys got her into an ambulance and came back to the house. Hamilton rode in the ambulance with her to the hospital and I met him there after we had secured the prisoners and remaining female hostages, and finished processing the scene."

"Describe the moment when you first met Miss Gomez."

Malcolm's steady dark gaze slid from Val to Rowan for a moment before he answered. "She was in the back of the ambulance, wrapped up in a blanket Hamilton had found for her."

The team members had found her naked in the woods, with—

"She had a rusted old collar and chain hanging from around her neck."

Because those animals had chained Miss Gomez to the fucking floor in a shed out back of the property so no one could hear her scream when they took turns with her.

Rowan's stomach clenched at the mental image but Val nodded and scribbled down something on his pad of paper. "Did you speak to Miss Gomez at the hospital later?"

"Just briefly. Hamilton and I tried to question her about Ruiz to see if we could get a lead on him but it was way too soon. She was in bad shape. Deep in shock, in pain and still scared as hell. The only person she seemed to trust was Hamilton. She wouldn't let go of his hand."

Oh, that made Rowan's heart hurt. That Miss Gomez would reach out to a near stranger for comfort and reassurance after suffering so horrifically at other men's hands.

"So he stayed with her while the medical staff treated her injuries, but had to leave before FBI and agency officials questioned her. I went in to get him when they arrived," Malcolm continued.

"Did Miss Gomez say anything of importance to you before you left?" Val asked.

Malcolm nodded. "As we were walking to the door. She said Carlos Ruiz was the man responsible. She'd been investigating him and he'd gone after her to make a statement that he was untouchable. His men killed her entire family while they were having dinner at her parents' place one night, then took her. She said he came to look at her a few days before we raided the property. And I remember her last words to us exactly. She said, 'He should have killed me that night with my family. Because now I'm going to bury him'."

Rowan stared at him, a shiver skittering up her spine. To have that sort of resolve and inner strength in the face of everything she'd gone through... Victoria Gomez was her new hero.

Even Val appeared affected by Malcolm's words, a slight smile tugging at his mouth. "She said that?"

"Yes."

"Well, good for her." Val exchanged a glance with her. Miss Gomez hadn't told them this. Maybe she didn't think it was important, or maybe she didn't remember that chunk of time in the hospital. That was understandable. She'd been medicated, so it was possible.

But it was more powerful testimony they could present to the judge, whether in a trial, or in a victim impact statement should Ruiz want and accept a plea bargain. Rowan and her office had to be prepared for either scenario.

They would check Malcolm's story against Agent Hamilton's when they interviewed him in a little while. Every eyewitness piece of information they collected on Ruiz was another nail they could use in the courtroom to pound into the lid of his richly deserved coffin.

They all turned when someone knocked on the conference room door. Rowan put a hand to the back of her neck, hid a wince as the tender muscles protested.

Commander Taggart poked his head in. He nodded at Freeman, then settled his gaze on Val. "Sorry to interrupt. Can I have a minute?"

"Of course." Val stood. "Back shortly," he said to them, and left.

As soon as the door shut behind him, an awkward tension took hold of the room. Rowan steeled herself and turned back to face Malcolm, meeting that dark chocolate gaze across the table. He had a way of looking at her that made her feel like he could see right through her. It made her squirm inside.

He folded his arms casually, emphasizing the thickness and power in his biceps as the sleeves of his dress shirt pulled taut across the muscles there. He looked amazing in a pair of jeans and a T-shirt, but in a suit, he was irresistible. It made her imagine him tossing the tailored jacket aside, those long, strong fingers undoing each button on his shirt one by one as that dark, intense gaze locked on her.

She swallowed, trying and failing to shove the image aside. He'd been wearing a suit the night she'd met him, too, at the veteran's charity event here in D.C. last summer. She'd noticed him from across the room as soon as she'd walked in, and when her brother had introduced them soon after, the mutual attraction was undeniable.

Looking at him right now, recalling the way he'd touched her, kissed her, it was hard to remember all the carefully thought through reasons why she'd decided to end things with him. She'd enjoyed his company, and she'd had fun with him too. Dates where they'd gone to see the latest action movie, late night dinners that had cost her sleep but had been so worth it, and of course braving the coasters he loved so much.

She'd thought breaking it off early would be easier for them both, had been as gentle about it as possible, but she'd still hurt him. She was sorry for that.

She searched her mind, trying to think of something to say that would dispel the unspoken tension simmering between them. "So—"

"You gonna cut a deal with Ruiz?"

The abrupt change in topic took her aback for a second. She couldn't read his expression, or his tone. "Maybe. There are a lot of variables to consider."

He studied her a long moment. "A guy like him, he'll want a deal." This time there was no mistaking the disdain in his voice. Whether it was aimed at her or Ruiz, or both, she wasn't sure. It stung to think he might think badly of her and her job now.

"It depends on how strong a case we can build against him, and what he's willing to give us in exchange." Malcolm understood how this worked. And that she couldn't divulge any details about it.

Sometimes her job meant doing things she didn't like to protect the greater good, but she'd known that going in and had learned how to put aside her personal feelings. In this case, if Ruiz could give them something solid that would lead investigators to *El Escorpion* or even give them something to take down the other lieutenants in the cartel, Rowan would view it with the hard-nosed professionalism that was expected of her and cut a deal that would reduce Ruiz's sentence. Even though she'd rather see him serve a long sentence before dying behind bars for what he'd done.

Malcolm shook his head slightly, his eyes burning with an almost merciless light. "You weren't there that night. I was. I saw what he and his men did to women. Just... Whatever happens with this whole thing, promise me he won't walk."

An answering anger smoldered inside her, the need to see justice done. "No. He won't walk." She and everyone else working on this case would make damn sure of that.

THE FIRE IN her sapphire blue eyes when she said those words triggered something deep inside Malcolm. A tingling, bone-deep awareness he couldn't ignore no matter how much he wanted to.

She wanted Ruiz to pay for what he'd done. It must turn her stomach to offer deals to pieces of shit like him. It would Mal's.

He'd never seen her in work mode before that meeting a few weeks back. She was so different here in her professional element, even that tailored pencil skirt suit hugging her lean curves like a suit of armor, concealing the true woman from the rest of the world.

There was so much more to her than her profession.

In the short time they'd dated he'd gotten to know the other her, see some of the softer layers hidden beneath that professional exterior. Her dry sense of humor, how impassioned she became when she talked about something that excited her. She was smart and kind. The way she'd smiled whenever he reached for her hand or wrapped his arm around her.

The woman in front of him now was determined, driven and self-assured. A little cool and reserved. Sexy as hell in her own right. But the woman he'd gotten to know a year ago, the one who had laughed with him, clung to him and melted under his kisses...she was beautiful, inside and out. He missed her.

She'd kept the keychain. He'd noticed it as soon as he'd leaned over to get her insurance papers this morning. It was just a damn keychain, had cost him five bucks. Yet she'd kept it this whole time. Why? It wasn't because she hadn't noticed or was too lazy to throw it away. Rowan was as hard working as they came, and didn't do anything by accident.

Sitting here across from her was a special kind of torture. She was sore from the accident, he could see it in her restricted movements, the way she kept rubbing at the back of her neck. His natural inclination was to help somehow. He would have run to help anyone involved in the accident this morning, but when he'd seen her car get rear-ended and then that asshole slam into her passenger side before taking off, all his protective instincts had roared to the surface, strong as ever.

He'd tried to tell himself he was over her, and had been for many months. Now he realized he had to call bullshit on that. She was the one who got away. He still cared. Still wanted her, even if she didn't want him. And that wanting wasn't going away anytime soon, no matter how much he wished it would.

Showing the first signs of discomfort under the weight of his stare, Rowan cleared her throat and pulled a bottle of pain relievers from her purse. He bit back the words of concern he wanted to say, along with the urge to go around the table to knead the sore muscles in her neck and shoulders. She wasn't his, hadn't been for a long time.

Hell, she'd never really been his in the first place.

All the old questions he'd tormented himself with in the weeks after she'd broken up with him came rushing back now as he watched her down the pills with a few sips from her bottle of water. Did she miss him? Think of him at all? Regret her decision even a little?

Right from the start he had known how special she was, that she was different from any other woman he'd ever dated. He'd been ready to dive headfirst into their relationship, give himself completely to her. Then bam. She'd pulled the plug, and to him it had seemed so damn easy for her to walk away.

He hadn't seen it coming. Still couldn't understand why she'd done it.

Rowan was the first woman he'd been with whom he could see himself having a future with, and the first one who had known what he did for a living. She understood what his job entailed, the effort and sacrifices it took to be a FAST member. Her rejection had stung not only his male ego, but hurt him more than he'd ever admit to anyone, triggering all the old insecurities he'd carried around as a kid.

He stared at her now, wishing he could see what was going on in her head. *Why wasn't I good enough for you?*

Deep down he'd already feared he wasn't when he'd asked her out. Her breaking up with him so suddenly had confirmed it, and worse, that she obviously didn't think he was good enough for her either.

Mal kept his expression impassive as she set the water down and made an attempt at small talk. "How's your brother?"

"He's good. How are your grandparents?" she asked in her soft Georgia drawl. He'd always loved the sound of it.

Maybe small talk was a bad idea. He had no interest in talking about personal shit with her. Just like he no longer had the right to be involved in her life, she didn't have the right to know about his. "They're both fine."

Her smile was a little strained. "That's good."

He nodded once. He'd grown up in a rough neighborhood in Detroit. After his mother had died of complications due to diabetes, her parents had taken him in. They'd been strict. Pops was a preacher who demanded integrity and high standards in everything from manners to school to how Mal treated people. He'd been tough but fair, and ultimately was responsible for Mal becoming the man he was today. And even though he'd overcome the odds and made a success of his life, Rowan dumping him brought it all back.

"Your whole team must be extra busy with all these meetings and interviews we're adding to your load, huh?" she asked.

"It's fine." What the hell was taking Taggart and her boss so long? Christ, he just wanted the hell out of here. Being forced to see her, talk with her, especially alone, made it seem like there was a concrete slab sitting on his ribcage.

She opened her mouth to say something else, and relief swept through him when her boss walked back in. "Thanks for coming in, Agent Freeman. I think we've got what we need for now." Val's gaze shifted to Rowan. "You up for a meeting over at the prison?"

Rowan hid her surprise well, shoving the bottle of pills into her purse as though they were some sign of weakness. "Yes. Why?"

"Ruiz wants to see us. He wants to see what kind of deal we can offer him."

"All right." She was up and clearing her things off the table in a heartbeat, only a subtle stiffness in her movements giving away her physical discomfort. Then those gorgeous eyes met Mal's, and his damn heart squeezed at the flicker of wistfulness there. As though the thought of not seeing him again made her sad. But why the hell would that be, when she'd been the one to walk away? "Bye. It was good to see you."

For his sake, he hoped it would be the last time. "Yeah, you too."

When the door shut behind her, Mal expelled a long breath. Their paths probably wouldn't cross again anytime soon.

This ache in his chest was only temporary, so he wasn't going to waste time torturing himself thinking about what might have been. He wasn't going to wish things were different. Or wish that he could be there for her tonight. Drive her home. Make her dinner. Rub her neck and shoulders. Put her in a hot bath before tucking her into bed beside him. Take care of her.

He wasn't going to wish she was *his*.

In fact, starting right now, he wasn't going to think about her at all anymore.

Chapter Three

———◇◇◇◇———

Carlos Ruiz sat with his spine ramrod straight in the chair in the prison interrogation room as he waited for the U.S. Attorney to arrive. The orange jumpsuit was uncomfortable and smelled musty, his ankles and wrists shackled, and they wouldn't allow him the use of his cane. Ridiculous overkill procedures designed to make a prisoner feel like a trapped, whipped dog.

There was good reason why he and the other cartel members would do anything to avoid being extradited to face trial in the United States.

This wasn't anything like being imprisoned in Mexico. Here he couldn't easily bribe or threaten his way out. Couldn't run his operation from behind bars the way he was used to. Here there was nothing but the monotonous daily routine of the incarcerated. A mind-numbing cage designed to break his will and spirit.

That would never happen. He was stronger and more resourceful than they gave him credit for. And even though he faced the probability of being convicted of most charges laid against him, he was not defeated.

His lawyer shifted beside him, anxious. They couldn't talk openly here. Everything was being recorded and watched. Not that it mattered. Carlos still had his ways of finding out what he needed to know, even in here.

The door opened behind him. He refused to turn around, sat perfectly still facing the far wall with its two-way mirror while the federal lawyers came around the table and took their seats. A fifty-something man with a paunch and pasty skin that told Carlos he rarely left his office.

And a hot, raven-haired beauty around thirty or so, her firm, trim body outlined so nicely by a snug skirt and tailored jacket. Classy. Attractive enough that she would have fetched a nice profit from one of his Asian buyers.

Setting a pile of folders on the table in front of him and leaning back, the male lawyer regarded Carlos with a no bullshit expression before introducing himself and the woman. She wasn't his assistant, as Carlos had assumed. She was an Assistant U.S. Attorney.

Rowan Stewart.

He would remember that name, and her face, for later. If he ever got out of here while he was still vertical, *after* he got even with the people who had put him here, he would punish both these bloodsuckers as well. For building a case against him that could keep him behind bars here in the U.S. until the day he died.

The man he'd have killed in a creative way that made an impact. The female, he'd make wish she were dead.

"Since you asked for this meeting," the man went on, all business, "I assume you've got something new and important to give us."

"What are you prepared to offer my client in exchange?" his lawyer countered. He had instructed Carlos not to say a word. Not to give a hint of emotion during this meeting. So Carlos stared at his current adversaries, letting the rage burn inside him.

"Nothing, until he gives us something we can use on *El Escorpion* and the cartel bosses."

Carlos repressed a snort as his lawyer shook his head and answered on his behalf. "You know that's impossible. No one within the cartel even knows *El Escorpion's* true identity."

"So he's a myth, then," the female said, a Southern kind of drawl doing nothing to soften the disdain in her voice. "A figment of everyone's imaginations."

"He's real," Carlos's lawyer said. "But my client has never met him. His only dealings with him have been over the phone."

"Then this meeting's pointless. If he gives us nothing, he gets nothing," she finished.

Carlos squeezed his hands into fists beneath the table, seething inside, both from his current predicament and the female's attitude. If he had anything on *El Escorpion*, he would give it to the Americans willingly.

Someone from inside the cartel—high up inside it, where he used to be until recently—had turned on Carlos prior to his arrest. It was the only explanation for how the Americans had known he was on that plane.

His source here at the prison had told him the rumor was *El Escorpion* himself had been behind it, out of disapproval over the kidnapping of a DEA FAST member's young daughter. Apparently the secretive head of the cartel had decided that damage control was in order and cut Carlos loose, handing him over to the Americans like a naughty dog that had pissed in its own bed.

Carlos would do *anything* to destroy the traitorous bastard.

The male attorney drummed his fingers impatiently on the file folders before him. "So why call us down here, then? Wasting our time and not cooperating with the federal investigation isn't going to do your client any favors."

"He can't give you what he doesn't have," Carlos's lawyer answered.

"Then what?" the woman demanded, raising her coal-black brows in a haughty expression Carlos longed to wipe off her face.

Her arrogance was so like another woman who'd thought herself untouchable. An American investigative reporter named Victoria Gomez who had learned the opposite in a way she wouldn't soon forget. It galled him that she was walking free instead of living a life of sexual slavery in Asia as he'd planned, likely a star witness for these same two prosecutors while he was trapped in this shithole they called a prison.

His patience snapped. "Nieto," he snarled, stretching his legs out beneath the table to help alleviate the deep ache in the right one. Not that it helped much. The bullet wounds had healed but the nerve and soft tissue damage was permanent. A permanent reminder that the bitch reporter Victoria Gomez had nearly cost him his life in a shootout with the DEA.

Carlos shook off his lawyer's warning hand on his shoulder, holding the female's intense blue gaze. To hell with legal advice, to hell with all of them. He was stuck in here, and likely wouldn't be getting out. But he was far from beaten.

"What about him?" the female said.

"I can give you whatever you want on him. In exchange I want a transfer and a reduced sentence."

"A transfer to where?"

He gave her a cold smile. "Somewhere more befitting my status and importance to this investigation."

She tilted her head, watching him. Analyzing him. Because she thought she held all the power now.

Oh, how he longed to prove her wrong. Spring a trap that would wipe that infuriating superior look right off her face and replace it with one of stark terror. In here, he had one thing in abundance. Time. Plenty of time to fantasize about the revenge he could wreak against all those who had betrayed him.

"That all depends on what you've got." She paused a beat. "Start talking."

Carlos did. He told them everything he knew about that traitorous son of a bitch Nieto. A nobody interloper who had moved in the moment Carlos had been arrested, to take over his hard-won territory.

Reaping the fruits of Carlos's years of work without a qualm.

Beneath the anger and resentment, a warm glow of satisfaction spread through his chest as he talked. Because now Nieto's daughter and mistress were missing. He would be frantic to find them—and stop them from talking.

But Carlos knew things about him that Nieto's only child and mistress did not. He'd already begun meting out punishment on his rival from right here, right under the American's noses. "I know all his operations," he began. "Because they used to be mine."

Him being locked up didn't mean he was out of the game. On the contrary. He was still a lethal threat to his enemies. As they would all learn soon enough, in order of insult to him. First Nieto. Then *El Escorpion*. Victoria Gomez. These two fucking smug federal lawyers. And the fucking DEA.

Time was on his side. He intended to use it well.

Sooner or later, he'd make every last one of them pay.

****

"Stop," Taggart commanded from high overhead on the catwalk situated alongside the shoot house hallway. He sounded pissed. The overhead lights came on, signaling an immediate end to the exercise. "Do it again. Freeman, you still wanna be our point man, or what?"

God dammit.

Suppressing a sigh, Mal took the criticism and turned the frustrated snarl inside his head back on himself as he shoved his NVGs back up on their helmet mount. Because this was on him. Again. "Yes, sir," he called out, then turned at Hamilton's signal to start over from the top.

One by one all nine of them filed back down the narrow, five-level staircase to begin the drill again. Their fourth run in the past forty minutes, because all of them had been shit so far, this last one culminating with Malcolm missing an armed suspect hidden behind the door in one of the rooms. If it had happened in real life, he or one of his teammates might be dead right now.

Taggart didn't ask questions or demand a debrief of what had gone wrong, instead stalking back down the catwalk to the starting point without a word. Fourth in line with his teammates, Mal mentally berated himself on the way back down the final flight of stairs. They'd started out the day at the gym together at 06:00, followed by breakfast and intel briefings on the latest goings on with the *Veneno* cartel before moving here to practice various CQB scenarios.

As a former SEAL and the second most experienced operator on FAST Bravo, Mal had held the position of being the team's point man for the past four years. Although you'd never know it from today's sloppy performance. His fucking head wasn't where it needed to be.

Because of Rowan.

He'd lain awake all last night thinking of her. Of what might have been.

It wasn't like him to let something personal affect his mental state to this extent, and never while at work. And yet it was. No matter how much he wanted to get her out of his head, he couldn't. Seeing her again yesterday had somehow brought back all those unresolved feelings. All those unanswered questions. He wanted closure, and wasn't going to get it. His brain was having a hard time accepting and compartmentalizing that.

Back at the starting point in front of the building's façade, he maneuvered a new door onto the hinges and locked it with a bolting mechanism while other agents inside the building moved everything else around. This scenario called for them to do a tactical breach and clear the building of armed hostiles on each floor. They were using live ammo and dummies this time rather than paper targets.

Training that way upped the stakes for everyone involved, allowing for zero margin of error. They trained as they meant to operate, because out there in the field, his and his teammates' lives depended on them getting it done right the first time. Which was why he was so damn pissed at himself right now. There was no excuse for his shitty performance today.

Hamilton, the team leader, eyed him with faint amusement as Mal took up position behind Rodriguez, who was responsible for blowing the door open with a battering ram. The moment it opened, Mal was always the first guy through it. Everyone else followed him, reacted to his actions and decisions. That was his role. They all depended on him being sharp.

"You need a nap, or what?" Hamilton asked him.

"I'm good." Lack of sleep wasn't any kind of excuse, for any of them. Hell, he'd gone days without sleep during his days in the Teams and managed fine. He was only thirty-four, so it wasn't like he was getting too old for this line of work.

"Okay. Think we can get it right this time? I'm getting bored."

Embarrassed, annoyed with himself even though his team leader was only giving him a hard time, Mal set his jaw and nodded once.

Hamilton gave his shoulder a good-natured nudge with an elbow. "Just jerking your chain, man." He turned to the others. "We ready to do this for real now, boys?"

A chorus of affirmatives answered, so Hamilton strode to the end of the stack and awaited Taggart's command to begin the assault. The lights went out.

Mal pulled down his NVGs and narrowed his focus to his immediate surroundings, his gaze locked on the door before them.

Taggart gave the signal.

Seconds later, Colebrook's hand landed on Mal's right shoulder and squeezed. In turn, Mal did the same to Rodriguez, who pulled back the battering ram and slammed it with all his considerable might into the bolting mechanism.

Wood cracked. Rodriguez rammed the door once more, splintering the lock. Mal charged through it, M4 up and ready.

This time Mal was on his game. They executed the assault perfectly.

"Third floor's secure," he announced over his mic. *Thank fucking God.*

"Building's secure," Hamilton informed their commander, "all tangos in custody."

Taggart didn't answer, but the lights suddenly came back on.

Switching off his NVGs, Mal met Hamilton's gaze in silent question, and the team leader gave a casual shrug. "'Kay, boys, good job. Everyone back downstairs in case we have to do this again."

Before Mal had made it two steps toward the stairs, Maka was there next to him, clapping him on the back with one huge, gloved paw. "'Bout time you brought your A-game, *brah*," he teased, always ready with a ribbing. "Was starting to think we might need to replace you."

Mal grunted at him and trundled down the concrete stairs with the others, allowing his mind to wander. This thing with Rowan was driving him nuts. Trying to forget her hadn't worked. He wanted answers. To know the real reason she'd ended it.

At the bottom of the stairs, he craned his head back to search for their commander. Taggart was still up on the catwalk, but he wasn't paying any attention to them, his back to them as he spoke on his cell phone at the far end. Mal milled around by the doorway as the team waited for further instructions.

"Freeman. Lockhart."

They both looked up at Taggart, who now stood staring down at them with his hands braced on the metal railing at the edge of the catwalk. "Need to talk to you both a minute."

He and Lockhart exchanged a puzzled glance before heading up a wooden staircase that took them to the catwalk. Their boots thudded on the plywood floor as they strode to the end to meet their commander.

Taggart slid his phone into his pocket and folded his arms as he regarded them. "Something's come up with the Nieto case," he said in a low voice. "The daughter and mother are refusing to enter WITSEC at this point, and nobody knows what the hell to do with them. Until it's all sorted out, the FBI wants us to provide temporary security for them."

Malcolm's eyebrows shot up. "Us?"

Taggart nodded. "I've volunteered you two."

What? Oh, hell no—

Taggart held up a hand. "I realize this isn't going to make either of you jump for joy, but it's only for a few days."

"Like, how many?" Lockhart asked, suspicion written all over his normally taciturn expression. A former sniper, the guy was notoriously quiet and impossible to read if he didn't want to be. Even Mal, who'd known him for years now, didn't know what went on in Lockhart's head most of the time.

A shrug from Taggart. "They just told me a couple. Two days, four, I dunno. You're assigned to the daughter," he told Lockhart, and then shifted his gaze to Malcolm. "You're with the mother. I don't have any other details for you yet."

Mal frowned, not liking this one bit. This didn't make any kind of fucking sense. "The mother doesn't even speak English, does she? And my Spanish is limited to ordering a beer and a taco." Not even well, at that.

The corner of Taggart's mouth twitched in the hint of a smile. "So it should be nice and quiet for you over the next few days, then. Think of it as a kind of vacation if you want."

Vacation? Not. Mal bit back a groan, sighed instead because he couldn't help it. "Rodriguez would be a better choice, don't you think?" His Spanish was flawless.

"Rodriguez is flying back to California this afternoon to visit his mom for a couple days. He got a call that she's not doing well."

Oh, damn. That sucked. She had advanced MS and had been declining recently. Why hadn't Rodriguez said anything to them this morning?

"Besides, you're good with people," Taggart said, giving Mal's upper arm a friendly slap. "So you'll do just fine."

"Hamilton speaks some Spanish," he couldn't help blurting. "More than me."

Taggart's turquoise eyes twinkled with amusement. "So he does. I'll keep that in mind for next time." He pulled his phone back out of one of the pockets in his cargo pants. "You've got ten minutes to shower and grab whatever you need to cover you until the weekend. We're meeting your principals at the U.S. Attorney's office in thirty."

Now Malcolm did groan. *Christ.* This day was already the shits, and now he had to go to Rowan's office again on top of everything else?

Arguing was futile, so he didn't bother. He'd survived worse over the years than having his heart broken and having to babysit a cartel boss's mistress. Might as well suck it up and take it on the chin like a man.

Chapter Four

———◇◈◇◈◇———

Rowan struggled to keep her professional demeanor in place as she faced Oceane and her mother from across her paper-cluttered desk. The FBI was currently scrambling to make arrangements for some security for the two women, who still refused to see reason. It was as mystifying as it was frustrating.

They'd been over this same issue a half dozen times already over the past few days, and each time Rowan thought the women were about to agree to enter WITSEC, they dug in their heels again. Out of desperation, because of his rapport with the ladies, her boss had personally tried to sway them to go into the program an hour ago. Now, in a last ditch effort to change their minds, he'd tasked Rowan with trying to sway them.

"I understand that this must be scary and overwhelming for you," she began to Oceane in as calm a tone as she could manage.

Everything about this day sucked so far. If she'd been sore yesterday, today she was in serious pain. Every muscle in her neck, shoulders and upper back was exquisitely tender. The extra strength Tylenol she'd taken for her headache hadn't touched the pain, and she was bone-deep tired.

When she'd finally made it home from the office last night, her father had shown up just as she was falling asleep—because apparently even whiplash wasn't a good enough excuse to avoid signing the paperwork for him. Now she had a small mountain of work piled on her desk and another twelve-to-fourteen-hour day ahead of her before she could drag herself home in her rental car and finally crawl back into bed.

She held Oceane's blue-gray gaze as she continued. "But the only real way to guarantee your safety until the authorities figure out who was behind the attack on you and neutralize the threat, is for you both to go into the WITSEC program." Why couldn't she see that?

Oceane sighed in impatience and pushed some chocolate-brown curls away from her face. "I have already told you, we're not doing that." Her accented voice was calm, her tone final. "The FBI agent I spoke to this morning said he would find us another option."

"Maybe, but that option won't be as secure as having a team of highly-trained U.S. Marshals guarding you in an undisclosed location." No one could force either of them to enter the program, however. It was voluntary. Oceane had been annoyingly tight-lipped about their reasons for refusing to enter WITSEC.

"I understand." Her mother nudged Oceane with an elbow, said something in rapid Spanish that Rowan didn't have a hope of catching. Oceane nodded and turned to Rowan. "Have you heard anything new in the investigation? About who attacked us?"

"*Fue* Ruiz," the mother said in an adamant tone, her face set, and though Rowan didn't speak much Spanish, she understood her meaning well enough. The woman blamed Ruiz for what had happened to them.

"The investigators are looking into every possible option," Rowan said, not willing to give anything away. New information and leads seemed to be coming in hourly, but federal authorities were tight-lipped about what they'd found. Only rock solid evidence pertinent to the case against Ruiz was passed on to the U.S. Attorney's office.

From what Rowan had been told, so far Oceane and her mother had been frustratingly reticent to share information about Nieto and the cartel. She got the sense that Oceane was still in the dark about a lot of it, but the mother definitely knew things, and she wasn't talking until she got what she wanted: federal protection of some kind *outside* of WITSEC, and a guarantee from the government that they would be allowed to remain in the U.S. after the Ruiz case was over. A tall order, considering they were both Mexican nationals. For the government to give them residency or citizenship, the women were going to have to give them something big.

At least three different agencies were currently working on their case, each frantically trying to find a lead that might help investigators unravel what was currently going on within the cartel. Information was sketchy.

From a string of recent attacks on labs and other operations in Mexico, it seemed as if Nieto had declared war on what was left of Ruiz's territory. Everyone involved in the case hoped that at least one of those threads might lead back to *El Escorpion*, whoever he was, so they could begin dismantling the *Venenos'* sprawling narcotics empire.

The pounding at the base of her skull got worse as Oceane and Anya didn't respond to her point, merely stared at her.

Her patience snapped. Her attempts to be the nice guy hadn't worked. Time to put some pressure on. "Here's the deal. You expect our government to jump through hoops to protect you, then you need to give us something solid today, or you'll both be deported back to Mexico." She stopped, glanced up when someone knocked on her door and pushed it open. Val raised his eyebrows at her in question and she gave a subtle shake of her head, the motion intensifying her headache.

Val's mouth tightened in a frustration she understood all too well. "Just got a call from Commander Taggart. The temporary protective detail will be here in a few minutes."

Surprised, Rowan blinked at him. Taggart? The DEA and FBI were calling in a FAST team on this? "Oh. Who is it?"

"No idea."

As he started to pull the door shut behind him, her cell phone rang from the corner of her desk. She glanced at it, expecting it to be the body shop calling with an estimate about repairs to her car, but instead her brother's picture popped up on the screen.

"Excuse me," she said to the women. "I need to take this." Well, actually she needed a few minutes' break from this futile argument, and more pain relievers. As soon as the women left her office, it was back to the mountain of paperwork she still had to wade through.

Stepping out into the hall, she answered the call with a tired sigh, rubbing the back of her sore neck. "Hey."

"Wow. Bad day already?" Kevin asked. "It's only eight in the morning."

"Don't remind me," she muttered, turning the corner so she could talk in a little alcove for some privacy. "What are you up to?"

"I'm at Mom and Dad's. He had some banking stuff and whatever that I had to sign."

That was promising, their father adding Kevin to his bank accounts as he restructured his estate. Things had been strained between them until recently. "I did that last night."

When Kevin had first come out to their parents officially five years ago, it hadn't gone so well. Their dad had taken it especially hard. Either due to his alpha male ego, archaic beliefs, or maybe embarrassment, he'd refused to accept it.

Over the last eighteen months or so he and Kevin had mostly stabilized their rocky relationship, but only because her brother had adopted a "don't ask, don't tell" policy about his personal life with their parents. Kevin told Rowan everything, though. They weren't just siblings, they were the best of friends.

"How are you feeling? You sore?" Kevin asked.

"More than I bargained for. I would give anything to crawl back in bed and stay there."

He made a sound of sympathy. "And I bet you're working late tonight again, huh."

"Every day from now until I die, yes," she said with a wry chuckle, only half-joking. "I've signed on for a lifetime of indentured servitude."

"A chip off the old block. Dad must be so proud," Kevin teased, and Rowan winced inside. She'd certainly done her best to follow in their father's footsteps, but he left a wide trail to follow and she wasn't sure she would ever be able to match it. Deep down, she didn't want to. "How about I bring you dinner there later on? I'll get takeout from that Greek place you love."

He was so good to her. "This is why you're my favorite brother."

"I know. You're lucky to have me."

"And you never let me forget it." She was two years older. "And I still think I won the sibling jackpot."

"Just for that, I'm bringing crème caramel for dessert. And I'll even take the takeout containers home with me when I leave."

"You're a saint."

"I know. See you at six?" He worked at a pharmacy a few blocks from her office. They had lunch together at least once a week, unless she was preparing for a big case like this one. She missed just spending time with him; he always made her feel better about everything. And she wanted to confide in him about Malcolm, since he'd been the one to introduce the two of them at that veteran's charity gala last year.

"Perfect. See you then."

Back in her office, she gave up trying to sway the women to enter WITSEC and tried instead to get more information about Ruiz from Oceane, who translated for her mother. Anya had detailed her account of the attack on her home in Veracruz, as well as given some information on Nieto's finances that the FBI was looking into as a means of tracking him. But nothing else about his operations, what she knew of his criminal activity, and nothing on the cartel itself.

Rowan wasn't yet sure if either of the women would be needed to testify against Ruiz, since their contact with him had been minimal, but they were the investigators' best chance of cracking the *Veneno* cartel wide open.

A knock at the door stopped their conversation. All three of them looked over as it opened, and the sight of Malcolm standing there in the doorway was a punch to Rowan's senses.

He wore a pair of dark jeans that hugged his powerful thighs, and a pale blue button down that stretched across his chest and shoulders. He'd worn it on their first date, when he'd taken her out to a fancy restaurant on the waterfront. The echo of excited butterflies stirred in her belly at the memory of that night.

"I'm here for Anya," he said, then looked at Oceane and pushed the door open wider, revealing another big, fit man beside him with dirty blond hair and pale blue eyes, wearing jeans and a T-shirt. One of his teammates. "This is Special Agent Gabe Lockhart. He's been assigned to you."

Oceane cast an uncertain glance at Rowan before speaking to her mother in Spanish and standing. "You're our bodyguards?" she asked Malcolm.

Rowan was surprised as well. Why had two FAST Bravo members been tasked with this assignment? And did Malcolm even speak Spanish?

He nodded, his expression grave. "For now. Are you finished in here?" he asked Rowan.

"Yes, for the moment," she said quickly, covering a wince as she pushed her chair back and got to her feet.

He gestured for Anya to follow him. "This way."

Rowan trailed after them into the hall, overcome by the strangest sense of abandonment as Malcolm walked away from her. Part of her wanted to call him back.

The thought came out of nowhere, taking her completely off guard. Why did she feel such a strong desire to hold on to him now, when she'd been the one to let him go?

"What about our things?" Oceane asked him as she walked beside her mother. Agent Lockhart followed them, and Rowan behind him.

"Another agent will bring them to your safe house later." Malcolm stopped and addressed Oceane, ignoring Rowan. For some reason that hurt, though she understood why he didn't want anything to do with her, and he was here in a professional capacity, not a social one. Except it confused her, his apparent one-eighty after being so concerned and caring after the accident. Now she had two kinds of whiplash. "We'll give you a minute to say goodbye," he said, looking between Oceane and her mother.

Oceane's blue-gray eyes went wide and she gasped as his meaning sank in. "Goodbye?"

He nodded once. "Protocol dictates you'll be transported to the secure location separately for your own safety."

Uh oh... Rowan glanced at Oceane, already knowing how that would be received.

"No." Oceane darted forward to grab her mother's upper arm and step in front of her, raising her chin. "We will not be separated."

"Yes, you will."

At that hard voice they all looked to the left as Commander Taggart strode toward them from the direction of the elevator, his expression set. "My men have been tasked with your protection. For everyone's safety, you and your mother will be taken in different vehicles." There was absolute steel in his tone.

Oceane shook her head, panic bleeding through in her expression, clearly believing this was a trick. That she and her mother would be separated for good. "No." She spoke in rapid Spanish to her mother, whose eyes filled with horror at the news, then launched into her own tirade.

Taggart put up a hand to stop her. "I realize it's not what you want. But it's the way it is. It's all documented right here." He pulled out a letter from his back pocket and handed it to her. Oceane scanned it, her brows knitted together.

Malcolm finally looked over at Rowan as the two

women continued arguing and pleading with Taggart, one in English and the other in Spanish, and she
could tell by the resigned look on his face that he
hadn't volunteered for this assignment. She felt a
twinge of sympathy for him, but as far as Anya's
safety was concerned, the woman couldn't be placed
in better hands.

"I want to speak to the agent in charge of our
case," Oceane said.

"You can speak to him on the way to your safe
house," Taggart answered, "but right now, you're going. Individually."

"My mother doesn't speak English."

"That won't affect Agent Freeman's ability to
protect her."

When Oceane opened her mouth to argue again,
Rowan stepped in. "If it helps, I can guarantee these
men's word. You'll both be taken to the same location, I promise, and you'll both get there safely.
Agent Freeman served in the military before joining
the DEA, and with all his training and experience,
he's well qualified to be your mother's security detail," she said, without giving too much about his
background away.

She could feel Malcolm's dark stare boring into
her, didn't have the guts to meet his gaze as she continued. "Agent Lockhart works with him and is also
former military," she added, not wanting to come
right out and say they were teammates, or in what
capacity they worked together.

Most of what FAST Bravo did was classified.
Oceane and her mother didn't have the security clear-

ance necessary to know more. The only reason Rowan knew what she did was because of her history with Malcolm and her involvement with the Ruiz case, and even her knowledge was limited. "You and your mother will both be in good hands with these men until other arrangements can be made."

Oceane stared at her in uncertainty, a worried frown pulling her brows together. "You know Agent Freeman personally?"

"Yes." *At least, I used to.*

The frown didn't ease. "And if you were in my place, you would trust him to guard your mother, and not take us away from each other?"

"I would trust him with my life," she answered without hesitation.

It was true. In Oceane or Anya's shoes, Rowan absolutely would trust him to keep her safe. Malcolm was not only a former SEAL, he was a man of integrity and strength. He was a professional, and highly skilled at what he did. None of that had any bearing on why she'd chosen to end things between them. She'd had her reasons. Solid, practical reasons she didn't want to think about right now.

While Oceane continued to study her, Rowan felt the continued weight of Malcolm's stare pressing on her. Again, she didn't look at him, not willing to risk it because she couldn't bear to see coldness or anger in his eyes.

"And remember, this is only temporary," she added, trying to sell this solution to her skeptical witnesses. "Maybe even as little as a few days until this all gets sorted out." *Until you give us something good on Ruiz and Nieto, or come to your senses and enter*

WITSEC.

Oceane exhaled a ragged breath, cast a worried look at her mother, then gave in with a nod, her shoulders relaxing a little. "All right." She pulled her mother into a fierce, protective hug, murmured something soothing to her in Spanish.

During the lull, Rowan could no longer ignore the force of that magnetic stare locked on her. Steeling herself, she met Malcolm's gaze and the breath stopped in her lungs at the mix of raw emotion burning there. Surprise. Frustration. Maybe even a measure of gratitude.

But he masked it quickly, breaking eye contact as he switched his attention to Anya and raised his eyebrows. "Ready?"

The woman nodded, cast a tearful glance at her daughter, as though afraid it might be the last time she laid eyes on Oceane, and followed Malcolm. Lockhart and Oceane went next, with Taggart on their heels.

Standing alone in the hallway when they disappeared around the corner, Rowan blew out a deep breath and rolled her head from side to side. Now her chest ached as much as her head. Why couldn't she stop the longing Malcolm generated inside her? Why did watching him walk away hurt so damn much when it's exactly what she'd wanted a year ago?

"You are a *magician*," Val said as he stepped up beside her. "Thought for a minute there we were going to have a screaming match. How'd you smooth everything over?"

Rowan shrugged, her sore shoulder muscle screaming in protest. "Just told them the truth."

But not all of it. Because the whole truth was, she missed Malcolm like hell.

Chapter Five

Manny set his cell phone down on the kitchen table and rested his head in his hands, elbows propped up on the polished antique wood surface. Almost a week now since the attack on Oceane and Anya, and no word yet on their location. As far as anyone could tell, they were somewhere in the States. He'd barely slept since, worry and fear eating at him from the inside out.

He knew who the culprit was, however. Ruiz. That fucking bastard.

Manny should have had him killed years ago and taken over his territory, saved everyone in the organization a lot of embarrassment and spared Oceane and Anya suffering. Instead he'd bided his time, playing it safe and living his double life until Ruiz's capture by U.S. officials had made it impossible to sit back any longer.

His cell rang, the familiar ringtone alerting him

that it was his accountant calling. He stared at it for a few seconds, wasn't going to answer at all, but a niggling in his gut made him pick up. "Yes?" He sounded every bit as tired as he felt.

"Is this a bad time?"

"No." He always projected a calm front. It was absolutely necessary for a man of his position in this deadly business. He was surrounded by power hungry men and rivals who would love to do the same to him as he'd done to Ruiz. No matter what, he had to appear to be calm and in control at all times. Make everyone believe he was unshakable. All while letting his enforcers do the dirty work they so enjoyed. "What is it?"

"I've just been alerted by our contact at the international bank. Some of your offshore accounts have been frozen."

"What? By who?"

"The FBI. Just this morning."

Fuck. "The FBI froze my accounts."

"Yes."

He sat up, dragged a hand over his face. They'd been so careful with his finances. Burying them so deep it should have taken years for anyone to trace them back to him. "Which accounts?"

When the man told him, Manny's stomach dropped. The accounts he used for sending money to Anya and Oceane. All three were compromised. "They've been talking to the Americans," he murmured, feeling ill.

"It would appear so. Or…someone's forced the information out of them."

God. "Of course." He stood, paced aimlessly

across the kitchen, not even noticing the beautiful mountain vista out the floor-to-ceiling windows of the house he'd paid a fortune for.

Of course someone must have forced Anya and their daughter to tell them about the money. They would never betray him willingly. They had fled to the States for safety, out of desperation, but instead of finding temporary refuge there, the Americans must have taken them. The thought of them imprisoned in some American prison while investigators interrogated them day and night about him and his activities was more than he could bear.

"What do you want me to do?"

"Create new accounts in Switzerland under a new company and sell whatever shares you need to make up the amount lost. When they return home, they'll need the money."

"All right." The accountant paused. "Are you going to stay in Mexico?"

"For now." Soon he would slip into Panama and wait there until the immediate threat against him was over. But not until Anya and Oceane were returned safely to Mexico. Until then, he had to pretend everything was as it should be. He had to fool *everyone*, not let anyone see him sweat.

"All right. You'll keep me updated?"

"Yes. Call me when you've arranged everything." He ended the call and immediately dialed his lawyer, a man he paid handsomely to be at his beck and call. "The Americans have Anya and Oceane," he began abruptly.

They were deep into conversation about what needed to happen next, to protect him, the women and his assets, when the front door opened into the grand foyer off the kitchen. Glancing over his shoulder, he watched his wife sail through the door, her hands loaded with boutique shopping bags, a pair of designer sunglasses hiding her eyes.

"I have to go," he said to the lawyer. "Call me later when you have more details." He hung up without waiting for a response and put on a smile for Elena as she swept into the kitchen. "Have a nice day?" he asked, taking the bags for her and setting them on the counter.

She seemed happier now, more like her old self. Things had been strained between them recently. Maybe a couple of months. He wasn't sure what he'd done, but she'd been distant and cool to him until maybe a week ago, around the time when this latest crisis had happened.

"I did. You?"

He shrugged, slipping into his acting role as comfortably as if it were a second skin. Over the years, he'd perfected it. "Just some business things I had to deal with."

She stopped, sliding her sunglasses up onto her head to study him with those miss-nothing brown eyes. "Is there trouble?"

He smiled again. "Nothing I can't handle." Elena didn't know about Oceane. She thought that his trips to Veracruz were business-related only, and out of respect for her as his wife, he'd been careful to keep both Oceane and Anya out of her life and never speak about them in her presence.

Elena had been just eighteen when they married, a naïve, uneducated peasant girl from a neighboring village, and he twenty-three. He'd been a nobody back then. A farmer's son with work-roughened hands who did the occasional illegal deal to get ahead. She'd been loyal to him from day one, long before he had power and money. He owed her for that. Would give her anything.

But try as they might, they'd never been able to have a child. And after he'd fathered Oceane, the possibility of adopting a child with Elena hadn't appealed to him in the least, so he'd quashed the idea and they'd made peace with the reality that they would never have children. Elena had let it go as well and now filled her time with travel, volunteer work, and her social circle.

"And that's why I admire you so much," she said, her hips swaying as she walked over and wound her slender arms around his neck with a sigh.

It gave him a measure of relief to know things were back to normal between them again.

Lifting one hand, she trailed the backs of her fingers down the side of his face, still as beautiful as the day he'd married her. "Such a handsome man you are, even with this new addition of silver," she added, stroking the streak of gray at his temple.

He squeezed her waist, leaned in to kiss her gently. "You spoil me with your compliments."

"I only say the truth," she whispered, sliding her fingers into his hair as she deepened the kiss. His cock reacted instantly, his blood heating when she pressed that lush, female body to his. Almost thirty years together, and she could still make his body hum with a single touch.

She pulled away, a sultry smile on her lips. "I

bought you something."

"Did you? What?"

Dropping her hands to her sides, she turned away and went over to dig something out of one of the bags. A small black bag, just big enough to hold something the size of an apple. "It's outside," she said, a smug gleam in her dark eyes as she held the bag out to him.

He raised an eyebrow and took the offering from her. Opening it, he found a key. He grinned when he saw the logo on it. "A Jaguar?" He'd been eyeing a particular model over the last few months, to add to his collection of sports cars.

"Mmm, you'll have to see."

Hooking an arm around her waist, he walked to the front door with her. She paused there a moment, gave him a smile and threw the door wide open. A sleek, silver Jaguar sports car sat parked under the porte-cochere, a huge red bow on the hood.

He couldn't help but chuckle. "It's not even close to my birthday."

"I know." She squeezed him once then gave him a push toward the car. "You've been working so hard recently, I thought you deserved a present."

She thought it had to do with business deals or cartel business, not because his daughter and former mistress had been attacked and he'd been frantically trying to find them. Even with all his money and contacts, he hadn't found them yet.

He gave a sideways nod at the Jag, watching Elena. "You wanna come for its inaugural spin?"

"Already did when I drove it here." Tossing him a grin, she sauntered back toward the front door.

"Have fun."

Manny took the bow off and climbed into the driver's seat, the heady scent of rich, new leather filling his nose. He pressed the start button, and the powerful V12 engine roared to life.

A sense of exhilaration pumped through him as he shot down the long, private driveway. The frustration and uncertainty gnawing at him eased somewhat beneath the flood of adrenaline. But even the thrill of racing down the road in his new Jag couldn't take away the lingering weight of worry in his chest.

Oceane didn't know much about his business, but Anya did. What had she told the Americans? He'd have to start emergency procedures immediately to limit the damage. Liquidate some of his larger holdings, create new shell companies just to be safe, change locations of his most important operations and switch up the people in his organization.

A call came in as he turned onto the main road a mile from his place. He set it on speaker, both hands busy, one on the wheel and the other on the stick shift. "Yes?"

"It's Hector. I...I have bad news."

One of his most trusted business advisers. Manny braced himself. "Tell me."

"Our main lab outside Guadalajara was just destroyed."

Manny gripped the wheel tighter. *God dammit.* The fourth one hit in the past week. "*Federales*?"

"No."

He clenched his jaw. "Ruiz," he growled, rage surging through him. First that bastard had dared to attack Anya and Oceane, force them into running.

Manny would see he went to hell for that alone. But this guerilla turf battle Ruiz continued to wage would not go unanswered, either. Manny would hit back hard, obliterate all remaining traces of Ruiz's organization.

"*Si*. We think so."

"Can any of it be saved?"

"No. It's a write-off."

Hijo de puta. The Guadalajara operation was one of his biggest, taken from Ruiz after he'd been captured. Manny had modernized it, spent a few million giving it extra security and camouflage and hired the leading drug mixers to produce his trademark product—Asian heroin cut with just enough carfentanyl to ensure addiction, but not kill the majority of its users.

Dead users meant fewer customers and less demand for his product. Manny was okay with some risk in his business dealings and didn't mind the body count his drugs racked up as long as he created more addicts than he lost.

Now it was gone, and he'd have to scramble to replace it somewhere new before supply was completely disrupted.

"Call Montoya." His chief enforcer. "He'll deal with it." Ruiz wanted war? Manny would snuff out his pathetic resistance in the most brutal way possible. Brutality was the only language an animal like Ruiz understood. How the hell was that stupid fuck attacking him from the inside of a U.S. prison, anyway? Manny wanted every last one of the bastards still loyal to Ruiz dead. As for Ruiz, it would take time to get to him in a U.S. federal prison. But it could still be done.

"All right."

Manny punched the end button and stomped on the brake and clutch, simultaneously cranking the wheel to the left, swinging the Jag around in a tight 180 that made the tires squeal. He gunned it, heading back to the house. There was a phone number hidden in his office safe there, one he'd never used before. The only contact number he'd been given for *El Escorpion*.

He'd held off on calling it after Oceane and Anya had fled because Manny's position in the cartel was new and a little precarious as he was still proving himself. He'd gone to great lengths to downplay to cartel insiders the seriousness of what had happened, spreading a rumor that Oceane and Anya had merely gone on vacation after the attack.

El Escorpion had a ruthless reputation, though neither Manny nor anyone else in the cartel had actually met the organization's leader. If you embarrassed the cartel in some way or did anything to make him question your loyalty, you and your family were wiped out on orders from *El Escorpion*.

The only exception was Ruiz, who'd been taken alive by the Americans, and now that bastard was a continual thorn in all their sides.

As soon as he got into his office Manny would call that number because things had gone too far. It was time to bring in whatever assets he could to get Oceane and Anya back, then destroy Ruiz's lingering grip on this country.

Today was the beginning of the end of this turf war.

****

Fernando Diaz paused with the bite of huevos rancheros poised halfway to his mouth when the ring of a phone came from down the hallway. The only landline in the entire *hacienda*.

All conversation at the breakfast table ceased instantly, his mother, wife and two young children staring at him expectantly. They all knew what the phone signified, though not all of them knew what it was used for.

Wiping his mouth with a crisply pressed linen napkin, he pushed his chair back and stood. "Excuse me for a moment, darlings."

As usual, his mother's light footsteps sounded behind him on the tile floor as he headed out of the kitchen and down the hall to the locked office at the end. *El Escorpion's* private domain.

The phone continued to ring as he looked into the retinal scanner installed beside the door and pressed his right hand to the keypad so it could read his palm and fingerprints. Seconds later the elaborate electronic locking mechanism flipped open. The door snicked open.

Pushing it aside, he strode for the desk, looked back at his mother as she shut the door and stood watching him. She raised a silvery eyebrow at him. "Are you going to answer that?"

A call at this hour meant bad news. He'd had his fill of that lately with Ruiz and was tired of dealing with infighting bullshit.

He picked up the receiver, hit a button to put the

conversation on speaker so he wouldn't have to relay everything to his mother afterward. She might be in her seventies, but she was still as sharp and nosy as ever. The line was heavily encrypted, the technology updated weekly to avoid hacking attempts by the Mexican and American authorities.

"Yes?" A state of the art program would synthesize his voice so it couldn't be identified by any computer systems. Or so he was assured.

"It's Nieto."

"Manuel. What can I do for you?"

Fernando listened as Nieto described what had happened with his daughter and former mistress. Or current mistress, Fernando never had understood the nuances of their complex relationship.

"It's Ruiz," Nieto said flatly. "Has to be. I don't know how he's doing it, but his network is still active."

Fernando met his mother's stony gaze, noted the telltale set to her jaw that he knew so well. Carlos Ruiz had been a pain in the ass and a proverbial thorn in the cartel's side for too long. Fernando had mistakenly thought that being locked up in an American prison would end the problem. "You have permission to go after what's left of his organization, and the cartel will back you up if necessary."

"Thank you. I truly appreciate your support in this."

Fernando liked Manny. Far preferred him to the likes of Ruiz, and yet *El Escorpion* was far too wise and experienced to fully trust any of the cartel's lieutenants. "You're welcome. But make no mistake, Manuel, the organization will not tolerate any further risks to its operations. Do you understand?"

"I understand."

"Good. Now I've got to get back to my family." He ended the call, set the receiver back into place and looked at his mother again.

Because of Ruiz, the cartel was in far too precarious a position at the moment. Anyone causing more trouble would learn firsthand how *El Escorpion* ruled this empire like an iron fist.

Chapter Six

When another knock came on her office door that evening, Rowan glanced up expecting to find her assistant standing there. Instead her brother grinned at her. "I come bearing sustenance," he said, holding up takeout bags.

"Yay!" She got up, her stiff muscles protesting each movement, and rounded her desk to hug her brother. "It's good to see you. Thanks for bringing me food."

"Welcome. I'll think of a way for you to make it up to me."

"I'm sure you will," she said with a laugh, pushing piles of papers out of the way to clear a corner of her desk.

"Damn, it looks like a war room in here," Kevin said in a sort of horrified fascination, taking in the state of her office.

She huffed out a laugh. "It really does. And as of right now, it seems like the good guys are losing the battle."

"I'm not worried. You'll prevail in the end." He set the bags down on her desk, moved a couple boxes off to make room for them to eat, then eyed her. "You really sore still?"

"I've felt better," she said, dropping back into her chair and reaching for the first bag. The savory, garlicky smell of whatever he'd brought was making her mouth water.

He came around behind her to rub her neck and shoulders. She stopped what she was doing, sagging back and letting out a moan. "Your shoulders are rock hard," he admonished, digging his fingers in while he made gentle circular motions.

"Not surprised," she muttered, closing her eyes. "Oh my God, don't stop. Since when can you give a massage like this, anyway?"

"Just another skill I picked up from Nick. I can now melt away muscular tension *and* build a cabinet with my bare hands."

"I knew I loved him." He and her brother had been dating for seven months now, and just moved in together a few weeks ago. "How's shacked-up life treating you so far? Still amazing?"

"Yep. I've definitely found The One."

The happiness in her brother's voice made her smile. Kevin had dated a few not-so-nice guys before meeting Nick, so she was even happier for him. "I'm glad. He's a sweetie."

"Yeah. And before you take a bite of your dinner, let's get another dose of whatever pain relievers you have down you."

"Good call. It's so handy, having a pharmacist in the family." She took the bottle out of her top drawer and downed two as her brother kneaded the back of her neck. "Believe me, I'm loving this, but can we eat now before I starve to death?"

"To *death*? Ah, we can't have that." He stopped and dug them both plates out of one of the bags. "Let's do this."

Within a minute she had a plate piled high with chicken souvlaki, veggies and tzatziki. "Yum," she mumbled around the first bite.

Kevin's deep blue eyes sparkled with laughter. "You're so easy, Ro. I'll have to make sure the next guy you date knows that one of the quickest ways into your heart is through your stomach."

She made a face and swallowed her bite. "Don't go telling my secrets, now. Not that I have to worry about having anyone for you to tell, since I'm going to be buried alive under paperwork for the foreseeable future."

"Still no one on the radar?"

She broke eye contact and looked down at her food, thinking of Malcolm. "No."

He paused at that and lowered his fork, watching her. "There *is* someone," he said, sounding captivated.

She shook her head, speared another piece of chicken. "No, there's not."

"There totally is," he insisted, and shifted his chair closer. "Who? Come on, tell your little bro." He leaned an elbow on the desk and propped his cheek on his fist, waiting.

Rowan sighed and finished her mouthful, debating whether she should tell him. Her office door was shut. No one could overhear them, and she told her brother everything anyway. "He's not on the radar. Not like that. Well, he kind of…reappeared on it all of a sudden, and it feels like our paths keep crossing lately." She couldn't help but think there must be a reason for that.

"Interesting. Who is it?"

She hesitated only a moment before answering. "Malcolm."

Her brother's eyes widened. "What?"

"I know. He's involved with the case I'm currently working on. We've seen each other a couple of times recently, but always for business. Except for yesterday after the accident."

"He was there?"

"He all but ripped my door off its hinges to make sure I was okay."

"Aww," he said, sitting up to put a hand to his heart. "And then what?"

"And then he left for a meeting here, and has done his best to ignore me ever since."

Kevin narrowed his eyes. "But you still have feelings for him."

She cleared her throat, pushed a piece of carrot around her plate. "I thought they would go away, but I guess not."

"You should know better than that." He folded his arms across his chest, cocking his head a little, his expression almost disappointed.

Yes, I should. It wasn't easy to admit she'd made a mistake. Even though she'd cared about Malcolm a lot, she could see it wasn't going to work out in the long run. Their jobs made it impossible, for one, and she figured the sensible thing was to make a clean break early on, before he got hurt.

Instead, they'd both gotten hurt. And her reasons, the ones that had seemed so definite and important at the time, seemed flimsy now. Sometimes hindsight sucked.

She frowned. "It's my own fault. I was the one who ended it." She'd been on her way to losing her heart. Ever practical, having seen the signs early on, she'd ended it with as clean a cut as she could manage.

"Yeah, and how'd that work out for you?"

A heavy pressure began to build beneath her breastbone. "I'm fine. I knew it was for the best, so I made the call and dealt with it."

"But you just said the feelings never went away."

There was no point in trying to put on the tough act in front of Kevin. He was the only person on earth she trusted with her deepest secrets. Her shoulders slumped. "All right. They're still there. And seeing him again makes me..." She tried to find the right word.

"Ache?" her brother suggested.

She met his eyes, a dark blue like hers. "Yes." She pushed out a deep breath. "I made a huge mistake when I broke up with him."

Kevin studied her for a moment. "Was it because of that jackass you shacked up with before him?"

"Partly." Her relationship with her asshole ex served as a cautionary tale for ever getting involved with another alpha male again. Malcolm had wound up an unwitting casualty of that decision. "Malcolm and I are both driven, and we both work too much. But we're also so different."

"So are Nick and I, and I've never been happier. I saw the sparks flying between you and Mal the night I introduced you at the gala, and anyone with eyes could see the connection there. I haven't talked to him since a couple weeks after you guys broke up, but—"

"Wait, you talked to him afterward? You never told me."

Kevin blinked at her. "Yeah, I called him up to see how he was doing."

"And how was he?"

"Why do you care about that now?" he challenged, raising an eyebrow. "I thought you decided you did the right thing by walking away."

She threw him a mock scowl. "Jerk."

He grinned, ripped off a piece of pita bread and stuffed it into his mouth. "He was hurt, Ro. He didn't come out and tell me that, of course, but I knew. And you must have too."

Somehow it was worse hearing it from someone else. "Yeah, okay, I knew. It didn't make sense to me at the time, though. We'd only been seeing each other such a short time. Hadn't even slept together." How could Malcolm have felt so strongly about her when they hadn't been intimate that way? She didn't understand that.

"Maybe not, but he was into you big time."

I was into him big time too. "He's pretty cold to me now. Strictly business, except for after the accident." He'd seemed so concerned then, and that hug, brief as it was, had been amazing. Didn't it show that he still cared about her on some level? God, she was so confused now.

"Male egos are fragile things, Ro. And when it's an alpha male we're talking about?" Kevin let out a low whistle and shook his head, then regarded her with a soft expression. "Look. I know how it is for you. How important your professional reputation is to you. How tough Dad has always been on you, and how hard you've had to push yourself your whole life to meet his standards and get here."

"He was hard on you too, and you've managed to overcome it."

"He and I have had other issues. But now I have Nick, so it doesn't matter."

Rowan envied his outlook. Would it be like that for her if she had Malcolm to have her back? Maybe. Though the idea of asking him whether he was open to get back together now seemed ludicrous. Because he was well within his rights to either laugh in her face or tell her off. And seriously, how embarrassing was it for someone else to know how desperate she was for her father's approval at this age?

"Just because I miss Malcolm and have unresolved feelings for him doesn't mean he feels the same way. I can't talk to him about it. I wish I could, but I can't." It was too terrifying, the thought of putting herself out there after she'd hurt him. Malcolm might lash out at her, wanting to hurt her as she'd hurt him. To get even. At least, that's what all her other exes would do.

"Okay," Kevin said with a shrug, and reached for another piece of bread. "It's your life. Do what you want."

Rowan sighed and aimed another mock glare at him. "I hate it when you do that."

His eyes twinkled. "What, give you some tough love and not care what other people think of me? Benefit of being in touch with my feelings. Took a long time to get here, but oh, so worth it."

Her little brother was brave, she thought in admiration. Much braver than her. How was that for a revelation? "I hate that you're better than me at relationships."

"And I love that I'm legit better at something than you, overachiever." His expression sobered. "And you do realize that work won't ever love you back, right?"

God, he was so right. "Can we change the subject now?" she asked, unprepared to deal with the emotional downer he'd just dropped on her. There was too much on her mind.

"Sure. What do you want to talk about?"

"Anything but my lack of a personal life, or Dad." The main driving force for her entire life, and not always for the better.

"Okay. Then how about I tell you about the idea I have for when I pop the question."

She gasped, lowered her fork to the desk. "You're going to propose?"

A small crease formed in his cheek as he grinned. "Labor Day long weekend. I've got it all planned out."

Rowan pressed her lips together as a rush of tears stung her eyes.

Kevin chuckled. "Come on, don't cry."

She shook her head. "I won't. It's just I'm so proud of you and happy for you." Her voice was all choked up. He was the best brother and friend anyone could ask for. "Nick's so lucky."

"That's true," he joked. "I tell him so all the time."

They finished dinner and talked about his plans to propose at an oceanfront resort down near Hilton Head. Their father was gonna freak when he heard the news, but Rowan had a feeling he would come around soon enough, once the initial shock wore off. Kevin could handle it, though, and he had the full support of her and their mom in addition to Nick and his family.

After eating, Kevin helped her tidy up and took the bags. "Oh, almost forgot," he said, pausing to pull a set of keys out of his pocket. "Surprise."

No way. "You picked up my car?"

"Yep. Nick dropped me at the garage. I'll take your rental back for you, too, so you can get some extra sleep tomorrow morning."

"God, you're the best." She threw her arms around him and gave him a big squeeze.

"Also true." He hugged her and traded keys.

"It's parked out front in my usual spot."

"Okay. Hey, it's even got a remote starter on it. How come the rental cars I get never have remote starters?"

"Because you're cheap."

"Frugal," he corrected on his way to the door. Once there, he stopped to glance back at her with a searching look. "Sis? There are no do-overs. We have to make every minute of this life count."

"Yeah, I know." His words were going to haunt

her. It seemed that while she'd been chasing down her goal of becoming a lawyer and being hired as an Assistant U.S. Attorney, she'd stopped living somewhere along the way.

Facing the mess on her desk after her brother left and shut the door behind him, that truth hit home harder than ever. A sinking feeling took hold in her gut and it was impossible to shake it off.

No, Rowan. You deliberately chose this. Just like you chose to walk away from what you might have had with Malcolm.

Regret settled heavy in her stomach, a hard lump she could no longer ignore. Yup, she'd made a big mistake with him. The question was, did she have the guts to try and fix it?

At least the food and pain relievers had made her feel better physically. Ready to put in another few hours, she sat at her desk and opened the file she'd been working on before Kevin showed up.

A loud boom from outside ripped through the quiet and shook the room, making her jolt.

"What the hell?" Heart hammering, she spun around in her chair to look out the window. What she saw made her heart lurch into her throat.

Down in the parking lot out front of the building, her rental car was on fire. And Kevin was lying crumpled on the sidewalk nearby it.

"Kevin, *no!*" Guilt and apprehension all but choked her. She shot to her feet, grabbing her cell phone to dial 911 as she raced for the door.

Chapter Seven

"Malcolm," Pops said on the other end of the phone, a warm smile in his deep voice. "Good to hear your voice, son. Wait, it's Tuesday. You got the day off?"

"No, I'm on a special assignment right now for my commander, but I had some downtime and thought I'd call home to check on you guys." He leaned against the safehouse condo kitchen counter, gazing out at the city view beyond the living room window. Lockhart was down in the lobby checking with the building's security team, and Oceane and Anya were settling into the bedrooms.

"Gram and I are both fine. What assignment are you on?"

"Protective detail," was all he said, because he couldn't say more.

"So you're bored to tears then, and decided to call to kill some time."

Mal grinned at Pops's dry humor. "At least I called." He and Lockhart were basically glorified babysitters for Oceane and her mother in this high-security condo not far from the capital. Out the eleventh-floor window on the east side of the unit, Mal could see the distinctive white dome of the capital building in the distance.

"True, and we'll take what we can get. When are you coming home for a visit next?"

Always the same question. "Hopefully a short one at the end of summer. Might be a bit later than that, before we deploy to Afghanistan this fall."

Pops grunted. "They keep you busy down there, that's for certain."

"They sure do." Except right now this assignment was making him nuts. It gave him way too much time to sit around and think about things he ought not to. Meaning, Rowan. "How's your blood pressure been lately?"

"Good."

"Pops. How is it?"

"It's fine," Pops growled in annoyance. "Gram makes me check it three times a day. She knows way more about all my bodily functions than any wife ever should."

"Because she loves you and wants to keep you around as long as possible."

Another grunt. "You know, before I met her I asked God for a strong, loving woman. And lord have mercy, that woman is *strong*."

Mal laughed. "She had to be, to hold her own with you." His grandparents were both strict but fair, and they'd provided Mal with a stable, loving home after losing his mother.

Pops was the disciplinarian. Mal had been expected to keep a tight routine while he lived with them, with bible reading in the morning before breakfast, grace before every meal, bible study after dinner, and prayers every night before bedtime. Church every Sunday without fail, staying to help with Sunday school and to serve and clean up the parish luncheon.

He'd hated Sundays with a passion back then, but in hindsight those community hours and scripture had helped forge the core of the man he was today. Pops had been the one to drive Mal with his schoolwork. He demanded respect and integrity, but he'd also given it back in return.

He'd also been the one to encourage Mal to join the military after high school, find a purpose and an outlet for the youthful energy and anger still burning inside him after his mother died so young. Without Pops there to push and guide him, Mal's life might have turned out very differently.

"Just goes to show you, son. When you ask God for something, be careful what you wish for."

"That's a good point, Pops."

"Another pearl of wisdom I'm passing on to you while I'm still here and have all my mental faculties."

"You don't have all your mental faculties," Gram called out somewhere in the background. "You haven't had them all for years."

"When I said strong, I didn't mean in the form of a sharp tongue," Pops complained to Mal.

The familiar banter between them, the bond that had been forged by nearly fifty years of marriage, set off a twinge in Mal's chest. They were both in their eighties now. He could lose them at any time, and even though he was a grown man with his own life hundreds of miles away from them, he wasn't ready to lose either of them. They were all the family he had, aside from his teammates.

"How is everybody on your team?" Pops asked.

"Great. Busy." FAST Bravo kept a breakneck pace in training and operational tempo. They had to, to remain sharp and ready to deploy at a moment's notice.

Sometimes the constant grind wore on him, although it wasn't much different from when he'd been in the SEAL Teams. Their mission profile was different now but the skill sets were mostly the same, and they operated in maritime conditions often. "Well, actually, one of our guys had to fly home yesterday to see his mom. She's got advanced MS and he doesn't know how much longer she has."

"I'm sorry to hear that. Gram and I will say a prayer for her."

"He'd appreciate that." He paused. "It got me thinking about how short our time on earth is."

"The lord has a plan for us all. He calls us home in his own time."

"Yeah." Pops's unshakable faith was one of the things Mal most admired about him. He even envied it a little. A faith that strong would have been a comfort to have in those long, horrible and lonely months after his mother passed away. Though he'd done his prayers and bible study and gone to church, he'd never believed in the same way Pops and Gram did. "Can I talk to Gram for a bit?"

"Sure. Hang on."

Gram came on the line and instantly demanded whether he was eating right, taking care of himself, and whether or not he was seeing a nice girl yet. "I'm not getting any younger, Malcolm. I'd like to see my great-grandbabies before I die."

"I'll get right on that, Gram," he said in a wry voice, but of course it made him think of Rowan. So far she was the only woman who he could see himself marrying and having a family with one day. So babies weren't even on the distant horizon for him now.

"Only after you find a good woman and enter the holy state of matrimony, young man. If you ever got a woman pregnant outside of wedlock I'd make you sorry you were ever born."

The threat made him smile, because he understood she was completely serious. There had been a time when that kind of threat made him roll his eyes and think his grandparents were uptight, religious zealots. There had been a time when he couldn't wait to be of age so he could move away and have the freedom he craved. Now he missed them like hell and wished he got to see them more often.

Funny how life worked sometimes. It didn't matter that he was thirty-four years old. He was her baby and always would be. "Yes, ma'am."

His phone beeped with an incoming call. Seeing it was his commander, he ended the conversation with Gram. "Sorry, I have to take this. As soon as my schedule clears up a bit, I'll see when I can come up for a visit."

"We'd love that. You take care, now. Love you."

"Love you too." He ended the call and picked up

Taggart's. "Sir."

"Freeman. I just got a call from the U.S. Attorney's office."

Mal's attention sharpened at Taggart's grim tone and he turned away from the window. "And?"

"There was an explosion outside the building about half an hour ago. They think it was a car bomb."

His stomach grabbed. "Anyone hurt?"

"Yes. Rowan Stewart's brother."

Shit. "What happened?"

"He'd dropped in to visit her and was about to return her rental car for her. He was fifty feet from it when it detonated."

Jesus Christ. "Is he alive?"

"As far as I know. They were transporting him to the hospital when I got the call."

God, Rowan would be frantic. And if someone had planted explosives in her vehicle, then she had been the intended target.

A shockwave of protectiveness blasted through him. "They have security on scene yet?" He needed to know she was safe.

"Yep, everything's locked down."

"What about Rowan?"

"She's at the hospital now with her parents."

"Have they got security there for her?"

"Not sure."

Mal didn't like it. Despite their breakup, he would never leave her vulnerable to a threat if he could help it. "Her brother's a friend of mine. I'd like to check on things personally." Well, more of an acquaintance now, but he needed a reason other than Rowan to go to the hospital.

"Why don't you put in a call to Hamilton, then. See if he'll cover for you with Lockhart while you go to the hospital."

"I will. Thanks." He ended the call and immediately dialed his team leader, impatience humming through his veins. He needed to get to the hospital right the hell now, see Rowan for himself and make sure she was safe.

****

SA Brock Hamilton spotted Victoria the moment he stepped through the door of the secure, private government gun range.

He had the entire day off, a rarity, and the first he'd had in a damn long time. He'd been looking forward to it for more than a week, planning to spend it parked in front of his TV with a few cold ones, and maybe even take a nap later on. Precious few things could have persuaded him to give that up, but then her text had come in this morning and he couldn't say no.

Because it was Victoria and he couldn't get her out of his mind.

She stood over in the far corner, back to the wall, constantly scanning the room. Assessing everyone in it to discern whether or not they were a threat, even with her U.S. Marshal security detail close by.

The two marshals spotted him first. He knew them, from the night they'd come to escort Victoria from the hospital to the WITSEC Safesite and Orientation Center.

Brock gave them a chin nod by way of greeting, then Victoria's restless gaze connected with his from across the room, and warmth spread through him at the relief that flashed in her deep brown eyes.

The corner of her mouth lifted a fraction, on the verge of a smile. The first hint of one he'd seen since finding her in the woods that night months ago, when he and his team had stormed one of Ruiz's hideouts down on the Gulf Coast. She'd been naked, beaten and bloody with a fucking collar and chain hanging from her neck, running for her life. He'd never forget that first sight of her as long as he lived. It had haunted him ever since.

Her happiness to see him surprised him almost as much as the text she'd sent him a few hours ago, asking him to meet her here. And damned if knowing the sight of him made her feel safe and at ease didn't compress something inside his chest.

He smiled back and closed the distance between them, careful not to move too fast. She looked like a completely different person now.

Her long, tangled brown hair was now cut into a sleek, jaw-length bob. She'd put some weight on since the last time he'd seen her. It looked good on her. Her body still too slender for her frame, but at least now she didn't seem half-starved, the hollows beneath her cheekbones less pronounced.

His eyes stopped on the light blue scarf wrapped around her throat. Since it was summertime and hot as hell outside, it wasn't a fashion statement. She'd worn it to cover up the scars around her throat from where that sickening metal collar had bitten into her tender skin. He'd seen the damage firsthand and watched the medical staff clean and dress her wounds. The bruises and cuts on her face had healed, the shadows under her eyes faded. But the shadows *within* them were still there, and might never disappear.

Brock stopped a foot or two farther away from her than he would someone else, so that she wouldn't feel crowded. "Hi."

Her lips curved up a little more. She was tall, around five-eleven or so, only a few inches shorter than him. He liked the way she looked him in the eye. "Hi. Thanks for meeting me."

"No problem."

She gestured to the marshals, who were standing a discreet distance away to grant them a semblance of privacy. "They only allowed this because I asked you to come. Apparently the powers that be really think a lot of you."

"Well that's good to know." He was proud of the reputation he'd built, both back during his SF days, and as a FAST operator. With a half-smile at her he cocked his head, intrigued. "So, what are we doing here?" She'd been mysterious about that. Meeting her at a shooting range wasn't something he'd ever thought would happen.

"I want you to teach me to shoot," she said, folding her arms and shifting her feet apart slightly.

Brock hid his surprise. "Yeah?" Why him?

She gave a decisive nod. "If you're willing."

Oh, she might be surprised to learn that he was willing to do a lot where she was concerned. "I might be. Depends on why you want to learn, though."

She broke eye contact, looking to the left at a

group of FBI agents Brock knew checking in at the counter. "You know why."

He thought he did, but that wasn't good enough. "I want to hear it from you," he added softly.

In the weeks following her rescue he'd become a bit of an expert on Victoria Gomez, reading everything he could find about her. Her investigative columns and articles in various newspapers and magazines. The two books she'd published on Mexican drug cartels, including one on the early days of the *Venenos*. The events leading up to the attack that had made her their prisoner.

He knew every detail about how she'd been taken, from various reports. Her entire extended family had been gunned down in front of her at the dinner table at her parents' place in Houston. Ruiz's men, acting on his orders as punishment for the article she had published and the book she was working on about him. They'd taken her to a hideout at a rural property on the Gulf Coast of Mississippi and subjected her to weeks of degradation and suffering that still twisted his guts to think about.

Now those deep brown eyes shifted back to his and held, the memory of that night an unspoken link passing between them. And the flash of fire he caught in her eyes gave him hope. Hope that she was stronger than what she'd endured. Strong enough to bury the assholes on the witness stand who'd done this to her, and then build a new life for herself. A safe, secure life somewhere new.

"I want to know how to protect myself properly. Because I never want to be a victim again," she told him.

Damn right, sweetheart. What she'd been through still kept him awake some nights.

Until her, Brock had never been affected like this by a mission. Maybe because for him, it was personal with Victoria.

He'd been the one to carry her out of the woods the night she'd fled her captors. He'd held her wrapped up in a blanket in the back of that van until the ambulance came. She'd been terrified, in shock and in pain. She'd clung to his hand on the ride to the hospital, and he'd stayed at her side until the medical staff had sent him from the room.

And when they'd finished treating her injuries and completed all the tests, he'd kept vigil at her bedside through the night, because she'd asked him to stay. It was possible she didn't even remember that, because they'd sedated her, but she had. Even though they were almost total strangers, on some level she must have instinctively trusted him to watch over her while she slept, even in a drug-induced haze.

Even if she did remember it, she had no idea how deep she'd gotten under his skin that night. No one did.

He forced his mind back to the present. "Okay. I'll teach you."

The fire faded from her eyes, replaced by gratitude. "Thank you."

"Of course." He paused a beat, keeping his eyes on her even though he wanted to catalogue every feature on her face. "You want your first lesson right now?"

"I was hoping for that, yes."

Spending his precious day off teaching her to

shoot so that she could regain some sense of safety and control sounded like the best thing that had happened to him in forever. "What kind of weapon are you thinking?"

"A pistol. Maybe a rifle too, but not until later. I want to see if I can get comfortable with a firearm first."

A lot of people who'd been victims of gun violence were afraid of them. Seeing your entire family slaughtered in front of you was something else altogether. He admired her courage for wanting to face this, take this step toward conquering her demons. And he loved that he'd been the one she had reached out to. "All right." He gestured to the registration desk. "After you."

He knew the clerk at the desk. Filling out the paperwork took only a matter of minutes. After grabbing a Glock, ammo and protective equipment for them, he led her through the door onto the sound-safe viewing area. She stayed close to him, stood to his left as he stopped where she could get a good view of one of the Feds shooting a paper target at the end of the lane.

"You'll need these," he said, handing her earplugs, earmuffs and protective glasses.

"Thanks."

He didn't miss the nervous way she kept darting glances at the Glock. "It's not loaded. Ammo doesn't go in until we're in position and ready to fire." He pulled back the slide to show her that the chamber was empty, then released the magazine to show her it was too.

She nodded and relaxed a little. "Okay."

He held it out to her. "Here."

She hesitated, glanced up at him a second, then gingerly took it, holding the pistol away from her body as if it was a coiled rattlesnake.

"Like this," he murmured, and maneuvered her palm and fingers into position around the grip. "Always keep the muzzle pointed downward and away from everything you don't want to shoot at, even when it's not loaded."

She nodded and studied the weapon. He explained all the parts, and what they did. Then he had her watch the fed shoot for a few minutes, pointing out his technique, giving her some tips.

"Ready to give it a whirl?" he asked.

Expression solemn, she nodded. "Ready."

Once they got their ear and eye protection on, he led her through to the range, to the last lane at the end, figuring a little privacy would make her more comfortable. He showed her how to load the magazine, slide it into position, then got her into a proper stance. She glanced at him over her shoulder, uncertain.

"I'll guide you through everything until you get the hang of it."

"Good. Thanks."

Moving in to stand mere inches behind her felt strangely intimate. He did it slowly, giving her time to adjust to having him in her personal space, in a position that had to make her feel vulnerable after what she'd suffered. He wanted to help her past that.

Reaching around her body to place his hands on hers in a gentle but firm grip, he guided her arms into position and adjusted her aim.

She stood rigidly before him, arms outstretched. As if her body and mind rebelled at having a big, powerful man so close, and in a position where she couldn't see him.

Brock didn't move, letting the tension slowly bleed out of her muscles. The fruity scent of her shampoo teased him, his awareness of her so acute that he could track each steadying breath she took, could see the elevated pulse throbbing in her neck. "Okay?"

She nodded, squared her shoulders, her attention on the target at the end of the lane.

"Fire one shot when ready."

She squeezed the trigger, jolted a little as the Glock kicked in her grip. Brock steadied her hands, helping absorb the recoil and preventing her arms from jerking upward. The round hit the extreme right edge of the target, missing the outline of the person's head and torso completely.

"Adjust your aim a little down and to the left, lock your wrists." He eased her hands into place and re-laxed his grip, cradling her hands this time rather than controlling them now that she knew what to expect. "Again. Fire when ready."

She squeezed the trigger. This time the bullet hit the target in the lower left abdomen.

"Good. Try again." He eased his grip even more.

Victoria adjusted her stance and aim and method-ically emptied the mag one shot at a time, the final few rounds hitting the target center mass in a ten-inch grouping. Brock counted out each shot, moving away from her little by little even as he wanted to stay close.

When the slide locked open on the final shot she stopped, lowered the weapon and turned her head to look over her shoulder at him. "How was that?"

Damn, that sparkle in her eyes was pretty. "That was pretty damn impressive for your first time."

The smile she flashed him squeezed his insides. "Can I do it again?"

If it meant putting another one of those smiles on her face, and him getting to be the recipient of it? "Absolutely. Release the mag, then you load it this time."

He supervised while she loaded in the bullets and slid the mag home. Once he set up a new target for her he stepped back against the wall and folded his arms to watch, part of him feeling guilty as hell for the way his gaze roamed over her body while her back was to him, taking in the long, lean lines of her.

Victoria faced the new target, aimed, and methodically emptied the mag, ending with another grouping center mass, tighter than the first. Lowering the empty weapon, she turned to face him, pulling off her eye protection as she gave him another smile she couldn't possibly know affected him so much. "That felt good."

He grinned, completely charmed and a hell of a lot more interested than he had any right to be. "It looked good." Almost as good as she did.

She broke eye contact, her cheeks flushing but the hint of a smile still in place. "I think I'm done for the day."

"You sure?"

She met his gaze once more. "Yes. I got what I needed." The look in her eyes told him she meant more than the opportunity to fire a weapon. "Thank you."

"Then I'm glad. And you're welcome." He took the empty weapon from her when she held it out, got the door for her as they stepped back into the observation area.

"Would you be up for doing this again sometime?" she asked, stopping near the bank of long, wide windows along the inner wall.

"Absolutely."

"Not sure I'm ready for a rifle yet."

The weapon Ruiz's men had murdered her family with. No surprise she wasn't up for firing one yet. "That's okay. Whatever you're comfortable with."

She watched him with those dark, shadowed eyes for a long moment, a subtle but unmistakable tension winding between them. A bone-deep, elemental awareness of each other that made him go still and his heart pound.

His cell phone went off, shattering the fleeting intimacy.

Cursing silently, he pulled it from his pocket and checked the display, prepared to ignore it. But it was his team point man, so he answered, ninety percent of his attention still on Victoria. "Freeman. What's up, my man?"

"You busy?"

Yes. "No, why?"

"Where are you right now?"

He met Victoria's curious gaze. "I'm at the range."

"I need a favor."

Brock blinked in surprise. Freeman never asked

anyone for anything, and wouldn't unless it was important. "Name it."

Freeman released a breath. "Just got a call from Taggart. Someone planted a bomb in Rowan's rental car in her office parking lot. Her brother was critically injured when it went off."

That drew Brock's attention off Victoria completely. "Oh, shit." Freeman was friends with the brother, and if Brock wasn't way off base, something had been going on with him and Rowan a while back, too. Freeman would want to go to the hospital, but he was currently stuck acting as temporary security detail for Nieto's mistress. "You need me to come take over for you there?"

"I would appreciate it."

"Done. Text me the address and I'll be there within the hour."

"Thanks, man."

"No worries. I'll call you from the road."

"Sounds good."

Brock ended the call and put his phone back into his pocket. Victoria watched him, her keen intelligence clear in those velvet-brown eyes. She catalogued everything, analyzing and drawing conclusions as naturally as breathing. It was easy to see why she'd been such a force to be reckoned with in the investigative journalism world. "One of my teammates. Rowan Stewart's brother was just injured in an explosion at her office." He only told her because she knew both Rowan and Freeman.

Victoria gasped. "Oh no, is he going to be okay?"

"Not sure. Sorry, but I've gotta go."

"Yes, of course." She stepped out of the way,

clearing a path for him to the door.

His phone dinged in his pocket, no doubt Freeman giving him the address where he needed to go. Ignoring it for the moment, Brock stopped in front of Victoria, unwilling to leave without a real goodbye.

An overwhelming need to touch her pulsed through him. To forge their connection in a physical way. He held out his hand. "Good job today."

The corner of her mouth twitched in amusement. "Thanks. You're a good teacher." She slid her hand into his, the skin of her fingers and palm cool and silky against his own. And she held his gaze, showing him another glimmer of that steely inner strength he'd witness the night of her rescue, and acknowledging their connection.

Whatever it was, she felt it too.

Brock squeezed gently then made himself let go. He'd never enjoyed a shooting instruction session more.

Damn, he hated to leave her so soon, wished he could have invented a reason to spend more time with her, get to know her more in a relaxed setting, just the two of them. Dinner, maybe. Or even a walk somewhere she'd be safe. "Text me whenever you want to do this again. If I'm in town, I'll make time to see you."

Searching his eyes, she nodded. "I'm definitely going to take you up on that."

I sure hope so. A smile curved his mouth. "Good." He couldn't remember ever being this absorbed in a woman. After today, it would be impossible to stop thinking about her.

He hurried for the door, aware with every step of

the way her eyes followed him...
And that he liked it. A lot.

Chapter Eight

———◇◇◇◇◇———

Rowan sat next to Kevin's hospital bed, holding his limp hand. On the opposite side sat Nick, Kevin's soon-to-be fiancé, though he didn't know it yet.

Staring down into her brother's swollen, battered face, she pressed her lips together and prayed he'd get the chance to live his happily ever after.

"He's gonna be okay," Nick said to her quietly, stroking his thumb over the back of Kevin's other hand. "The doctors had to sedate him to help him heal, that's all."

She nodded, not trusting her voice. The shock-wave from the blast had ruptured Kevin's eardrums and spleen. A surgeon had removed it and stopped the internal bleeding that had almost cost Kevin his life. He'd been conscious when they'd put him on the operating table, and all brain scans showed no sign of permanent injury, merely a concussion.

Beneath his closed lids his eyes were swollen out like golf balls, a hideous, almost neon purple. They wouldn't know about his vision until the medical staff reduced his meds and he regained full consciousness. Hopefully sometime tomorrow.

"You should take a break. Go get some coffee or something," Nick said.

"No." She was still full from the dinner Kevin had brought her. The thought of forcing anything else down her throat made her stomach gurgle. "I can't leave him." Her parents were outside the room talking to the doctors. They'd met her here within minutes of Kevin arriving in the ER.

Nick reached across Kevin's legs to cover her hand, bringing her gaze to his. His deep brown eyes were bloodshot, but full of understanding and kindness. "You didn't do this to him, Rowan. It's not your fault."

Her breath hitched on a strangled sob. "Yes it is," she whispered, her throat so tight she could barely get the words out.

"No. Honey, no."

She nodded stubbornly, refusing to let him try and assuage her guilt. "It should have been me." It would have been her, whenever she'd finally finished up for the night and gone down to her rental car.

God, who had planted the bomb? Logic dictated that it must be connected to the Ruiz case. But how would he pull something like this off from behind bars? Unless it was someone else from the *Veneno* cartel trying to send a message. Nieto maybe?

Investigators were working on it now. It scared her to death to know someone had tried to kill her, but seeing her brother lying so still and fragile in her place was far worse. Whoever had targeted her had clearly intended for her to die tonight. And they hadn't cared who else was caught up in the blast. Another clue. The sophistication of the operation, the method and the nonchalance about collateral damage bore all the hallmarks of the *Venenos*.

Nick squeezed her hand, his brows drawing together in a fierce frown. "Hey. Listen to me. It's no one's fault but the sickos who planted the bomb. The FBI will find out who soon enough. And when Kevin wakes up, he'll want to know you're safe."

She'd been holding it together really well given the circumstances, but at that her eyes filled. She blinked fast, staring down at her brother once more, impatiently swiped away the tears that fell. Nick was right. That was so Kevin. To wake up like this in the hospital after having major surgery, find out what happened and immediately worry for her safety, rather than his own.

Nick gave her fingers one more squeeze and released her, sitting back in his chair. "Kevin's going to be okay. And he won't be alone. I'm not budging from this bed until he wakes up."

She gave him a tremulous smile. "Not sure if I ever told you this, but I really love you, you know."

His answering smile was warm but tired. "Thanks. I love you too. I always wanted a sister. My brothers are total pains in the ass," he said fondly.

The door to the private room opened and her father appeared, his face drawn. "Rowan. There's someone from the DEA here to see you. Says he's a friend of Kevin's."

"Who is it?"

"Special Agent Freeman."

Surprise flashed through her, but Nick spoke first, sounding surprised. "Malcolm's here?" Nick had been there the night Kevin had introduced her to Malcolm.

Her father gestured down the hall. "He's out in the waiting room. Wanted to speak to Rowan privately."

She glanced at Nick in indecision. She wanted to see Malcolm so badly, but hated to leave her brother.

"It's okay, go," he told her. "We're not going anywhere."

"I won't be long." She let go of Kevin's hand, fought the stab of guilt that pierced her chest and stood. Her leg and back muscles were stiff from sitting hunched over for so long, and the headache was a dull pounding in her temples.

Ignoring her father's questioning look, she turned sideways to pass him in the doorway and headed down the hall toward the waiting area. Her mother was at the nurse's station asking more questions. Rowan nodded at her on the way by and quickly looked away, not wanting to invite conversation or field any questions at the moment. She wanted to find out why Malcolm was here.

The door at the end of the hall loomed larger and larger as she approached, her high heels clicking on the scuffed linoleum floor. If he was cold and distant to her right now she wasn't sure she could handle it. Not after this.

Taking a deep breath to collect herself, she braced for the moment when she saw Malcolm. Then she pushed the door open, the tattered remnants of her emotional armor gathered securely around her to protect her aching heart.

MALCOLM STOOD FROM his chair when Rowan entered the empty room at the far end of the intensive care unit. She stopped just inside the doorway, her posture stiff, her face pale. There was blood smeared on the front of her top and her knees were scraped, the dried blood visible just beneath the hem of her pencil skirt. She'd obviously come straight here from the scene and hadn't had time to change.

"Hi," she said quietly, her expression guarded.

He suppressed the snap of irritation that look caused. Now was not the time to wonder why she would feel wary around him. "Hey. I heard what happened and came as soon as I could."

She nodded, her eyes a little puffy and red. "It's fine. Thanks for coming."

The inane, overly-polite conversation was like barbed wire scraping over his skin. They were like two polite strangers facing each other. "Is he all right?"

"No. He just came out of surgery a little while ago. They took his spleen, fixed other internal bleeding. His blood pressure's low now, but it's stable. As far as brain injury, they think he'll be okay. Not sure yet about his vision."

Mal hid a wince. "I'm so sorry."

She exhaled and lowered her gaze to the floor. "Thanks."

"Is there anything I can do?" *Besides hug you.* God, she looked like she needed one, and he ached to wrap his arms around her, even if he never could again. Hugging her after the car accident yesterday had been pure reflex. He hadn't been thinking, had just been so relieved to see she was okay. A mistake.

A shiny lock of ebony hair brushed against her cheek as she shook her head. "No. But I appreciate you coming down here. It would mean a lot to Kevin, knowing you're here."

But what about you? He bit back the words before they could burst out of his mouth. They were done. He needed to accept it on every level and drop it.

The pause lengthened, filling the space between them with a brittle silence as they stood facing each other. Mal tried to think of something comforting to say. As hurt as he was, as indifferent as he wanted to appear to her, he still cared and hated to see her torn up like this. Hated even more that someone had targeted her in the first place.

His blood pressure had dropped fifty points when Taggart had told him about the explosion. It was shitty enough that Kevin had been so badly injured. But when Mal thought of Rowan being in her brother's place right now, when he imagined her walking out of the building juggling her briefcase and files and pulling out her keys to unlock her rental car...

The thought of losing her for good was incomprehensible. Okay, she wasn't his and never would be again, but the idea of her life being snuffed out in an instant and that precious light extinguished from the world forever just ripped him up inside.

"What happened?" he asked finally when he couldn't think of anything else safe to say.

Those deep blue eyes lifted to his. "He stopped by

my office with dinner. You know Kev, always taking care of people, and he knows how I get when I'm working on a big case like this."

Yeah, she went into pure workaholic mode. She didn't eat, barely slept. He'd seen that once firsthand during their too-short time together, when he'd come by her place after work and found her buried in papers.

Part of him admired her single-minded determination and work ethic. He understood what it meant to be driven. He totally got what it took to reach a life-long goal.

But there was something inside her driving her to those extremes that he didn't understand. Almost as if she pushed herself to the brink of her endurance because she was afraid of what might happen if she didn't. Like she still felt she had something to prove—whether to herself or someone else, he wasn't sure. He suspected it had to do with her father, but she hadn't kept Mal around long enough for him to find out.

"I'd left my car at the shop to get fixed yesterday. Kev picked it up for me on the way over as a surprise, then was going to return my rental for me when he left. He..." She faltered, swallowed and glanced away before continuing. "He hit the remote start button on the key fob when he got outside. It exploded." She drew in a steadying breath, still avoiding eye contact. "If he'd been in the car when he started it, he would have—" Her voice shredded, igniting a primal, frantic need inside him to comfort her. Make it stop hurting.

She pressed her lips together in a clear effort to

keep from crying and wrapped her arms around her middle, and Mal's resolve crumbled. He could no more keep his distance from her at that moment than he could quit breathing.

Without a word he erased the space between them and gathered her into his arms. She was stiff at first, her body rigid, arms remaining clasped around her own waist. He simply tucked her against his chest and rested his chin on top of her head without saying anything or pressuring her to talk.

After a few seconds, she unwound like a coiled spring, her arms winding around his waist, her cheek pressed to his heart. Her shoulders jerked and she made a soft, choked sound, like she was desperately trying not to cry. Afraid of appearing weak, even in front of him. Or maybe especially in front of him.

It shredded him.

Mal closed his eyes and sighed, twisted up inside. *God, sweetness, I'm not gonna hurt you.* He tightened his hold, slid one hand up to cradle the back of her head in his palm, keeping her close.

She shuddered, sucked in an unsteady breath, then let it out slowly and seemed to melt into his body. Her silent acceptance of his comfort soothed him on the deepest level. Her hair was cool and silky under his hand, her slender curves melded to his front, the sweet scent of her shampoo teasing him. She fit against him so perfectly, like she'd been made for him.

With effort he stopped the thought, refused to wish for something that could never be. If life had taught him anything, it was to live in the moment. So he would take this one and savor it, memorize every detail of it, because it wouldn't last.

He could have held her like that forever but all too soon she composed herself and straightened, pulling away to wipe her face and run a self-conscious hand over her hair. Mal's fingers itched to do it for her.

"Thanks. I needed that," she murmured.

Mal nodded, stuffed his hands in his jeans pockets. He didn't ask to see Kevin, because it was family only in the ICU. "Can I get anything for you guys? Call someone?"

"No, but thanks. We're planning to take shifts at Kev's bedside until he wakes up, although Nick has already told us he's not leaving—" She broke off when the door swung open.

Her father stood there in dress slacks and a button-down shirt, his gaze cutting from Mal to Rowan and back, a frown pulling his salt-and-pepper eyebrows together. "Rowan. Who's this?"

So she hadn't ever told her father about them. Not that Mal should have been surprised.

She opened her mouth to respond but Mal beat her to it, stepping forward and offering his hand. "Special agent Malcolm Freeman, Mr. Stewart."

"FBI?"

"DEA."

Those shrewd blue eyes exactly the same color as Rowan's studied him as they shook hands. "Have we met?"

"No, sir. But I know both Kevin and Rowan." *And heard plenty about you.* Not all of it flattering, either.

Her father nodded and withdrew his hand, switching his attention to his daughter. "The FBI agent in charge is here to talk to us."

Rowan sighed and rubbed a hand over the back of her neck, reminding Mal that she must still be sore from the accident. "All right."

Her father turned away for a second to wave someone in, and in entered Rowan's mother and the FBI agent, wearing the standard dark blue windbreaker. "He's got news about the case," he explained. "Agent Freeman, if you'll excuse us."

Rowan surprised Mal by putting a restraining hand on his shoulder, to stop him from leaving. "Actually, I'd like him to stay. He's involved with the case I've been working on, so he knows what's been going on behind the scenes."

Her father frowned again, gave Mal a cursory once-over, then dismissed him by turning to the Fed. "All right. Go ahead."

The forty-ish agent got right to it. "They found another device wired to the engine of your boss's car," he told Rowan.

She blanched, her stomach grabbing. "They were able to dismantle it, I hope?"

"Yes. A search of the other vehicles in the lot hasn't turned up any other devices so far, and of course we're checking the building and perimeter as well."

Rowan shook her head. "How did someone plant bombs in two vehicles right out in front of our office without anyone noticing? Without security noticing?"

"We're questioning the security members and reviewing video footage now. Your boss has been moved to a hotel for now, and both he and his family have police protection. We suggest you do the same."

She shook her head. "I don't plan on leaving here until my brother wakes up and I know he's going to be okay."

"We've got an agent posted on this floor for your family's protection. When you do leave the premises, a police officer will escort you. But for now we don't suggest going home."

Mal gave a mental snort. Police protection? Against the *Veneno* cartel? Screw that.

"She can stay at my place," he announced, and all eyes snapped to him in surprise. He held Rowan's for a long moment before speaking to the other agent. "I live in a secure building. I've been temporarily removed from my current assignment and can watch Miss Stewart until you get something else arranged. I'm not comfortable sending her outside of this hospital with nothing more than police protection."

Hamilton had assured him he would take over bodyguard duties for Anya until Mal had everything settled on his end. This wasn't about feelings he may or may not still have for Rowan. This was about doing the right thing and making sure she was safe.

The agent nodded once in acknowledgment, then glanced at Rowan and her parents. "Well?"

"If you're sure," Rowan began to Mal, seeming surprised he'd made the offer, "then I'll go with you."

"I'm sure." The surprise in her eyes annoyed him. Yeah, she'd hurt him more than she seemed to realize when she'd decided she was done with him. That didn't mean he didn't care about her wellbeing, and after something like this? No goddamn way he was letting some beat cop guard her when the *Venenos* might have her in their sights.

Not only that, he considered Kevin a friend, and it was the least Mal could do to look after Kev's sister right now. Besides, it would only be for a couple of days, tops. He was a big boy. He could grin and bear having her at his place that long to ensure she was safe.

Rowan's father's hard blue stare bored into him. "How did you say you know my daughter?"

"I met him through Kev at a gala," Rowan cut in, sounding exasperated.

"And how do you know Kevin?" he demanded, never taking his eyes off Malcolm.

"Dad, stop. It's okay. I trust him." She turned those blue eyes on Mal, and there again was that weird catch in his chest. Not really painful, more like pressure. As though invisible fingers were closing around his heart. "I feel safe with him."

That shouldn't have puffed up his ego so much, but it did. Mal nodded at her once. "I'll stay in here until you want to leave."

"Are you sure? I don't know how long it'll take for him to wake up."

"I'm sure." He could stretch out on the floor and sleep if he needed to. This room was more comfortable than a lot of places he'd bedded down in during his military and DEA career.

"Okay then. Thank you." She flashed him a grateful smile that set off a pang of yearning inside him before walking out after her parents, leaving Mal alone with his thoughts. Mostly they were telling him this was the right thing to do, but still a damn bad idea as far as his heart was concerned.

Having Rowan at his place, under the same roof. Her sleeping in the bed across the hall. Every time he saw her there, every moment he spent with her in his intimate space a reminder of what might have been.

Blowing out a deep breath, he sank into a chair and pulled out his phone to call Hamilton and Taggart. Only a few days, he told himself. Rowan would only be with him for a day, maybe two at most before they arranged a security detail for her.

The Navy had taught him how to mask his emotions half a lifetime ago. He could keep his true feelings for her hidden a couple days, no problem.

Chapter Nine

Rowan walked into the entryway of Malcolm's condo late the next morning and waited while he closed and locked the door behind them, the weight of exhaustion pressing down on her and a low-grade anxiety churning inside. Malcolm had waited to bring her here until after Kevin had finally woken up. The drive here from the hospital had been tense, neither of them saying anything.

It was strange to be here again.

The one time she'd come before was to have dinner with him one night about a week before she broke things off, the two of them eating at his kitchen table together. He'd cooked for her and set the table with candles, even though she could only stay long enough to eat and have a short conversation before returning to the office. He'd done it just so they could spend a little time together slotted into their hectic schedules.

Now the memory made her sad. He'd only offered this solution out of some sense of obligation to her or maybe to Kevin, though she was grateful no matter the reason because right now she didn't know where else to turn. While she was here she might be a little uncomfortable with the strain between them, but without a doubt she would be safe. Malcolm would make sure of it.

"One of my teammates will bring a suitcase over for you later tonight," he said, his tone brusque, all business as he hung up his windbreaker on a peg beside the door.

"Okay. Thank you." This was more awkward than she'd expected, and she was still worried about her brother. Kevin had come to briefly before she'd left, long enough for them to tell him what had happened. He took it all in, reached for her hand. *I'm glad you're okay.* God, she still had a lump in her throat from that.

"You can take the guestroom." Malcolm walked past her into the kitchen, his clean, citrusy scent drifting back to her. "Pantry's here, and help yourself to whatever's in the fridge. I don't have much in there at the moment, but if you give me a list I'll go grab whatever you need."

She was merely an overnight guest to him, and from his demeanor not an entirely welcome one. Rowan swallowed and squeezed the handle of her briefcase tighter, feeling uncharacteristically small and vulnerable as she stood there in his kitchen. "Thanks."

He stopped by the kitchen counter, faced her with his hands on his hips. Gorgeous, strong, masculine.

And completely unreachable across the chilly divide between them. "You hungry?"

"No." Shaken, lost and alone, yes. Definitely not hungry.

His expression softened slightly but he made no move toward her, his earlier attentiveness at the hospital long gone. His hot and cold routine confused her. Frustrated her. But she wasn't going to ask him about it. "Why don't you go get settled, then. Take a bath, maybe lie down for a bit."

She wanted him to hold her. Tight, like he used to. The way he had at the hospital. Like he still cared. She'd worked long and hard to establish a reputation for inner strength. The world saw her as strong, driven, not needing anyone else.

It was a lie.

Underneath that carefully constructed façade, she was lonely and missed the man standing across the room. And right now she was scared and worried and sick with guilt over her brother.

"Okay," she murmured, shoving her feelings deep down inside. What Kevin had said to her before he'd left her office was true, but she wasn't about to embarrass herself by throwing herself at Malcolm and getting her heart crushed when he rejected her. The man in front of her now was hard, remote. She didn't know how to deal with him.

The guestroom was at the far end of the condo, across the hall from his room. She shut the door behind her and faced the queen-size bed with its thick burgundy comforter, the window beside it looking out over the park behind the building. Setting down her briefcase, she let out a slow, deep breath.

Golden yellow sunlight streamed through the bright green leafy canopies of the oak and maple trees planted between the playground and the road. Young children played on the swings and teeter-totters or drew chalk pictures on the sidewalk while their parents looked on.

So innocent, oblivious to the dangers in this world. It was her job to ensure some of those dangers were put behind bars where they couldn't threaten anyone again.

Today, her lifelong goal had almost killed her brother.

Tears blurring her vision, she looked away from the park and took in the rest of the room. A long wooden dresser sat along the far wall, a giant mirror on top. It looked old, maybe from the early 1900s. Next to it was the door to the en suite. She would have liked a shower, but she had nothing else to change into and didn't feel like putting her blood-stained work clothes back on.

So she lay down on the bed instead and tried to get a grip on her turbulent emotions. Within moments, the lock on the box she'd shoved everything into shattered, hitting her in an unforgiving torrent. The tears she'd been holding at bay broke free, shaking her shoulders with their force. She was careful to stay quiet, not wanting Malcolm to hear her.

Finally the tears slowed, leaving her exhausted and taking in quivering breaths. She closed her sore, swollen eyelids, the sound of the children playing in the park coming in faintly through the window.

She must have dozed off, because the next thing she knew, she opened her eyes to see the walls of the room ablaze with orange and pink. Sunset.

She checked her phone, but no one had called or texted. No update on her brother, then. Her stomach growled. She glanced at the door, hesitating. Missing meals wouldn't kill her; she missed meals all the time when she was working. Except right now she could really use some company and wasn't going to hide in here all night simply to avoid Malcolm.

Pushing up, she went into the bathroom to wash her face and brush her teeth with the spare toothbrush she found in the drawer. When she opened the guestroom door a few minutes later, the muted sounds of the TV came from the living room.

Malcolm looked up when she came around the corner. He was sprawled on the couch still in his jeans and T-shirt that stretched across the defined muscles in his chest and shoulders, a decorative cushion beneath his head. He sat up, running his gaze over her in assessment. "Get some sleep?"

"Yes."

He got to his feet and walked into the kitchen. "My teammate Logan dropped by with a suitcase for you a little while ago. His girlfriend Taylor went to your place with him and packed it for you. She's an organizational wizard, so I'm sure you've got everything you need in there."

She followed him, took the bag he wheeled toward her. "Thank you. That was thoughtful of them."

"Welcome. You hungry now?"

"Have you eaten?"

"No. Grilled cheese and tomato soup okay?"

"Sure. I can make it, though." He'd done enough by bringing her back here, and she didn't want him going to any more trouble.

He shot her an annoyed look. "I got it. Go sit and watch something. I'll bring it out in a few minutes."

There was no point in arguing, so she took the chair beside the sofa and grabbed the remote. The first thing she flipped to was a newscast detailing the explosion. She quickly changed the channel, but the image made her relive everything all over again. Thankfully she found a romcom, watched it while Malcolm moved around the kitchen, though she couldn't pay much attention to the thin plot when she had so much else on her mind.

Malcolm came in a few minutes later with a plated sandwich and a steaming bowl of soup and set it down on the coffee table in front of her. "Soup's hot."

"Thank you," she murmured, avoiding looking at him as she tucked her hair behind her ear. She waited until he sat down with his own meal before starting.

They ate in silence, the movie the only sound in the room, and soon the growing tension began to grate on her nerves. If she apologized for hurting him when she ended things, would it help, or make things worse?

"Hear anything else from your family?" he finally asked her.

"No. Anything on your end?"

He shook his head, helping himself to the last half of his sandwich. "It's good that he came to on his own so soon. And he's got a lot of support to help him through the recovery."

"I'd like to see him again tomorrow. If it's not too much trouble," she added.

"Of course not. I'll take you over in the morning."

She let out a relieved breath. "Thank you."

He nodded but didn't look up.

She stared at him from beneath her lashes, her whole chest aching. *I'm sorry. I didn't mean to hurt you.*

She held the words back, sensing they would be yet another mistake where he was concerned. But Kevin's parting words at the office kept coming back to her, haunting her with their truth and multiple meanings about her and Malcolm.

There are no do-overs.

Yeah. Wasn't that the damn truth. And a helluva bitter pill to swallow.

Chapter Ten

———◇◇◇◇———

In the darkness of his bedroom, the glowing blue numbers of the digital alarm clock read 2:18 a.m. when Malcolm rolled over in bed to check it. Rowan was up. Her door had opened a few seconds ago. She'd tried to be quiet, but he was a light sleeper, something he'd picked up during his Navy days, because many times during a mission, his life had depended on it.

He scrubbed a hand over his face and sighed into the darkness. What the hell was he supposed to do with her? She'd been unusually quiet ever since the hospital, almost…deflated. At first he'd thought it was shock and worry about Kevin, maybe fear for her safety. But during that awkward dinner earlier he'd realized the way she'd closed up was at least partially because of him. He'd purposely been shutting her out, so that was his fault.

Her quiet footsteps faded on the hardwood floor

of the hallway. Had she had a nightmare? Gotten a phone call about her brother?

He lay there another minute, wrestling with himself. If he was smart he'd stay the hell away from her. It wasn't his place to be a shoulder for her anymore, but damned if he would leave her to deal with all of this alone right now.

Getting up, he snagged a pair of pajama pants and T-shirt from the closet, tugged them on, and walked down the hall to find her. She hadn't turned any lights on but there was a faint glow coming from the kitchen.

He found her sitting at the table, her back to him as she opened something on her laptop, a stack of files set next to it. Working at this hour? After everything that had happened?

"Hey," he said softly.

Rowan gasped and whirled in her seat, putting a hand to her chest. "God, you scared me."

"Sorry." He leaned a shoulder against the wall. "Couldn't sleep?"

Lowering her gaze, she shook her head. "Sorry I woke you."

"It's okay." He crossed to the table and sat across from her. She definitely shouldn't have to work right now. "Someone call?"

"No. I just can't sleep. I'd doze off for a bit, then my subconscious reminded me of what happened and jerked me wide awake again." She closed the laptop, leaving them bathed in light from the streetlamps in the park that streamed through the edges of the blinds on the kitchen windows.

No surprise she couldn't sleep, considering what

she'd seen yesterday. She was so confident and composed all the time, it tugged at his insides to see her this vulnerable. Her white-collar world was totally different from his. She had no training or experience to help her cope with what had happened, and it had shaken her badly.

"That's pretty normal," he said in a low voice. "Seeing something like that happen to someone you care about is hard." It never got easier, either.

She lifted her gaze, those sapphire blue eyes studying his. "How do you deal with it?"

"I put it in a box for later." The Navy had drilled that into them relentlessly. Now, he did it automatically. And it had always worked for him. Until Rowan.

She pushed out an aggravated breath. "Well I don't know how to do that. Unless you count burying myself in work as a way of compartmentalizing, and I can't even concentrate on that right now."

Malcolm leaned back in his chair, unsure what to say. Compartmentalizing shit wasn't always healthy, especially if it wasn't ever taken out of the box and dealt with. A box could only hold so much before it burst open and everything fell out. She needed to talk about what had happened, needed someone to tell her she wasn't to blame for Kevin getting hurt. "It wasn't your fault."

Pain filled her eyes. "Yes it was. They were targeting me. It should have been me, not Kevin."

The thought of her being caught up in that explosion, of lying so still and pale in a hospital bed right now sent a wave of ice through his veins. "It shouldn't have been either of you. And Kev's gonna be okay. You saw that yourself before we left."

"I know, but..." She dragged a hand through her thick, glossy hair. "I just feel responsible. Like I should have known somehow."

"Not your fault," he repeated, stifling the urge to reach across the table for her hand.

It was hard enough keeping detached from her. Having her here in his space, just the two of them, looking so alone and lost...it was killing him not to touch her. But he knew damn good and well where he stood with her and had no desire to get his heart mashed again by opening up to her now and having her walk out of his life when she left in a day or two.

Elbows resting on the table, she rested her forehead in her hands, her inky hair spilling onto the wooden surface. He wanted to stroke his fingers through it. Gather it into his fist and squeeze gently until her head came up and he could look into the blue of her eyes. Make her look at him the way she once had. As if he was the only man she wanted, as if what they had together would last.

"I'm not going to be able to go into the office for a while, am I?" she asked.

"No. Not until we find out who was behind this and whether the threat's over with."

She groaned softly. "I've got so much work to get done, you have no idea. And how am I going to visit Kevin outside of the hospital?"

"Depends on where he goes after he's discharged. If we can't get you over there in person, you'll have to make do with your phone or Skype for the time being."

"All right." She sounded resigned. Exhausted.

Silence spread between them when she didn't say anything else. He became aware of the quiet hum of the fridge in the background, the sound of her even breaths. He should do something to help her get to sleep. Something that didn't involve him touching her or being any closer to her than he was now. She liked peppermint tea, but he didn't have any. "Want some water or something?"

"Sure, thanks."

He got two bottles from the fridge, handed her one. She took a sip then set the bottle on the table and rolled it between her hands, the crinkling sound of the plastic becoming an annoyance after only a few moments.

If she were his, he would scoop her out of that chair, carry her to his bed and tuck her in close beside him. Then peel that tank top and pajama bottoms off her and make love to her until she came apart in his arms, until she was sated and drowsy with him there to hold her through the darkness.

"Wanna watch a movie or something?" he asked instead, trying his best to ignore the twin bursts of yearning and sadness the erotic image brought. She was so close, but he couldn't have her.

"No." She sat up a little straighter, watched him in a way that set his instincts on edge before she spoke again. "I'm sorry I hurt you, Malcolm," she murmured.

His stomach muscles contracted as if in response to a blow. "You didn't," he lied, not wanting to go there.

She shot him a look that said he was full of shit and crossed her arms. "Yeah I did. But I didn't mean to. Didn't want to."

She hadn't wanted to? What the hell did she think would happen when she metaphorically slammed the door in his face that day? "It was a long time ago, don't worry about it," he said as he shoved to his feet. Dammit, he should have stayed in his room when he heard her get up. "Ancient history."

"Then why are you walking away?"

That stopped him, the awareness that he was basically retreating rubbing him the wrong way. *Because I was falling in love with you, and I thought you were falling for me too.* No. He was sure she had been.

Christ it stung to realize just how wrong he'd been. "You should go back to bed and try to sleep," he said without turning around. Wasn't this a kick in the ass? Big bad former SEAL, and he didn't have the balls to face her again.

"There's no way I'm getting to sleep anytime soon," she said. "Much as I appreciate you letting me stay here, I don't want to invade your space if you're not comfortable with it."

It wasn't that he was uncomfortable. Fighting not to act on his feelings, that was the real problem. "Rowan, it's fine. I wouldn't have brought you here if I felt that way."

"Yes you would. That's just who you are. You're all about duty and honor and sacrifice."

Malcolm heaved out a breath. It was true and he couldn't deny it. He could never turn his back on someone he cared about. No matter what they'd done or how much they'd hurt him in the past.

He made himself turn around to face her. "I wanted you to feel safe. You told Oceane you would trust me with your life." That had surprised him, but he'd never forget it.

She nodded, holding his gaze. "I did. I meant every word, too."

Well, that was something. And damned if her complete trust in his ability to keep her safe didn't hit him square in his bruised, aching heart. "Good. That's all that's important right now."

"No, that's not all that's important. I can't leave things like this between us." Determination stamped her expression, but also a sadness that simultaneously made him angry and feel like an asshole.

Fine. "You really wanna do this now?" Because this had eaten at him for the better part of a year now, and he wanted to know the damn truth so he could put it behind him and move on. Or at least try to.

"Why not?"

Because you're scared and shaken up about your brother and I don't want to add to that? No. He wouldn't do that to her. If they ever had this conversation, it would be when they were both less stressed. He shook his head, exasperated. "Go back to bed, Rowan."

She stood so fast the chair legs scraped against the hardwood floor. She spun around to confront him, hands on hips. "No."

He dragged a hand over his face, fighting for patience. The right thing would be to walk away. Give her time to settle down, hopefully get some sleep. But maybe it was kinder to have this out here and now, get it over with and out of the way. Closure, for both of them.

"Fine. You want me to talk? Then you can start by

telling me why you up and walked away all of a sudden."

She swallowed, seeming taken aback by his directness. "Because I thought it was best, and decided it was kinder to end things before we got too involved."

Before they slept together, she meant. "So you saw us breaking up as inevitable right from the start?"

"Yes."

Shocked, he stared at her, trying to read her, to understand. "Why the hell is that?" It better not be because she didn't think he was good enough for her.

"Because I knew."

No. No way. He refused to believe it. She'd been just as into him as he was into her. "What did you know?"

"That it wouldn't last. That we were just too different."

Too different, my ass. "It wasn't because you didn't have feelings for me, and it wasn't because you didn't want me." He stared at her, daring her to deny it.

She didn't. And now that he was on a roll, he couldn't stop, all the frustration and pain he'd bottled up for so long bursting free. He refused to let her hide from the truth. Refused to let her believe whatever lies she'd told herself about why they wouldn't work.

"All you gave me was bullshit excuses about why it wasn't good timing for you. You were new to the job, had a lot of big cases lined up, didn't have time for a serious relationship. But you know what? Those aren't even close to being good enough reasons to walk away from what we had. So why?" If she'd been trying to let him down easy, it hadn't worked.

Her chin came up, the set of her jaw pure Irish stubbornness. "I told you. Because it wasn't going to work out long term."

He blinked at her. "Says who?"

"Me. And you'd have seen it too, if you'd thought about it."

"No, I wouldn't have, and you're still feeding me bullshit, so stop." He folded his arms across his chest. "Give me the truth. I deserve that much."

She seemed to falter a second, that tightly controlled lawyer façade cracking a little. "We're too different."

Yeah, she'd said that before, and he still didn't buy it. "Really? How?"

"Our jobs. Our backgrounds. Our goals."

It felt like she'd just punched him in the chest. "What, I'm too blue-collar for a high-class girl like you? Is that what you're saying? Because excuse me, princess, but you might remember your dear old dad once served in the Navy too before he made it big." Emotion swirled through him in a chaotic haze. Anger. Confusion. Hurt.

"No," she bit out, her eyes burning with frustration, "that's not what I meant! Believe me, I'm extremely aware of my father's military service. I spent my entire childhood moving from city to city every time he was assigned to a new post, and it wasn't until he got into the JAG corps and moved us to D.C. when I was in eleventh grade that I finally had a permanent home. It seemed to me like he was gone more often than he was around." She paused, set her jaw for a moment before continuing. "I hated that life then, and I sure as hell don't want it for my future."

What the hell? "Huh? I'm based out of Arlington. You wouldn't have had to move at all if we'd stayed together."

"I would if you got transferred someday, which is always a possibility while you're with a government agency. And you're gone all the time as it is. And," she continued, holding up a hand to stop him when he would have argued, "it's no secret that my father is a hard taskmaster. I had a good home with parents who loved me and we eventually had money once he left the Navy and his law career took off, but believe me, it came with a price."

She drew in a breath, kept going. "I had to work harder, longer than everyone else. At everything. School, piano, ballet, chores around the house. Charity work. Why the hell do you think I'm such a workaholic? Because I like it?" She shook her head. "Only the best was ever good enough for him. Growing up, if Kevin and I weren't out of bed by five a.m. every morning when he was home, there was hell to pay. And if we did anything that disappointed him, he withdrew his love and support until we fixed it and met his exceedingly high expectations. Kev was the smart one, he stopped giving a shit and got on living his own life when he graduated college. Me, not so much."

Mal struggled to keep his expression calm. "I know your dad was always tough on you, and I'm sorry you grew up like that. No parent should ever do that to a child. But what's that got to do with me? You're saying you think I would treat you that way?"

127

He raised a skeptical eyebrow.

"You hadn't yet, but it's in you. You were a SEAL, for crying out loud, and you guys take self-discipline and work ethic to a whole other level."

"Because we have to if we want to survive," he argued. "That doesn't mean we're controlling ass-holes when we come home. It's nuts that you would think that. What the hell, Rowan? That's not just un-fair, it's ridiculous."

She broke his gaze, studying her hand as she fid-dled with the edge of the table. He knew about her ex, but not the details or how the relationship had im-pacted her. "I also lived with a former military guy for a little while before I met you. He was Special Forces."

He'd known she'd dated a guy, but hadn't realized they'd been living together. "And?"

"*And*, things started out okay, but pretty soon he was riding me about every little thing I did wrong. Leaving a wet towel hung on the shower door, or not keeping the kitchen spotless. Not being out of bed at the crack of dawn every day or working out every morning or spending eighty hours a week at the of-fice. Nothing was ever good enough. It was like liv-ing with my father on steroids, and when I pushed back he acted all confused, like why was I reacting that way when all he was trying to do was help me live to my 'full potential'."

Now Mal was just insulted. "So the dude was an abusive asshole with OCD issues. That's not me." He waited until she met his gaze again. "That's not me, Rowan, and you know it. You think I give a shit if you leave wet towels all over the place? What time you get out of bed or if there are dirty dishes on the counter and in the sink? I never once did anything that would make you think I was like that. So why. *Why*, Rowan?"

Her eyes blazed at him. "Because you got too serious too fast!"

Chapter Eleven

◆——◇◆◇◆◇——◆

The shouted outburst shocked her as much as it did him, her eyes widening slightly because she hadn't meant to blurt that out. Yet even as she said it, the memory of the breakup played in her head.

She'd been distracted all day, thinking about him and their upcoming date that night once she got off work. Everything had gone downhill from there.

"Rowan?"

She jerked awake on her office couch to find her assistant standing over her, frowning. The ring of her phone alarm finally penetrated her awareness. "Oh, God, what time is it?" she muttered, sitting up to clear the cobwebs from her brain. She'd only meant to have a twenty-minute power nap.

"Almost one-thirty."

Rowan gasped. "What? Nooooo..." She leapt up and bolted for her desk, scooping up the paperwork and stuffing it into her briefcase. The meeting started at one-thirty, and she was at least twenty minutes away from the location. She stopped, glanced around. "Am I forgetting something? I feel like I'm forgetting something."

"Probably because you're only half-awake. Here." Her assistant shoved Rowan's high heels at her.

Rowan quickly slipped them on and grabbed her purse. "Tell Val I'm on my way."

"Okay. Hurry."

I'm hurrying. *She raced down the hall, took the stairs rather than wait for the elevator and rushed to her car. Of course there was an accident on the way over to the meeting location, putting her arrival time at forty minutes late. From the looks on her boss's and client's face, they were both pissed.*

"Late lunch?" Val said in a disapproving tone that made her cringe inside.

"Sorry. Here." She began laying out the paperwork, her heart lurching when she couldn't find one critical file. Crap, she'd left it in the damn photocopier before she'd lain down to nap. God.

The meeting was awkward as hell, and Val didn't mince words as they left together after.

"I don't know what's going on with you, Rowan, but I have to say I'm extremely disappointed in your lack of focus and effort lately."

She flushed in embarrassment, squirming inside. "I'm sorry."

"Every day this week you've left the office at four, even though we're gearing up for trial in another month." Val frowned. "Is everything all right?"

"Yes. I'm fine." Just distracted, and sleep deprived. Not that those were good excuses. She'd thought she could juggle her work schedule and her new relationship with Malcolm without a problem, but apparently not. It was embarrassing and a blow to her ego to be reprimanded by her boss. And not only had she allowed Malcolm to distract her, it scared her a little how easily he had gotten under her skin. Deeper every day, it seemed.

Val sighed. *"I don't want to take you off the case, but if you're not willing or able to put the necessary time in and get everything done when I need it, then I'll have to."*

"No, it won't happen again." She didn't dare mention Malcolm, or that she had to leave work by four-thirty today to meet him for their dinner reservation. God, this wasn't like her. She was driven. Dedicated. Married to her job. Had she really changed that much over the past few weeks because of Malcolm? *"I'll come in early from now on and stay late until we're caught up."* She hated to give up her time with Malcolm, but he would just have to understand. Right now her job had to come first. She would have to talk to him tonight, tell him they needed to stop seeing each other during the week.

Val nodded. *"Can you stay late tonight?"*

"I..." They'd already bought tickets to the movie. *"Not tonight, but starting tomorrow, I'm clear."*

He looked annoyed but didn't argue. *"Fine."*

By the time she got home and freshened up for their date, she was still suffering pangs of guilt about sneaking out of work early. But seeing Malcolm's smile when she walked up to the restaurant door at

*six and the feel of his arms around her as he pulled
her into a tight hug had gone a long way to temporarily pushing her worries away. She would talk
about slowing things down with him later.*

*"Everything okay?" he asked as they waited for
their appetizers. "You seem a little distracted."*

*"Just had a rough day at work," she said with a
dismissive wave of her hand. "How was your day?"*

*"Great." He talked about the team a little, a train-
ing exercise they'd done on vehicle takedowns.
"Commander let us break for lunch, so we headed to
this little pub I found a while back. There's an old
building across the street that's been newly reno-
vated and has a couple two-bedroom units for rent.
My teammate knows the landlord, says he can get us
a reduced rate. Price is reasonable, and it's closer to
work for both of us. Might save you about twenty
minutes commute time. You mentioned you might
want to move. Interested in going to take a look with
me this weekend maybe?"*

*Fingers tightening around her wineglass, Rowan
raised her eyebrows at him in surprise. He had not
just casually asked her whether she wanted to move
in together. After not quite three weeks of dating?
Who did that? "What?"*

*His broad shoulders moved in a casual shrug and
a slight smile tugged at his mouth. "I thought it might
be worth taking a look."*

*Unease stirred in her gut. She'd already been un-
settled about how intense her feelings were for him,
and how her performance at work had suffered since
they'd begun dating. But apartment shopping at this
stage? No. Things were moving way too fast and he*

was assuming too much. She'd just gotten out of a bad relationship with a controlling former military man two months ago. She wasn't ready for any sort of long term commitment; she wanted to keep things light and have fun. And it had been fun with Malcolm, up until a minute ago.

"I thought I was clear about wanting to keep things casual," she finally said.

Another shrug. "No pressure. It's just a good price in a great location if you were interested. Which you're clearly not," he added with a wry chuckle.

No pressure? Her smile was forced, brittle. "Thanks, but I've got my plate full with work right now. I can't even think about moving."

He let it drop, but she couldn't get past it for the rest of the meal. Or that the relationship was already interfering with her professional life. Her career was something she'd worked a lifetime to attain. She couldn't jeopardize that for a guy, even one as amazing as Malcolm. She also didn't trust her feelings for him, since she was on the rebound, had been reluctant to go out with him in the first place for that reason.

Then, later, as they were leaving the theater, she couldn't hold back the giant yawn she'd been fighting for the past hour. "Sorry, I've been burning the candle at both ends a little too often lately."

"Huh. Somebody keeping you up too late maybe?"

"Gee, I wonder who."

He grinned, his dimples appearing. "How about you spend the night at my place, then? I'll make sure you're tucked in and asleep by eleven. Okay, make that midnight."

Not a good idea. "No, I think I'll just head home." *She softened the rejection with a smile.*

He slung an arm around her shoulders. She liked the feel of it too much. Was tempted to ignore the niggling at the back of her head and risk taking things to the next level. "You sure?"

"Yes. I need a good night's sleep and if I want to keep my job, I have to be in the office early and stay late the rest of the week."

Before she could tack on that she could only see him on weekends, he hugged her into his side and said, "Come on, you only live once. And you can sleep when you're dead."

He was joking, that was clear in his tone, but she stiffened, cold sluicing through her as the words triggering memories of life with her ex.

Sleep is for the weak, *Carter used to say. He'd turned out to be controlling and possessive. Always pushing her to get his way. Nothing she did was ever good enough. God, she'd dreaded coming home to him near the end. And Malcolm was a former SEAL. He had that same relentless, never-quit attitude ingrained in him too.*

In that moment, any confusion she'd had about ending things evaporated. They were done. Part of her had been hoping for a clear sign to help her figure out how to handle this, and she'd just gotten it. She didn't want to go there again with another military alpha male. Been there, done that, still had the scar.

She stopped in the middle of the sidewalk, her

mind made up. "Malcolm."

He stopped too, looked down at her with his arm still around her shoulders, a slight frown pulling his eyebrows together at her tone. "What?"

How the hell did she say this without hurting him or coming across as a total bitch? "Look, things at work are crazy right now, and you're leaving for four months overseas soon. I need to focus on my career and not let distractions get in the way." She pulled away from his embrace, unable to say the rest with him touching her. "You're a great guy. I like you a lot, and I've enjoyed our time together." Until to-night. "But I'm not ready to be in a committed rela-tionship again yet, so I think it's best if we stop seeing each other now, rather than drag things out."

Her heart thudded in her ears as he stared at her, disbelief in his dark eyes.

"Is this because I brought up the apartment?" he said quietly.

Partly. But mostly because this would never work in the long run. She knew that from past experience. "No, it's just that the timing is bad for me. I'm really sorry." When he didn't say anything, just kept watch-ing her with that are you serious *look on his face, she bolted. "You don't need to drive me home, I'll grab myself a cab."*

Without waiting for him to respond, she spun around and hurried to the curb to hail a cab and didn't look back.

The memory hung over them now like a heavy thundercloud, oppressive and dark.

"Too serious," Malcolm repeated in a low voice, that same stunned look on his face as when she'd walked away that night.

She raised her chin a notch, her fingers twitching at her sides. Yeah, she'd really left him standing there on the sidewalk, thinking she was making the right decision. God, how wrong she'd been. "Yes. We'd only been dating a few weeks and I was just out of a bad relationship, and you were calling me every day, wanting to see me every night even though I was swamped with work, and then you asked about looking at that place together." Her baggage about Carter wasn't Malcolm's fault, so she didn't add that, although it had been a factor at the time. "Way too much, way too fast."

"Then what about the keychain?"

What the hell did that have to do with anything? "What about it?"

"It's a stupid keychain. Why keep it all this time if it was so easy for you to walk away?"

"Because…" *Because I missed you and wanted something to remember you by.* "It doesn't matter. The point is, you came on too strong, too fast." Her tone was defensive, but she couldn't help it. He was chipping away at her arguments the way she did with a witness in the courtroom.

For a moment Malcolm simply stared at her in incredulity. Then his expression turned shocked and his mouth opened slightly. "Oh my God. You were scared," he said, his voice barely above a whisper.

Her face went stiff. "No I wasn't." *No, I was terrified.*

"Yes you were," he breathed, and took a step toward her. She edged back but had nowhere to go, her fingers curling around the edge of the table. "You were scared to death of what I made you feel. Weren't you?"

"No," she whispered, the sheer vulnerability in that one word almost splitting her heart open.

"Yeah, you were." He shook his head in wonder. "God, you hid it so well beneath that strong, independent exterior, even I missed it."

She gave a tiny shake of her head, in fervent denial, the movement jerky, convulsive as she leaned back more.

But unlike a year ago, there was nowhere for her to go now. No escape. And his insight was dead on.

Scared.

Rowan tested the word as she clutched the edge of the table, denial shrieking in her head and her heart slamming against her ribs. Busted, she stared at him, unable to think of a single thing to say in her defense.

How? *How* had he seen through her, realized the truth when even she hadn't until the moment he'd said it?

Malcolm prowled toward her slowly, that dark, magnetic gaze impossible to break, his intense expression so full of hunger that it made her knees wobble.

Hell yes, she'd been afraid. Spooked by what he'd made her feel, and even more terrified of risking her heart and having it broken down the road. Because Malcolm would have broken it in a way that her ex never had. She'd never truly loved Carter. But Malcolm? No, he had the ability to tear her heart out.

Right now, facing off with him in his dark, quiet kitchen, she was more vulnerable than ever, the invisible barrier between them gone, destroyed by his uncanny insight.

Malcolm came right at her, stopping mere inches away from her. Close enough for her to breathe in his addictive scent and feel the heat of his body licking along the front of hers. He stared down into her eyes, this powerful, magnetic man who held the power to break her if he so chose.

She held her breath as he raised a hand, brushed a lock of hair away from her hot cheek, her pulse thudding hard in her throat. "You're shaking," he whispered.

Automatically she locked her knees and clamped her jaw to stop the embarrassing tremors. She didn't dare touch him, didn't dare act on the need humming through her. If she did, there was no going back.

"I'm only gonna tell you this once, so listen up," he murmured, the pads of his fingers skimming down the side of her face, raising goosebumps all over her body, tightening her nipples to hard points under her tank. "You don't ever need to be afraid with me. Not of anyone ever hurting you. And never of what I make you feel."

She swallowed and stared up at him helplessly, all her senses on overload, unable to form a single coherent response. It took all her strength not to reach out and take what was right in front of her.

Those deep brown eyes delved into hers for a long, breathless moment before they dropped to her mouth. He stared at it intently, dragged the pad of his thumb across her lower lip, making her whole body tighten with need. She vividly recalled how he'd turned her inside out with his kisses. Was dying for him to do it now, aching to finish what they'd started so long ago, what she'd only allowed herself to imagine with him.

"No more running," he said, taking her face between his big hands. "I won't let you this time."

Even if she wanted to, there was nowhere to go, trapped against the table by over two hundred pounds of smoldering, protective male. But she didn't want to run. She wanted Malcolm.

She choked back a moan of pure need as his lips molded to hers and let go of the table to grip his wide shoulders, her fingers digging into the powerful muscles there. He held the back of her head in one hand, slipped his other down her spine to press on her lower back, pulling her tight into his body.

Her insides clenched at the feel of the thick, hard length of his erection pressed against her belly. So many times she'd fantasized about what it would feel like to have him inside her, feel the weight and strength of his body as he pinned her in place and buried himself in her.

All her thoughts scattered at the heat and hardness of him, the hungry, almost desperate kiss. Malcolm made a low, hungry sound and kissed her senseless, nibbling at her upper lip, sucking at the lower one before stealing his tongue inside to stroke hers.

She came up on her toes, arching into him with an incoherent sound muffled by his tongue. He stroked hers, sucked it, tightening her nipples, the blazing heat deep in her belly spreading to the pulsing throb between her legs.

All too soon he broke the kiss and buried his face in her hair, breathing hard.

Rowan couldn't catch her breath, her heart racing,

pure need thrumming through her veins. He still cradled her head in his hand, the other dipping under the edge of her tank to caress the sensitive spot at the small of her back.

The last functioning bit of her brain warned her that they were on the brink. One more move by either one of them, and they would wind up naked on the kitchen floor.

She shook the tempting image away. Too soon. Way too soon when there was still so much unresolved between them to take that disastrous step.

Malcolm drew in a deep breath and pressed his cheek to hers, his body eerily still, tensed, the muscles under her hands coiled as if he was about to pounce. Or explode. "God dammit. I didn't want this," he whispered in a ragged voice. "Swore I wouldn't fall under your spell again."

At that, the haze of arousal evaporated like fog under a blinding ray of sunlight. She stiffened, tried to push away.

"Don't," he said, his hold tightening. She stilled, closing her eyes to better absorb the feel of him. It would be so easy to give into this need. But it would be another mistake.

After a moment she found her voice. "So what happens now?" she whispered.

It was as if her words broke some spell they'd both been under. Malcolm straightened and released her, taking a step back to put some distance between them. In the dim light filtering through the kitchen windows his expression was unreadable.

"You go back to bed and get some sleep," he said gruffly, as though he hadn't just made every nerve ending in her body come alive. "If you want to go to the hospital we need to be there early, before the shift change."

Before she could answer he turned and walked away, leaving her body and heart crying out for him.

Chapter Twelve

In his private office at his estate, Manny locked the door so no one would disturb him and turned to face the window that overlooked the pool and garden, the mountains a pale gray-green in the distance. He tightened his grip on his cell phone and sought the inner well of calm that seemed to have deserted him.

"What?" he rasped out, his entire body rigid with disbelief.

"Oceane and Anya went to the Americans on their own," Juan Montoya, his chief enforcer said. "They're aiding the FBI and DEA in their investigation on the cartel right now."

A strange, hollow ringing filled Manny's ears. He sank woodenly into his richly upholstered leather desk chair, his bones and joints suddenly stiff as unoiled hinges. "They can't be." They wouldn't betray him, no matter the circumstance. "Oceane doesn't know anything—"

"But Anya does, and she's obviously told Oceane certain things that they're feeding the Americans," Montoya added in a flat tone.

"You have proof?" Without irrefutable evidence, Manny refused to even entertain the thought that his daughter and mistress had betrayed him.

"I finally got a signal from the tracking device."

His muscles tightened. The Americans must have missed it, then. Maybe there was still hope for him to recover Oceane. Or, the Americans had found it and this was a trap. "When?"

"Yesterday afternoon. I followed it. And do you know where it originated from?"

Dread congealed in the pit of his stomach. "Where?"

"The U.S. Attorney's office in D.C."

Manny shot out of his chair and began pacing the length of the room, his mind racing. "They might have been forced into talking."

Montoya made a disparaging sound. "I know you don't want to believe it. But it's true. The chatter is that someone close to you is aiding the feds. And it's not a coincidence that the FBI shut down your accounts connected to Anya."

Hijo de puta. He stopped at the window, ran a hand over his face, sick inside. "Did you follow them?"

"I waited as long as I could, but they didn't come out of the building. I found out who they've been talking to, though, and left a little parting gift for the lawyers involved."

"No one saw you?"

"No. I had my guys do it. Feds are all over the building now."

Annoyance speared through him. Montoya had his crack team with him in the States—mostly comprised of Mexican Special Forces veterans. Planting a car bomb was nothing to them.

But killing federal lawyers working on the case would bring unwanted heat and scrutiny, although Montoya wouldn't care. He was all about vengeance and maintaining his reputation as a sadistic, ruthless bastard who decimated anyone who got in his way. So far Manny had been able to control him, for the most part. How much longer he would be able to was…probably not that long.

"How are you going to track them now?" he snapped. There was no way Oceane would ever allow her and her mother to be separated. She knew better than that. What had Anya told her? How much did she know? What did she think of him now? It sliced him up inside to think that he might have lost her love. That she might think he was a monster now.

"I'll find them," Montoya said, arrogant as always. "Someone else triggered the bomb in the female lawyer's car. Both she and her boss are still alive."

A spark of hope lit inside him. "Get one of them, or both." If Manny couldn't find his daughter, he'd use the American lawyers to find her for him. A lawyer was a far easier target at this point anyway. "Find out where my daughter is."

Once he got her back, he would explain everything. He was a gifted businessman. His daughter was gifted with handling finances. He could pull this off, make her see the wisdom in why he'd protected her the way he had. Then she would understand. And then he could finally begin to show her the empire she had been born into.

He forgave her for being afraid. It was his fault for keeping her ignorant for too long.

****

Rowan rode up the elevator to the ICU with Malcolm in complete silence, every cell in her body tingling at his nearness. After tossing and turning for another hour following that knee-melting kiss in his darkened kitchen, she'd finally fallen into a fitful sleep, only to wake to Malcolm's brisk knock on the door an hour ago.

They'd barely spoken a word to each other on the drive over. Malcolm because he was unwilling to risk crossing that invisible line again, and she because she didn't want to make things any worse between them. But there was no way she could pretend she didn't want him, didn't want to be with him and give them a real shot. She just wasn't sure how to tell him, or whether he'd turn her down flat.

He's worth the risk. You know he is.

The ICU was quiet, the nursing staff moving about efficiently, an hour before shift change. One of them recognized her, gave her a little smile before returning to her paperwork.

Rowan headed straight for Kevin's room. After showing her ID to the police standing guard at the door, she tapped on it softly and cracked it open. No surprise, Nick was there, sound asleep in his chair

146

beside Kevin's bed, his neck torqued at a weird angle as he rested his head near Kev's pillow. Rowan's heart squeezed when her gaze landed on their joined hands.

She set a gentle hand on Nick's shoulder. He jerked up, his eyes springing open, focusing blearily on her. "Hey," he mumbled, wincing as he reached back to grab his nape. "What time is it?"

"Little before six," she whispered before focusing her attention on her brother. "How is he?"

"Good. He woke a couple times through the night and his mind seemed clear. They gave him some more pain meds through his IV about an hour ago, so he's out." He dropped his hand and covered a yawn. "Didn't expect you here today. I thought you were under twenty-four-seven protection for the next while."

She nodded at Malcolm. "I am."

Nick twisted around, gave a startled smile. "Oh, hey."

"Hey," Malcolm answered with a warm smile, and Rowan felt a twinge in her chest. She knew firsthand that not everyone was accepting of gay people. Malcolm was as alpha as they came, but from the get-go he'd accepted Kev and Nick's relationship without any hesitation or reservations. She loved that about him. She loved a *lot* of things about him, and hoped she still had a chance with him. "How you holding up?"

"Honestly?" Nick thought about it for a second. "Better than I thought. I even slept for a few hours."

"That's good to hear."

Rowan rounded the hospital bed and sank into the

chair opposite Nick. She met Malcolm's dark gaze where he was standing sentry at the door, his muscular arms folded across his ripped chest. And in that moment, it hit her. Hard.

He was right. She was a freaking cowardly idiot for ever walking away from him. The hot, pricking shame that washed through her was an unwelcome and foreign sensation. She had to fix things between them somehow. Or at least try. If Malcolm rejected her... She prayed he wouldn't.

Ripping her attention off him, she turned her gaze on her brother. "He looks pretty bad." Both his eyes were still swollen shut, the lids shiny because the skin was stretched so thin, and a deep, purplish-magenta. More bruises and cuts scattered across his face, and she could just imagine what his surgical incisions looked like. Thank God he was asleep and not in pain at the moment.

"Yeah. It's still Kev in there, though, thank God," Nick said. "Doc's coming to see him around eight or so. We'll get a better idea of what he's looking at in terms of rehab then."

He was going to have a long road ahead of him. "You want to go grab something to eat while we're here?"

"I could eat." He pushed to his feet, stretched with a grimace. "You want anything?"

"No, we're good."

Nick reached across the bed to pat her shoulder. "I'm leaving him in good hands."

The words made Rowan's throat tighten. When Nick closed the door softly behind him, she took in a deep breath and let it out slowly. "I want whoever did this to suffer."

"They'll find the perps," Malcolm said, still not moving from just inside the door. "They've got a short list to work with. Might be quick."

"Hope so." She twined her fingers through her brother's, watching to make sure she didn't wake him. He didn't so much as twitch. "It's still surreal that it happened. And that I was the target. It's scary as hell."

"Yeah, it is."

She looked over at him. A mountain of strength for her to lean on, if he'd let her. "Do you think the threat's over?"

"Probably. If it's the cartel, they've made their point. But we're not taking any chances, just in case." He squared his shoulders as he said the last part, his posture and bearing making it plain that he was more than willing to place himself between her and any further threat. That melted her even more.

Yesterday's violence terrified her. "If it is the cartel, they were either trying to disrupt the case against Ruiz by getting rid of me, or maybe it had to do with Oceane and her mom."

"They were trying to make a statement," Malcolm corrected quietly. "The why of it doesn't really matter."

She lowered her gaze to where she gripped her brother's hand. A day ago she'd been questioning whether or not she wanted to remain a U.S. Attorney long term. Yesterday had solidified it. "I'm scared, but I'll be damned if I cave and give them what they want. I'm staying on this case until I nail Ruiz to the wall for the rest of his goddamn miserable life, and whoever was responsible for this with him."

"I understand."

She turned her head to look at him. "Do you?"

"Yes."

Of course he did, he was a former SEAL and now a FAST member.

She shoved down the sudden spike in vulnerability and went for it. "But I don't want to go through this alone." It was as close as she could come to saying out loud that she needed him.

Malcolm's gaze sharpened. He held her stare for a long moment, not saying anything as the silence stretched out between them. It was impossible to figure out what was going on in his head.

Rowan glanced away, her stomach knotting as blood rushed to her face. He hadn't shot her down, but his reaction hadn't seemed that positive, either.

She was saved from further mortification by the nurse from earlier coming in. The petite woman gave her and Malcolm another gentle smile before checking Kevin's vitals and adding more medication into his line. Nick returned a few minutes later with a plate of food and a cup of coffee. "It's like funky-tasting dishwater, but it's hot and it has caffeine, so I'm going for it."

Rowan chuckled. "I'd offer to get you the real deal from down the street, but I'm already kind of bending the protection rules here, so…"

"It's okay." He plopped down into his seat and talked with her about logistics of what would happen once Kevin was discharged. A few minutes in, Malcolm pulled his phone from his pocket, glanced at the screen and slipped out the door.

The door opened a few minutes later and Malcolm only poked his head in. "We need to go," he said to her.

Alarmed, she shot to her feet. "Is everything okay?" What had the phone call been about?

He softened his demeanor at once. "Yes, everything's fine. But we should go now."

After saying goodbye to Nick and making him promise to call and update her on Kevin, she stepped out into the hall with Malcolm and followed him toward the elevator. "What happened?" she said in a low voice, tension pulling tighter and tighter in her stomach.

"Got a call from my team leader. Apparently they found a cell phone hidden in Oceane's room this morning. Her mother smuggled in the disassembled parts in the lining of her suitcase, and it was sophisticated enough that the X-ray machine missed it."

What?

"Turns out she's been in contact with one of her former bodyguards after she met with you the first time."

Rowan stopped dead. Arturo? Had to be. Oceane had made it clear how much she trusted him, that the bond was stronger than merely respect for and reliance on the man who kept her safe. It was almost like she saw him as an older brother or something. "So he knew her location this whole time?"

"Not the whole time, and for sure not the WITSEC facility, but he definitely knew she and her mom were at your office."

Disbelief hit her, followed by a red-hot wave of

fury. "Fuck," she snapped and turned to face Malcolm fully, her heart thudding. It was public knowledge that she and her boss were the main attorneys working on the case. Nieto's network would have known it as well. "So her bodyguard could have planted the bomb that almost killed my brother."

"Him or anyone skilled enough to pull it off. They're questioning her and her mom now."

"Where?"

"Headquarters."

Rowan hitched the strap of her purse up higher on her shoulder. She wanted answers. She wanted justice. And she would see that she got it. "I'm going there."

"We're *both* going there," he answered, and hit the elevator call button on the wall.

Rowan pulled in a calming breath, her mind spinning. If Oceane or Anya had anything to do with the bombing, there was gonna be hell to pay.

Chapter Thirteen

Oceane struggled to stay calm and not allow her anxiety to show. From an early age she'd been taught many things that she had assumed all kids learned, like the need to mask her emotions, never display any kind of fear, because predators sensed it and preyed upon it.

But it turned out not all kids learned those things. And she'd learned them long before she'd discovered that her entire life was a lie and her father was the most dangerous predator of them all.

"Where are you taking me?" she asked the man behind the wheel who was acting as her new bodyguard. DEA Special Agent Lockhart. From her position in the back seat where the doors wouldn't open from the inside, all she could see was the back of his head, and his military-short dirty blond hair.

Rowan had said he was qualified to guard her, but Oceane didn't know him. While she hadn't expected the American authorities to treat her with much kindness, she certainly had expected to be treated with respect and that was definitely lacking. Being treated like a criminal, a pariah, was a shock to her system that made her feel small and helpless. She would have given anything to talk to Arturo, ask for advice. He'd been there for her through hard times before, always kept her safe, even when her father's enemies had stormed her home.

Did no one here understand that she hadn't asked for any of this to happen? That she hadn't even known the reality of who her father was until she'd been forced to run for her life when the bullets had started flying outside her bedroom window? She'd bet none of the people assigned to her case had had their life ripped apart, only to find that everything they thought they knew was a total lie.

That hard truth bubbled like a pool of battery acid in her stomach.

Lockhart had been totally remote, curt and unfriendly since the moment he'd been assigned to her. She'd had bodyguards all her life in addition to Arturo, and they'd all warmed up to her within the first few days. But no matter how hard she tried to get Lockhart to thaw a little or try to engage him in a polite conversation, he wouldn't budge. Although to be fair, her former bodyguards had all been on her father's payroll. Lockhart wasn't.

"In for questioning," was all he said, not bothering to glance over at her as he answered, and there was a definite edge to his voice.

She didn't appreciate the attitude, or being kept in the dark. Not only that, the DEA bodyguards had split her and her mother up again.

All because they'd found the damn phone in her room where her mother had haphazardly hidden it. Why the hell had she even taken it out of its hiding place?

Oceane had been so careful to use it sparingly since entering the States—and only to stay in contact with Arturo—then disassemble and hide it in its secret spot. Another thing she'd been taught long ago, along with keeping a packed "go bag" hidden and ready to go at a moment's notice. For security reasons, because they had a lot of money from the legitimate companies her father ran and Oceane handled the finances for the ones belonging to her and her mother. Security reasons such as when those gunmen had tried to storm the gated home where she and her mother had lived.

So many things her mother had taught her over the years, things she hadn't thought much of at the time, were so clear to her now. Her whole life, her mother had secretly been preparing her for this in case it became necessary.

But why take out the phone and risk the DEA agents finding it? Her mother must have wanted to contact Arturo, maybe to let him know where they were being kept. It was the only thing Oceane could think of, and a disastrous mistake. Until now the U.S. government had kept its word about protecting them in exchange for information on her father and the cartel.

Now that they thought she and her mother might have been talking to people within the cartel and telling them God only knew what, the deal might be off the table. They could be locked up and charged if they found evidence. Or they might be shipped back to Mexico, to certain death at the hands of her father's rivals. Ruiz's men would love to capture them.

Oceane stared out the tinted back window of the SUV she had no doubt was armor plated, the traffic and landmarks of America's capital a blur even though she tried to memorize them for later. She knew too well the risks of what she was doing when she had fled to the U.S., but she'd been willing to accept them in order to protect her and her mother. Life as they'd known it had ended that night of the attack, and she couldn't seem to adjust to this new reality.

Except fleeing to the U.S. had been their only option.

Already she missed her mother. Her home, her work. Dammit, her *life*, which she had been blissfully living until a short while ago. She wanted things to go back to the way they had been, before she'd had the blindfold so painfully and suddenly ripped from her eyes.

She would gladly have lived in the bliss of ignorance for the rest of her life instead of knowing the things she did now. What was going to happen to her? Her mother?

The ring of a cell phone filled the brittle silence and Lockhart answered. "Yeah, I'm bringing her in right now. We'll meet you there," he told whoever he was talking to, then hung up.

"Meet who?" she asked, not really expecting an answer.

"One of your lawyers wants a word with you."

Surprised that he'd responded at all, much less answered her question, she asked another. "Which one?"

"Rowan Stewart."

Her anxiety eased slightly. Good. She wanted to talk to Rowan and plead her case against these accusations, explain her side of the story to one of the only people here who seemed to give a damn about her.

Lockhart drove her into the underground of a fortress-like building. As soon as he stopped, stern-faced agents were there to rip the door open and haul her toward the elevator.

"Where's my mother?" she demanded, digging in her heels. Little good it did her, because the men merely carried her along as though she weighed no more than a doll.

"You'll see her when we're done," the older of the two dragging her said, not slowing his pace.

Her brave front faltered as they neared the elevator doors. From the location and biometric scanners outside it, this wasn't an ordinary elevator. They were taking her to somewhere ultra secure, maybe a holding cell, and once they put her in it she might never get out again.

The ability to mask her fear crumbled. "*No*," she shouted, twisting in their grip. She started babbling, didn't even realize she'd slipped into frantic Spanish until Lockhart stepped in front of her and halted the other agents.

Piercing, pale blue eyes locked on hers. "Calm down."

Normally anyone saying that to her would make

her bristle, but his tone was so calm it snapped her out of her momentary panic. And, if she was honest, he wasn't hard to look at with those angular features and sculpted muscles stretching his T-shirt.

Not that she intended for him ever to know that she found him attractive. The man had been as cold as ice to her so far. She stared back at him now, still wary but willing to listen to him, because he had been tasked with her safety, and he didn't strike her as a man who would take his job lightly.

"We're taking you upstairs for questioning. Your mother is being questioned as well. When you're both finished, you'll see her. So the sooner you settle down and cooperate, the sooner you'll see her."

He could be lying. But she considered herself to be a good judge of people's character—except when it came to her father, who she now realized she'd never actually known—and Lockhart seemed sincere. Her gut said she could trust him, at least in this.

Relaxing slightly, she nodded once. "All right."

Rowan was coming. She would be able to fix this whole mess.

The agents took her into an isolated room at the end of a guarded hallway. The windows were frosted so she couldn't see out.

Her heart thudded erratically and her palms were clammy as she sat in the chair indicated. They left her alone except for Lockhart, who stood guard next to the door to her left, his arms folded across his chest, feet braced apart. Even though he didn't say anything, she took comfort in his presence. If he stayed with her, they wouldn't hurt her. Instinctively she knew he would protect her from harm, no matter what his personal feelings toward her were.

A few minutes later two people came in, a man and a woman, both wearing business suits. They sat opposite her, opened a folder and began the questions. Or rather, the interrogation. That's what it felt like. Back and forth they went, firing question after question at her, trying to trip her up, get her to falter on her story. Where she'd gotten the phone. Who she'd been in contact with. What she'd told her former bodyguard. Where Arturo might be now.

Oceane stayed firm on her version of events, because it was the truth. Their tech people were analyzing the phone right now. Even with its encryption, it was only a matter of time before they cracked it. They would be able to trace every call from the device, and where each originated from. Now that they knew about the phone and her contact with Arturo, she had nothing more to hide.

The truth shall set you free. That was the saying in English.

In this case, a version that was close to the truth would do the same. That way she could protect her mother and still come across as truthful. Yet another useful lesson she'd been taught at a young age.

Finally the agents paused, both of them watching her, expecting her to sweat. She was far calmer inside now than she had been when they'd brought her here. They weren't going to torture or starve her. But she was afraid of what they might threaten her mother with if Oceane didn't cooperate fully. So she gave as much information as she dared, as close to the truth as she could.

A knock on the door interrupted the staring contest. Oceane glanced over as it opened and Rowan strode in. Her posture was rigid, her expression the furthest thing from friendly as she turned her gaze on Oceane.

"You're up to speed?" the male agent asked her.

"I heard everything," Rowan said, the chill in her voice sending a thread of warning winding through Oceane. Rowan stepped behind the two agents and faced her, that deep blue gaze penetrating. "You know what happened last night?"

Oceane glanced between her and the agents in confusion, then shook her head. "No, what?"

Rowan's eyes turned cold. "Someone planted a bomb in my car while I was working."

Cold fingers wrapped around Oceane's stomach and squeezed. "Oh…"

"My brother was nearly killed in the explosion. He underwent emergency surgery last night and is in the intensive care unit right now."

Oceane blanched, even as her heart beat faster. "I'm so sorry."

Rowan's jaw clenched and she drew a deep breath, never breaking eye contact. "You told your bodyguard about me."

Because she trusted Arturo more than anyone here. "Well, yes—"

"He found out where my office was."

"I—"

"And then funny enough, my car gets bombed."

Oceane shook her head slowly, a fresh wave of anxiety building inside her. They thought she was behind it. That she had helped set this up. "I knew nothing about this. And it wasn't Arturo."

"And why are you so sure of that?" the male agent demanded.

Oceane met his gaze. "Because he would never harm an innocent, and he wants to protect me. He would never do anything that might jeopardize my safety." He wasn't stupid. And he was as loyal to her as she was him.

"But you said he used to work for your father," the man pointed out.

"Yes, but that was years ago. He's been with me since I was fifteen. He wouldn't risk my safety here by doing something like that."

"Not even with the amount of money your father was privately paying him?"

"No. *Never*."

The agents and Rowan looked unconvinced. She risked a glance over at Lockhart, still posted beside the door. He was watching her too, but his expression was thoughtful instead of cold.

"The FBI and DEA are going to find out who planted that bomb," Rowan said, drawing Oceane's attention back to her. "And if they find out you were involved, any deals made with you and your mother are null and void."

"Do you understand what that means?" the female agent asked.

Oceane flushed. She may have an accent, but her English was excellent, and she was far smarter than anyone here appeared to think. "Yes."

"Not only that," Rowan continued, "you'll be prosecuted to the full extent of the law. If convicted, you'll do hard time in a Federal prison. The same goes for your mother."

Oceane's chest constricted. They wouldn't find any evidence linking her or Arturo to the bombing. But her mother? She didn't know. Since that awful night of the attack she'd seen a whole new person emerge in place of her mother's laid-back, affectionate self. Could she have done this? Leaked information to someone within the cartel or even contacted Oceane's father? Because from what she'd learned in the past few days, he was certainly capable of ordering the assassination of a federal attorney.

"It could have been Ruiz," she protested.

"He's been locked up tight in a federal penitentiary for months now," the male agent said.

"If he's still alive, then he can still get orders out."

None of the others argued the point. Because everyone knew a man like Ruiz was still dangerous, even behind bars.

"Our agents are exploring all avenues," the male agent told her.

"Is there anything you'd like to add to your statements?" the woman asked.

"No. When can I see my mother?"

"When we decide neither one of you were involved in the bombing."

A heavy weight pressed down on her chest, slowly compressing her ribs. She'd run here to save herself and her mother, in the hope of starting a new life. Instead she'd run into a trap that was closing in on her with every passing hour.

Chapter Fourteen

"So do you believe her? That she wasn't involved with the bombing?" Malcolm asked Rowan as he drove them back to his place. The first thing he'd said to her since leaving DEA headquarters ten minutes ago.

Glad that the stony silence was broken, she answered honestly. "At this point I don't know what to think."

Every time she thought of Oceane or Anya being part of this nightmare, a fresh rush of fury shot through her veins. But as far as Rowan could tell, Oceane's reaction to the question of involvement had been real, and so had her surprise about the bombing. Either that, or she was the best damn actress Rowan had ever seen. The FBI was going to polygraph her and her mother, so if either of them was lying, they'd find out soon enough.

But *someone* had tipped off the *Veneno* cartel that

Oceane and her mother had been meeting with Rowan and her boss. If not Oceane or her mother, then who?

Adding to her irritation, Malcolm remained polite but remote, acting like they were mere acquaintances forced to spend time together, when last night he'd practically set her on fire with his kisses. Part of her was too exhausted and overwhelmed with everything else to attempt to break through the wall he'd put up between them. But another, larger part was desperate for him to let her in.

"We'll get some answers soon," he said.

"Not soon enough for my liking." She stole a glance at him out of the corner of her eye as he drove. His left hand was on the steering wheel, his right forearm on the center armrest between them. If she reached for his hand, would he yank it away? She couldn't take that kind of blatant rejection right now.

Where did she stand with him? He wanted her physically, but that was all? She couldn't believe that. Not after all he'd done for her the past few days, the way he'd stepped up and volunteered to keep her safe. If it had only been physical for him, he could easily have brushed her off. So it had to run deeper than that.

She wracked her brain for the rest of the drive, trying to figure out where to go from here.

He opened the door for her and she walked inside, kicking her heels off and heading straight for the hallway, intending to go to her room and shut herself away for some privacy until she decided what to do about her and Malcolm.

The door locked behind her. Her stride faltered.

No.

The word reverberated in her head, so loud and clear it startled her, stopping her there at the start of the hallway.

Her entire body was on edge, all her emotions a chaotic, roiling mass in her chest. Seeing Kevin today, battered and far worse for wear but deeply in love with his partner despite their father's obvious disapproval, had solidified something for her. For too long she'd lived her life towing the nearly unattainable line to gain his approval. His love.

That wasn't love; it was a form of hostage situation.

For years she'd focused solely on school, then work, all in a pathetic and misguided attempt to make him love her. In the process she'd given up everything else, barely making time for her family, hardly ever seeing her friends, and had no one to come home to at night.

Now, outside of work, she really had no life. And when a good man like Malcolm had come along, what had she done? Shoved him away because she hadn't known what to do with him and panicked like a frightened child. Worse, she hadn't even recognized it for what it truly was until Malcolm had forced her to confront the truth last night.

She was no coward. And she was sick and tired of living a half-life, denying herself the chance of happiness when the only man she wanted was right behind her. Literally standing there behind her, and he not only was still attracted to her, he must still care about her on some level or he wouldn't have gone to all this trouble.

Heart pounding, Rowan screwed up her courage and spun around to face him. Malcolm froze in the act of shrugging out of his shoulder holster, his body preternaturally still as he met her stare. Watching her warily, correctly reading her intent.

Just the sight of him set her pulse racing. And God it was sexy, knowing that he'd willingly placed himself between her and any danger to her safety.

Her bare feet were almost silent on the hardwood floor as she walked toward him, her steps slow, measured. Without breaking eye contact he slowly set his holster on the kitchen counter. His posture was tense, his expression unreadable as he watched her.

She walked right up to him, ignoring the quiver of uncertainty in her gut. It was time to be bold, take what she wanted, and go from there.

"Rowan..." he began in a warning tone.

She ignored that too, reaching up to curl a hand around his nape as she lifted on tiptoe and pressed her mouth to his, the need to restore their connection obliterating everything else. His lips were smooth and firm beneath hers, the shape of them so familiar as she poured her feelings into the kiss.

Malcolm resisted for a second, then made a deep, dark sound and plunged his hands into her hair, his mouth slanting over hers as he took control of the kiss.

Rowan moaned in combined pleasure and relief, letting the sensations cascade through her. At least he wanted her as much as she wanted him.

The kiss was all heat and hunger, his tongue stroking hers with urgent need. He was hot and hard all over, the unmistakable ridge of his erection stretching the front of his jeans. No more waiting. She was finally going to do all the things she'd fantasized about him over the past year. Explore the kind of intimacy she'd craved but had been too afraid to risk.

Her free hand curled around the sculpted contour of his muscled shoulder, the coiled strength beneath her fingers making her dizzy with arousal. She'd meant to turn him, flip their positions and press him back against the island to take control back, but her brain short-circuited the moment he fisted a hand in her hair and pulled her head back, his wicked mouth sliding over the sensitive skin at the side of her neck.

Before she could gather a single coherent thought, he locked an arm around her hips and popped her off her feet, carrying her a few steps to the nearest wall where he pinned her with the strength and weight of his body.

A shaky, startled moan bubbled out of her at the raw show of dominance. Before, he'd kept this side of him tempered, hiding it beneath a hot tenderness that she'd enjoyed, but ultimately had left her frustrated. *This* was what she'd sensed beneath the surface. This forceful and passionate side of him was what she'd been craving all along.

Now she couldn't get close enough. Rowan grabbed hold of his wide shoulders for balance, frustrated by her snug skirt as she fought to wind her legs around his hips.

Malcolm captured her jaw in one hand, bringing her eyes to his. His burned with a primal light that made her shiver. "I didn't want to want you anymore," he rasped out, his jaw taut with residual anger or resentment.

Her heart stuttered, the fear of rejection rising sharply, but then immediately covered her mouth with his, his tongue plunging between her lips in a claiming that sent a hot bolt of arousal through her. The fear receded.

She met him stroke for stroke, arching into his body, every nerve ending fizzing like champagne. She was already wet, aching for him, her breasts swollen and sensitive, rubbing her hips against him to ease the ache between her thighs.

Breathing hard, Malcolm lifted his head a moment later to stare down at her with molten chocolate eyes. "But I can't keep my hands off you," he half-growled, his voice laced with accusation.

"Good." It was a start. Something she could use to crack through his defenses. He stilled, his body going rigid as she slid one hand down his chest, over his clenched abdomen, watching his eyes. Then lower, to the thick bulge in his jeans. She had to reach him, had to touch his heart, and if this was the only way he'd allow it to happen, then she would take it.

He sucked in a sharp breath that sounded almost tortured. "Fuck. Rowan." He dropped his head to the side of her neck, his ragged breaths hot against her skin. Fighting his need.

She wouldn't allow it. Wouldn't allow him to shut her out or turn away now.

Unwinding her legs, she let her feet slide to the floor to give her more room, her mouth busy nipping at the edge of his taut jaw, the pulse hammering in his throat. A low, warning growl rumbled up from his chest when she slid the button at the top of his fly undone. But he made no move to stop her.

Emboldened, she slid her hand beneath the denim, inside the cotton of his underwear to grasp his hard, thick length. He was hot in her hand, swollen to bursting.

His breath halted, his hips surging forward when she squeezed him, dragging a helpless moan from somewhere deep in his chest. She'd imagined this moment so many times, couldn't wait to feel him inside her, filling her, taking away the empty feeling and replacing it with pleasure.

The sound of their quickened breathing filled the air. He pulsed in her grip, triggering an answering empty ache between her legs. She continued kissing his neck, dragging her tongue up the side as she stroked him with her fist, remembering how he liked it. They'd done this before, a long time ago in a heated rush in the front seat of his truck, but there were so many other things she'd wanted to do to him and never gotten the chance. Tonight, she wasn't stopping until she had all of him.

Malcolm stood stock still before her, his chest rising and falling with each rapid breath while she worked him, her other hand shoving his T-shirt up so that her mouth could slide over the flexed power of his pecs. She paused to dart her tongue across one tight nipple, dragging another groan out of him, sucked lightly before trailing down, down, sinking to her knees in front of him, her back and hips bolstered by the wall.

Nipping at the tense muscles in his abdomen, she glanced up at his face. He stared down at her with an expression of pure masculine hunger, his flexed fore-arms braced on the wall, hands knotted into fists.

He wanted this. So badly that he couldn't pull away now. Clearly fighting the need to shove his pants down, grab her head and bring her mouth to him. She didn't want him to fight it.

Her heart thundered against her ribs as she held his gaze and reached up to grasp his left arm, pulling it down. When it was level with her head she turned her face into his hand and nuzzled him, rubbing her hot cheek against his palm.

Telling him without words what she wanted, she set his hand on her hair and tugged the denim and cotton down, freeing the thick length of his erection to her ravenous gaze.

Malcolm hissed in a breath and tangled his fingers in her hair, tugging at her scalp, the slight burn increasing the tension humming between them. Breaking his gaze at last, she curled her fingers around the wide base and parted her lips as she bent to him, determined to mark him, drive him out of his mind with pleasure.

Slowly, slowly she closed her lips around the swollen crown of his cock. His fist clenched in her hair, the muscles in his thighs and belly locking tight. A heady wave of feminine power and arousal sizzled under her skin.

He let out a low, strangled groan, the feel of her hot mouth engulfing him making that powerful body shudder. The scent of his soap, the salty taste of his arousal filled her senses.

God, she loved this. Loved going down on him, making him insane.

His thigh tensed beneath her left palm as she closed her eyes and slid her mouth down on him, taking as much of him as she could, her tongue stroking, cheeks hollowing as she sucked. A ragged sound of pleasure tore from his throat.

He tightened his hold on her hair, pulling, forcing her to slide up his shaft before locking her head in place and surging his hips forward, driving back into her willing mouth. Rowan whimpered and shifted restlessly around the ache of arousal between her thighs, reaching around to grab his tight ass with her free hand, sucking him eagerly, unable to get enough.

"Oh yeah, sweetness, more." The deep, dark timbre of his voice was like a caress to her senses, the approval and enjoyment creating a melting sensation inside her. But sweetness. That was something only he had ever called her, and it made her believe she might be breaking through the barrier around his heart.

Sliding back up his length, she opened her eyes to watch his reaction as she tightened her mouth and twirled her tongue around the sensitive crest of his head. Bracing his free arm against the wall, Malcolm propped his forehead on his clenched fist and took what she so willingly offered, sliding in and out of her mouth. Low, almost inaudible groans filled her ears, mixing with the thud of her heart.

He couldn't stop this now, he was too far-gone. She wanted him riding the edge of his control, ready to explode.

Fighting for control, he squeezed his fist in her hair, slowly withdrew from her mouth. She released his shaft to grab his ass with both hands and tried to lean forward to take him back in, but he wouldn't let her, instead dragging her up and wedging her against the wall. He was so damn hard, his entire body strung taut, and she wanted to push him over the brink.

But Malcolm fused their mouths together before she could utter a single protest, claiming her mouth as she wanted him to claim her body. Needed him to.

The buttons on her blouse popped free when he tugged the two halves apart, and he broke the kiss long enough to drink in the sight of her breasts encased in ivory satin and lace, her hard nipples pressing against the fabric. With a hungry sound he hauled her higher up the wall, lifting her off her feet to bury his face between her breasts.

She gasped and arched her back, pushing into his face, his searching mouth, the faint stubble on his cheeks and jaw abrading her pleasantly. Impatient, he yanked the cups of the bra down, revealing her tight pink nipples that made him groan.

He flicked his tongue over one, teasing it while she moaned and twisted in his grip. Malcolm held her in place while her fingers bit into his shoulders, his scalp. Holding on for dear life while the world spun around her. Finally he darted his tongue over one sensitive peak, rolling around that sensitive flesh before at last closing his lips around it.

She made a mewling sound and panted, straining in his arms as he suckled. All too soon he switched to the other, using his weight to hold her to the wall, seeming to revel in her every little cry, each desperate gasp, while he trailed his right hand down her ribs to the bare skin of her inner thigh, exposed by the hem of her skirt he'd hiked up.

Rowan bit her lip and closed her eyes, dying a little as she waited for the touch she needed more than the air to breathe.

Firm, deft fingers slid over the damp lace covering her core, tugged the center aside to slide beneath to the wet, soft folds awaiting him. "God, you're soaking wet," he breathed, pressing his scalding hot cock to her bare thigh at the evidence of her arousal.

Rowan whimpered in response, unable to speak, fighting to roll her hips against his hand with the limited space he'd given her, needing more than he was delivering. She wanted him with every fiber in her being. Wanted to know she wasn't alone in her feelings for him.

Then he pulled his hand free.

No!

He snaked a steely arm around her hips, smothered her babbled protests with another hot, searing kiss as he shoved her skirt all the way up to her waist. Tongue tangled with hers, he reached between them to grab the side of her panties and yanked, tearing the flimsy fabric.

She shuddered and moaned, shifting her legs to wind them tighter around his hips, opening herself to him completely as she ripped her mouth free. "Please, I need—"

"Shh." With one hand he dove into his pocket for his wallet, managed to drag out the condom before it fell to the floor.

He ripped it open with his teeth, let her take it from him and reach between them to smooth it down his hot length. Gritting his jaw as she gave him a slow, firm stroke with her fist, his eyes went heavy-lidded, that luscious mouth mere inches from her own.

Ready to beg for what she wanted, Rowan held on tight and wiggled her hips, rubbing the open folds of her sex along his taut abdomen. He made a rough sound and held her tighter against the wall, then levered her up enough to nestle the length of his cock in her tender folds. Rowan caught her breath at the heat of him, licked her lips and stared down into his eyes, her body tensed. Waiting.

Now. Please now...

Malcolm held the rest of his body absolutely still as he eased the weight of his torso off her slightly, allowing gravity to do the work. Mesmerized, Rowan held his gaze while the hot, thick head of his cock eased into her. She bit back a groan, her eyes widening a little at the breadth of him.

A flare of alarm flashed through her as she eased down farther, her body opening, stretching to the slow, heavy pressure. She grabbed hold of his shoulders, her body automatically tensing as the pressure turned into a burning. A soft, plaintive sound came out of her and she pushed up on his shoulders with her hands, trying to escape.

His arm tightened around her hips, a steely band that allowed no quarter. "No," he ground out, his voice ragged, features tense. "Take it."

Rowan froze at the low command, the erotic edge to it. Her heart thundered beneath her ribs. He didn't just want her body. He wanted her surrender.

And she wanted to give him both, she realized with startled insight.

Gazing down into his eyes, she drew a deep

breath, then deliberately relaxed. Surrendering to him. Allowing her body to open for him, for her weight to sink down on him.

This slow, intimate penetration was so much more than sex. Twice as hot, so fucking good she could barely breathe. He watched her the whole time, seeming just as transfixed as he filled her, inch by aching inch. Pushing through her body's lingering resistance. Branding and claiming her as his own.

When he was buried inside her to the hilt, claiming total possession of her, Rowan sucked in a breath and shuddered. Her inner muscles fluttered around him, fighting to adjust to the thick intrusion, the burn fading slightly but the unsatisfied ache more intense than ever.

Unable to articulate what she was feeling, afraid for him to see her stripped so bare, she dropped her head onto his shoulder and turned her face into his neck as she clung for dear life.

Chapter Fifteen

⸺◈◇◈◇◈⸺

Mal was dying.

At least, that's what it felt like to finally be enveloped in the tight, slick warmth of Rowan's body. He'd wanted this for so damn long, could barely stand the burn at the feel of her rippling around him.

He was too damn close already, had somehow managed to hold off while she'd sucked him like he was her favorite treat. Another time—if there was another time—he'd let her finish him off with her mouth. Right now, he wanted to pin her beneath him, stare down into her face as he took her, claimed her as no man ever had or ever would again.

Her core clenched around him as she shifted in his arms, sending pleasure rocketing up his spine. She drew in an unsteady breath, her fingers flexing on his back.

A wave of tender possessiveness flooded him as

she clung to him, her face hidden in his neck, tiny little quivers running through her. Something caught in his chest.

You're mine, sweetness.

The domineering, possessive thought was clear in his head, and irrefutable. She could fight the idea of them together all she wanted, but once he was through claiming her tonight, she was his. And his alone.

Her whole body was tense, her breathing shallow and rapid. He'd caught the flare of pain in her eyes as she'd started to slide down on him, some primal part of him getting off on the act of surrender she'd shown him. But as hot as this was, he wasn't taking her against the fucking wall this first time.

Wrapping his arms around her, he gathered her close and turned them, striding for his room. With every step down the hall his cock shifted inside her, the friction making sweat break out along his spine. Rowan made a soft, helpless sound and squirmed in his hold, unable to do anything but go along for the ride.

His room was almost dark with the blinds pulled down, so he left the door open, providing just enough daylight spilling in from the window at the end of the hall for him to see her face as he lay her down on the sheets, still buried inside her. Then he stretched out on top of her, gently pulled her head from his shoulder and smoothed the hair back from her forehead.

Her eyes were clear now, no longer heavy-lidded with arousal and hunger, while he was ready to come out of his skin from the way she squeezed and flexed around him. That wouldn't do at all.

With single-minded intent he set about rebuilding her need, rocking slowly inside her while he sucked at her lips and toyed with her nipples. She met him stroke for stroke, her eagerness easing the knot in his chest. When she moaned and flexed her body into him a few moments later, fighting to get closer, he slid a hand between them to find her clit with his thumb, rubbing the side of it gently.

She wriggled under him, angling her hips, then let out a gasp and grabbed the back of his neck when he added a little more pressure. "Oh, yeah, there," she breathed, rocking against his thumb.

He was rock hard inside her, tingles of pleasure intensifying at the base of his spine. Mal kept her pinned beneath him, allowing her only a limited range of motion with her hips while he maintained the slow, deep rhythm.

Jesus, the way she moved, the sounds she made were about to make him come unglued. Being inside her was even better than he'd imagined, and he didn't see how he was going to keep his distance from her now. He'd wanted to play it cool, stay remote. She'd just smashed through his barriers with her surrender.

He fought the climb to release, catalogued every hitch in her breathing, every tiny cry in response to his touch, memorizing what she liked best. Soon she was panting, her thighs wrapping tighter around his hips, her hands clutching at his back.

All mine. You're all mine.

The thought almost sent him over the edge. Clamping his jaw tight, Mal shoved the pleasure back through sheer force of will and drove into her harder, angling his hips to hit her inner sweet spot.

His gaze remained riveted on her face, drinking in every last detail of her response.

Four more strokes and her eyes squeezed shut, an expression of unspeakable ecstasy filling her face as she neared the edge. "Malcolm..."

Oh, fuck, the sound of his name in that pleasure-drenched voice. "God, you feel so damn good."

"I'm so close..." Her teeth sunk into her lower lip. Seconds later she bucked and started coming, her slick core clenching around his cock, head thrown back, that lush mouth parted on a wild, keening cry of release.

God. He'd never seen anything so beautiful in his life than Rowan coming undone beneath him. Once would never be enough. He was addicted now, would always want more.

He continued to ride her through it, drawing out her pleasure as long as he could, slowing only when she sagged back against the sheets, her grip relaxing on his hips and shoulders, her body going limp. Mal's heart hammered against his ribs, his breathing ragged, pleasure searing every nerve ending, the need to come so intense it hurt.

But he waited for her eyes to open. For that post-orgasmic haze to fade from those blue depths until she focused on him.

Only then did he slide both hands into her hair and surge deep, a hard, hungry rhythm while the sensation grew and he savored every slick glide of his cock in her sweet heat.

Rowan shifted her legs higher to wind around his waist and clamped her inner walls down on him, her fingers caressing his cheek. The combined gentle touch and steady eye contact was so intimate, so intense.

And he was lost. Lost to everything but her and the pleasure she gave.

Burying his face in the curve of her neck, he let go, his whole body shuddering as the orgasm hit, pulse after pulse of ecstasy ripping through him. Gasping for air, his muscles like soft wax left in the sun, he sank into the cradle of her body with a groan and lay in her arms, destroyed.

He'd never felt like this before. Never felt so connected to a woman. Never needed anyone the way he needed her.

Through the fog of oblivion, a flicker of dread ignited in his chest. He'd just let his guard down for her, in an even bigger way than the last time. Now what? If she decided she wanted to move on, pretend that this wasn't everything, what the hell was he going to do?

Rowan's soft, sleepy sound jerked him out of his thoughts. Realizing he must be crushing her, he reluctantly eased off and out of her warmth. Quickly dealing with the condom, he returned to the bed and stretched out alongside her.

She was on her back, her face turned toward him, eyes open. Watching him. There wasn't enough light for him to read her expression.

In that instant, cold, brutal reality hit him.

He'd just laid himself physically and emotionally bare to the woman he'd wanted forever, yet he had no idea where he stood with her. It was disorienting as hell and he didn't have the energy to deal with it right now. They would iron out where they stood to-morrow. He'd rather focus on the here and now, hold onto this moment for as long as he could. In case it didn't last.

Determined to enjoy the closeness between them, he cradled the side of her face in his hand, swept his thumb across her cheek as he leaned in to kiss her. Her lips were soft, inviting, parting for the tender glide of his tongue.

And when he rolled her onto her side and tucked her into the curve of his body, she snuggled up with a contented sigh while he pulled the covers over them. In the dimness he kissed the top of her shoulder, breathing in her clean, feminine scent. "Can you sleep now?" he murmured.

"Not sure," she mumbled drowsily. "Maybe if you hold me like this the whole time."

His heart lurched and he tightened his arms around her. "I will." *I'll hold onto you forever if you let me.*

Chapter Sixteen

"Rowan Stewart. Where is she?" Manny stalked across the carpeted floor of his home office, his agitation so strong he worried he might explode if he didn't keep moving. How the hell hard was it to find such a high profile lawyer?

"No leads yet."

No leads. No answers. No fucking information whatsoever for the past forty-eight hours.

From what he understood, the female lawyer was the one in closest contact with Oceane and Anya. Of anyone, she would know where they were. "She couldn't just have up and disappeared into thin air," he growled.

"Oceane and Anya both did," Montoya pointed out.

"No, they didn't. And we're only having trouble finding them because the DEA or FBI is hiding them." It infuriated him. None of his contacts had come back with a location yet.

"So, you talked to *El Escorpion*?"

"Yes."

"What did he say?"

"He said to take care of it," he snapped, annoyed. What did Montoya think the man would say?

After Manny had told *El Escorpion* about the situation with Oceane and Anya, the conversation had been brief. That weird, digitally altered voice that was supposed to help keep *El Escorpion's* identity a secret from even the top cartel members had instructed him in clipped Spanish that he had best deal with the situation poste haste, or prepare to be dealt with in turn.

Manny had no desire to die. He was doing everything he could to mitigate the damage done and recover his daughter and mistress.

"He didn't say anything about Ruiz?" Montoya asked.

"Yeah, he's going to help us shut the last of Ruiz's network down." So some good had come from his call.

"That's good. Means the boss still thinks you're valuable and wants to keep you around."

Manny grunted. He was many things, but stupid wasn't one of them. *El Escorpion* was only going to keep Manny around so long as it suited his and the cartel's purposes. To make sure that happened, Manny needed to get this shit cleaned up immediately. For that, he needed a lead on the female lawyer, who would hopefully give him one on his daughter and mistress.

"Nothing more from the tracking device?" The damn thing had cost him a fortune when he'd paid for it a couple years ago. Maybe it wasn't functioning properly anymore. The technology was outdated. Had the Americans found it and disabled it?

"No. It was a long shot that I found it last time. And after last night the lawyers' office is locked down tight. There's a security perimeter up, and nobody's getting in or out without extra screening. I've got eyes on the place but no one's seen the female lawyer or her boss since last night. They've been moved into a secure location by now. They'll have their own security details."

Manny scoffed. "Nothing's ever totally secure. Find Oceane and Anya. Find the lawyer if you have to."

"Trying. I've got eyes and ears all over this city. If I hear anything, you'll be the first to know."

"Not good enough. I want this dealt with *now*, do you understand me? Send your best man in to find a lead. Pay whoever will help us, offer whatever it takes. Just take the woman if that's easiest, find out where my daughter is, and then make our problem disappear. Got it?"

Montoya was quiet a moment. "How much you willing to spend?"

"I told you. Whatever it takes. You understand?" Even if this phone line was secure, he wasn't going to come right out and say something that might incriminate him later. Montoya knew *exactly* what he meant.

"Yeah, I understand." Montoya's voice held an undercurrent of anticipation. His most lethal *sicario*, about to have his leash cut and turned loose to do what he loved most.

It was probably going to come back to haunt Manny in the end, but at this point, he was willing to risk it because he didn't have any other option. He needed this taken care of immediately or risk losing everything.

Once again, letting Montoya do what he loved best was Manny's best chance of getting what he wanted.

****

Rowan's new phone rang a little before two that afternoon. She glanced at the screen, couldn't help but smile when she saw the number on the display. "It's Malcolm," she told the male agent, who had stopped reading his newspaper to look at her.

When he nodded his consent, she got up and walked from the kitchen into her new bedroom for the foreseeable future, wanting at least the illusion of privacy.

"Hey," she answered, relieved that he'd called. Things had still been somewhat unsettled between them when she'd left his place a few hours ago. Part of her had worried that he would pull away now that they'd slept together, that he'd withdraw from her emotionally. Him reaching out to her now was a good sign.

"Hi. How are you settling in? Your new detail okay?"

Just hearing his voice made her feel better. "They're fine." Remote but professional. "I'll be honest—I liked my last detail way better."

"Yeah, I liked my last assignment better too."

Her smile turned wistful. They'd been woken from their post most-amazing-sex-ever nap just before eleven that morning by a phone call from Commander Taggart, informing them that a new detail was being sent over for her within the hour, and Malcolm was to relieve Hamilton and return to guarding Anya.

Agents had arrived shortly thereafter and whisked Rowan off to a new safe location, where she'd been given an update on the state of the investigation. After undergoing a polygraph test, both Anya and Oceane had been cleared of any wrongdoing with the bombing and released back into protective custody this morning. A huge relief for Rowan, to know that the women she'd been trying to help hadn't been involved.

FBI analysts assigned to the case had found exactly what Oceane said they would on her phone, but her bodyguard was long gone, might even have slipped back into Mexico. Surveillance footage from the cameras outside Rowan's building had shown nothing about the bombs being planted in her and her boss's cars, because someone had disabled them for a critical ten-minute window.

Whoever had done it, they were pros. The type of explosive, the method and timing, however, all pointed to *Veneno* involvement. Ruiz had denied having anything to do with it. And no one knew where the hell Manny Nieto even was. Which one of them was responsible?

"How long do you think you'll be there?" Rowan

asked, missing him already even though it had only been a few hours. This morning had been amazing, and being able to fall asleep in his arms had soothed her on the deepest level.

Except they hadn't had time to talk about things, and what each of them wanted and what would happen going forward. She wasn't sure if having a reprieve was a good thing or a bad thing. Them being separated didn't help either. Too much time and distance might allow him to pull back and put that wall back up between them again.

"Not sure. Depends on what happens." He paused a second. "How are you holding up?"

"Okay." *Except I miss you like crazy.* So much she ached, especially since things were still up in the air between them. She wanted another chance at a real and lasting relationship with him, to make up for the mistakes she'd made last time. Now that Malcolm had made her face and own her fears, she was willing to work past them.

Because he was worth fighting for, and she didn't want to remain trapped in this lonely existence she'd created for herself. The only benefit of her work right now was that she had a ton of it, and it would keep her mind occupied.

"I'm going to call Nick in a little while and find out how Kevin is, then talk to my parents," she said. "I won't be going into the hospital anymore until this is resolved."

"That sucks, but it makes the most sense given what's going on."

"I know. I just hate being away from my brother right now."

"He'll understand. And he knows you would be there if you could."

"Yes." She rubbed her palm over her denim-covered thigh, anxious about asking the next question yet not being able to contain it a moment longer. He hadn't brought it up, but they couldn't dance around the obvious forever. And she was under enough strain right now without the extra anxiety of worrying about losing him on top of everything else. "So, I have to ask this, because it's driving me insane not knowing."

"Not knowing what?"

"About us." She paused a beat. "What do you want to happen between us from here on out?"

He was quiet a moment, and she held her breath, all her secret fears bubbling to the surface. "We won't be able to see each other while I'm on this assignment," he finally said.

She pushed back a frustrated noise, forced her insecurities back into the box they'd escaped from. "I know, but I mean after that. Are we...was this morning a one-off for you, or..."

"Or?"

"Or do you want more?" *Please say yes.* She couldn't bear it if he said no.

"I guess that depends on you."

She blinked, surprised. "Why on me?"

He sighed. "Look, now isn't the best time to have this conversation. We'll talk about it later."

She didn't care if it was a bad time. With everything going on, if they waited for a good time, it might never happen. If that's what he was hoping for, too bad for him. "No, tell me what you meant."

"You want the truth?" He made it sound like she might not like it.

An invisible weight settled on her chest, pressing her lungs. Her heart thudded in her ears. "Yes."

"I think I made it clear where I stood a year ago, but that's not what you wanted. I won't do that to myself again unless I know you're in this for real this time."

The pressure eased even as her heart swelled, a tentative smile tugging at her lips. "I am."

Another pause. "How do I know I can trust that you mean it this time?"

She flinched inside, hating how much she'd hurt him. "Because now I can admit that I made a mistake back then, and I also realize that my reasons for walking away were bullshit. I've missed you, and I want to be with you. Just you," she added, in case that wasn't clear. It was hard to put herself out there like this in the face of possible rejection, but it had to be done. "I want you in my life. To come home to you, lean on you, and for you to lean on me."

"You sure?" He didn't sound completely convinced.

"Yes. I've never been surer of anything in my life." She could understand why he would have reservations about trusting her again, though.

"Well...good, then." There was a smile in his voice. "Then let's hope this assignment wraps up fast, huh?"

"God, yes." She laughed, feeling like half the weight she'd been carrying around on her shoulders had suddenly been lifted. She wanted to talk about them more, make sure everything was spelled out clearly, but wouldn't push him right now. For the moment it was enough that he was willing to give them another chance. "I really miss you."

He chuckled softly. "Miss you too. I gotta go now, but I'll call later if I can."

"Okay. Bye."

"Bye."

Rowan set the phone down in her lap and drew the first full breath she'd taken in days, the relief crashing over her so acute that her entire body sagged. Against all odds, it seemed that Malcolm was hers again.

As long as she had him by her side—even if it was only in a metaphorical sense while they were separated—she could get through anything.

Chapter Seventeen

————◇◇◇◇◇————

Astream of rapid Spanish burst through the room along with feminine crying when Oceane and her mother were finally reunited at the secure condo location that afternoon. Mal stood at the far end of the kitchen to give them a semblance of privacy and met Lockhart's long-suffering gaze as his teammate walked in and locked the front door behind him.

Kill me now, Lockhart's expression said, and Mal bit back a smirk of sympathy. They'd both rather be doing a *lot* of things right now than guarding a cartel lieutenant's daughter and mistress. Most of all, Mal would give anything to trade places with one of the agents placed on Rowan's new detail.

Their phone call earlier had helped a lot. This morning had been amazing, yet part of him had still been worried that he'd made another huge mistake in letting her back in. He'd opened himself up to her

191

once before and gotten his heart smashed to pieces for his trouble.

She seemed different now, and not just because she'd let her guard down and they'd finally slept together. Although being with her that way had been ten times better than he'd ever imagined it would be. It helped that she was taking ownership of her former actions, and that she'd said she was willing to work on things.

He just hoped she would live by those words, because honest to God if she bailed on him again it would fucking crush him.

Lockhart joined him and together they moved to the living room off the kitchen. After the phone incident, they'd been ordered to maintain an eyes-on policy except for bathroom breaks and when the women slept, although Mal and Lockhart would check on them at intervals through the night.

Mal sank down onto the end of the couch nearest the kitchen. Close enough to keep watch over the women and see what they were doing, but not so near that they felt imprisoned.

"Man, Taggart owes us for this," Lockhart muttered in a low voice, removing his customary ball cap to scrub a hand over his dirty blond hair.

"He knows it." Their commander was a good guy, and fair. He'd probably do something to make it up to them later. "So, the inquisition's over?"

"For now. She cleared her poly with flying colors."

So had Anya.

Lockhart shoved his hands in his jeans pockets and leaned against the wall. "You sweep the place?"

"FBI techs checked for bugs, and I went through the place myself just before they brought Anya back." There was no way in hell Mal would have been able to stomach guard duty for her now unless she'd been cleared of any involvement with the bombing, or of leaking Rowan's name. To the point that he would have taken a temporary leave of absence to avoid it, and taken whatever consequences came from Taggart and the DEA.

Lockhart grunted. "Helps that you and she don't speak the same language."

Mal couldn't help but grin. "Silver lining."

"Lucky bastard. Wanna swap?"

"Nope."

The hint of a smile tugged at the corner of Lockhart's mouth. "So. How's Rowan?" he asked casually.

She's holding my heart in her hands without realizing it, and I hope the hell she won't break it again. "Doing well, all things considered. New security detail took over this morning."

His teammate nodded. "Any leads yet?"

"Not a solid one. Apparently the two parking lot security guys at the U.S. Attorney's office disappeared at the same time the video feeds went dark, and haven't turned up since."

"Perp paid them off, then. My bet is they're either already out of the state and thinking of how to leave the country, or floating facedown in the Potomac."

"My money's on the second." That's how the *Venenos* operated. Total warfare, didn't matter who got in their crosshairs. They used whoever they could to get what they wanted. And if they saw a threat, they eliminated it immediately, be it man, woman, or child.

Speaking of threats... He shifted his gaze back to the two women, who were walking toward the kitchen table now, Oceane's steadying arm wrapped around her mother's shoulders. "They're damn hard to figure out, aren't they?" he said quietly so only Lockhart could hear him. It wasn't their job to analyze the women, but he couldn't help but wonder about them.

"Christ, yeah. And after that stunt they pulled with the phone, they're both lucky they're not locked up or being deported right now."

"Must have given the agency some good intel, to warrant them this kind of protection."

Lockhart gave another grunt. "Honestly? I think they gave only exactly as much as they had to, and the government's keeping them safe in the hopes of getting something even better later on." He watched the women as they sat next to each other at the table, speaking in low tones, Anya's spiral-curled head resting on her daughter's shoulder. "The daughter's smart. I think way smarter than a lot of people are giving her credit for. She's using that."

Mal cocked his head, intrigued by the observation. Lockhart had been a Ranger sniper. And snipers were the world's best observers, seeing things most others didn't. "What makes you say that?"

"I've been watching her. Those gears in her head never stop turning. I can't figure her out. At times she seems so young and naïve, and at other times she's guarded. She's careful in what she says and does, and she knows how to mask her emotions better than most people."

Huh. "You make it sound almost like she's had training."

"Oh, I'm betting on it. But I'm not sure she even realizes what she's been taught."

"You don't think the agents figured that out while they were questioning her?"

"Yeah, but I think they're still underestimating her."

Interesting. Mal looked back at the two women. Oceane's eyes flicked up, moved from him to Lockhart and held for a moment on his teammate, almost as if she was assessing him before lowering her eyes again. Even more interesting.

"What's their reasoning for not joining WITSEC now?" Mal asked. Because surely to God, by this point someone as intelligent as Oceane must see the wisdom in it.

"Part of her is still worried it might be a trap, something our government would use to separate her and her mom permanently. Not only that, they both still want to be able to return home when the dust settles one day."

Mal scoffed. "That doesn't sound so intelligent." They likely wouldn't last a day back in Mexico. The *Venenos* had eyes and ears everywhere. The moment they set foot back on Mexican soil, someone within the cartel infrastructure would know. Then they'd be walking targets for anyone looking to push Nieto out of power.

Lockhart shrugged, his pale gaze trained on the women. "It's because she's still not sure what the hell's really going on. From what I've heard, she knows next to sweet fuck all about her dad, except that he's rich and powerful. He and her mom basically kept her in the dark about his operations this whole time. I think she's still hoping he'll be able to pull enough strings and throw out enough money to make it safe enough for them to return home."

Hard to believe any child of Nieto's could remain ignorant as to who and what he really was for twenty-four years, but that wasn't Malcolm's problem. His job was to keep the women safe, Anya specifically, and ensure there were no more breaches in security. Which meant that as long as he was on this assignment, the women were on lockdown.

When it was clear neither Oceane nor Anya intended to leave the table for a good long while yet, Mal and Lockhart lounged back on the couches, keeping an eye on them while picking up only snatches of what was said. Lots of feminine whispering, then long minutes of silence as they sat huddled together before the conversation started up again.

"You getting any of this?" Mal murmured to Lockhart finally. His teammate had way more Spanish than Mal did.

"Bits and pieces. They're talking about their options from here. Weighing the pros and cons. And Oceane just told her mom that she doesn't see any way they'll be able to go home again."

That would explain the weeping. Anya had her face buried in her daughter's shoulder now, her body jerking with the force of her tears, while Oceane was more composed, pressing her lips together and taking unsteady breaths.

How trustworthy they were, Mal didn't know.

How much of an asset they were to the U.S. government, Mal didn't know.

Their heartbreak, however, was real. They could never go home again. Their lives as they'd known them were over. Dead and buried along with any hopes and dreams they'd had in Mexico. Their only option now, after they were released from government protection, was to start new lives either here in the States, or abroad. He hoped they realized that soon enough.

When fatigue began to creep up on him, threatening to weigh down his eyelids, Mal got up and moved around the room. Lockhart remained planted on the couch, his long legs stretched out in front of him, arms folded across his chest as he listened to the quiet conversation going on at the table. Mal was just starting to think about getting something to eat when a kitchen chair scraped over the floor.

Oceane stood to face them, her creamy-brown skin pale, her blue-gray eyes full of sadness. Her mother sat at the table mopping her eyes with a tissue, her shoulders shaking with residual shuddering breaths.

Mal stopped walking. Lockhart stayed exactly where he was, both of them watching Oceane. She walked into the living room, chin up, with the intrinsically proud and elegant bearing of a woman raised in the lap of untold luxury—and a former security that had been completely, irrevocably shattered.

"We've talked it over," she began in accented English, her voice soft but steady. "And we've decided that it's best if we enter the WITSEC program."

Oh, thank you, Jesus. Mal shot a relieved look at Lockhart.

His teammate still hadn't moved, watching her, expression giving nothing away. His almost preternatural stillness was a dead giveaway to his sniper background to someone with military training. "I think that's a good decision," Lockhart said.

Oceane took a deep breath. "So will you call them and let them know?"

"Sure." With that, Lockhart was up and off the couch, phone in hand as he dialed someone. Probably Taggart. "Better go get your stuff together," he told her. "Once we pull the trigger, things are gonna move fast."

Unable to not feel a slight twinge of sympathy for her and her mother, Mal gave her an encouraging smile and gestured for her to head to the bedroom so she could start packing while he watched.

She might not see it now, but this was the best decision for everyone. WITSEC would give her and her mother the best protection available. It also meant Mal was free to rejoin his team—and find a way to see Rowan the first chance he got.

****

"It's done?" Manny said into his phone as he left his lawyer's office, where he'd just finished a meeting about his estate and Oceane.

At the curb, two of his men were standing guard beside his new Jag, which gleamed in the afternoon sunlight. Elena was out at one of his charity's auctions and wouldn't be home for hours. Manny was looking forward to having the house to himself for the rest of the day and not worrying about her overhearing anything she shouldn't.

"Oh yeah," Montoya replied enthusiastically from the other end. "Killed every last one of the fuckers."

Manny frowned in annoyance and climbed into his car, quickly slamming the door shut behind him. Body count was of little importance to him. Results were. "What about the operation?"

"Main lab and all the outbuildings are in ashes. Along with the homes and businesses of anyone suspected to support Ruiz."

He pinched the bridge of his nose and drew in a deep breath. "Please tell me you kept it to the known suspects."

Montoya snickered. "Yeah, them too."

God. Manny sank into the plush leather driver's seat, suddenly bone weary, and leaned his head back. Too much collateral damage would bring unwanted heat down on him and the cartel. Bribing and blackmailing officials down here was common practice, but every once in a while he ran into someone who wasn't corruptible. That made his work a lot harder. "I told you to be careful. You were to have your guys take out the operation and those responsible for it *only.*"

"Which I did, mostly. But it never hurts to send a message, does it? Besides, we had a little help from *El Escorpion.*"

At that Manny opened his eyes and lowered his hand to his lap. It was rare for the shadowy head of the cartel to get involved on that level. "He sent men to assist?"

"A few. Mostly weapons and logistics stuff."

So then *El Escorpion* would be briefed directly about the op, and probably knew all the details already. Including the collateral damage and body count. *Shit.* "Send me a report through the secure channel asap."

"You got it, boss man."

Manny glanced out the driver's side window. This business district of downtown was quiet, people going about their day and not paying him much notice. He basically owned this entire town, and the smaller surrounding ones as well. He paid his people well and gave enough back to the community that every man, woman and child for miles around here considered him a hero philanthropist. He couldn't afford for them to find out all the things he'd ordered and allowed in order to make and keep that money.

"What about my daughter?" he asked.

"No sign yet. Obviously no financial or social media activity we can use. I've got others out using the scanners around the city. Should be able to detect a faint signal from around a kilometer out. If they get a signal on the tracking device, they'll let me know."

Manny shoved out a hard breath and started the engine. "Let someone else handle the upcoming operations on Ruiz's people. The only thing I want you to do is find them and bring my daughter back to me."

He paused, his heart heavy, an uncomfortable ball of guilt squirming in his belly. If there had been any other way to handle this, he would have. But he was out of options and out of time, so it had to be this. He would contact Arturo and initiate everything. "You know what to do."

"Looking forward to it, boss man."

Yeah. That's what worried him.

Chapter Eighteen

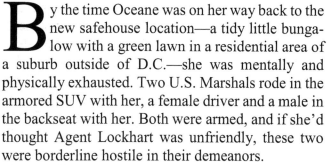

By the time Oceane was on her way back to the new safehouse location—a tidy little bungalow with a green lawn in a residential area of a suburb outside of D.C.—she was mentally and physically exhausted. Two U.S. Marshals rode in the armored SUV with her, a female driver and a male in the backseat with her. Both were armed, and if she'd thought Agent Lockhart was unfriendly, these two were borderline hostile in their demeanors.

The marshals had arrived soon after Lockhart had placed the call to his commander. They hadn't messed around. Within minutes of them walking in the condo, they rushed her and her mother down to separate vehicles waiting in the underground parking lot, where they'd been blindfolded and driven to this little house. A special arrangement made at the last moment for them.

The U.S. Marshals Service had told her that normally people in the WITSEC program were taken to a kind of orientation center in D.C. where they stayed with other federal witnesses until the trial they were to testify at was over. Then they were given a new life in a different city under carefully constructed aliases.

In her and her mother's case, that couldn't happen because of a particular snag. Victoria Gomez was also in WITSEC, at the orientation center, and officials didn't want them all at the same facility for security reasons. Miss Gomez would be testifying directly against Ruiz in the upcoming trial, whenever that happened, so for now Oceane and her mother were here in this little house.

She'd had just enough time to unpack and get acquainted with the layout of the place before her security detail had whisked her off to DEA headquarters for another meeting, while her mother stayed at the house. The FBI and DEA no longer believed she was involved with the bombing at the law office, but they were pressuring her to help them find Arturo. Unfortunately, she had no idea where he was, and even if she had, she wouldn't tell them. Arturo was a trusted protector and friend. She wouldn't turn on him after all he'd done to protect her.

They arrived back at the house around dinnertime. The neighborhood was quiet, only a few young mothers out walking their babies in strollers or kids riding their bikes up the sidewalks. Watching them, Oceane envied their freedom and carefree lives. But there was no point in wallowing in self pity or wishing things could be different, because her situation was fixed now and there was no going back.

She'd lost a lot by coming here, but she and her mother still had each other, and that was the most important thing. That would have to be enough to sustain them both through whatever came at them from here forward.

The driver pulled into the driveway and continued past the house, up to the fence that marked the edge of the backyard. Her mother had wanted to cook dinner rather than order takeout, so they'd arranged for someone to run out and grab the groceries.

Anticipating some good old-fashioned Mexican comfort food, her stomach growled hungrily as the male marshal, Smythe, opened the back door for her. He went to the fence, opened it, and stopped dead. The way he froze sent a burst of alarm through her.

He held out an arm to stop her. "Stay here," he commanded, and withdrew a pistol from his shoulder holster.

Frightened now, Oceane peered over his shoulder, wide-eyed as he stepped through into the backyard while his partner rushed up behind her, weapon drawn, and set a restraining hand on her shoulder. The back door to the house was open, sagging crookedly on its hinges.

One of the marshals tasked with protecting her mother lay facedown on the grass, arms flung out.

She sucked in a sharp breath, started to turn toward the female marshal behind her, but the gasp turned into a horrified cry as the ruined door flung open and her mother appeared in it, naked, blood dripping down her body from what looked like numerous knife wounds.

Her dark brown eyes were wide, glazed with terror and pain, but they locked on Oceane. "*Corres*," she yelled, her voice desperate, filled with a frantic urgency that raised the hair on Oceane's arms.

Run.

Oceane's scream was cut short as Smythe charged back to the fence, grabbed her by the shoulders and spun her around. She fought him, clawed at his restraining hands, needing to see what was happening with her mother.

A series of gunshots behind her shattered the soft evening air.

Wrenching her head around, Oceane cast a desperate glance over her shoulder in time to see a man burst out of the house holding a pistol. The female marshal fired. The man fell, clutching his chest. The female marshal was down too, and Oceane's mother had fallen into a bloody heap on the grass.

"*Mami!*" She screamed it, the word exploding from her as she struggled to tear free from Smythe. He tackled her to the ground and pinned her beneath him, issuing rapid orders via his earpiece.

A sound of rage and grief tore from her as she twisted and fought to get away. "Let me go! I need to get to my mother!" She was lying there just meters away, bleeding, helpless.

"Don't move," he ground out, and squashed her flat beneath his weight, rattling off more commands.

Running footsteps sounded to her left. Smythe swung around, raised his weapon and fired just as an armed man wearing a hoodie appeared around the side of the house.

More shots rang out. Bullets pinged off the side of

the SUV, inches from where she and Smythe lay on the ground. He grunted but didn't move. She gasped and covered her head with her arms, heart rocketing into her throat. Where were the other marshals? Were they all dead?

Smythe fired again, and the attacker's footsteps stopped. A quiet thud sounded, followed by a low groan.

Before Oceane could raise her head to see what had happened, Smythe hauled her to her knees and dragged her behind the cover of the side of the SUV. He reached up to fumble with the door handle, his breathing labored, and when she glanced down she saw blood running out from beneath the fingers he pressed to his side.

"Get in," he rasped, giving her a shove. "It's armored. Stay down and don't move until I say otherwise."

"No, my mother—"

"I'm going to her. Lock the doors and *don't move*."

She almost crawled across the seat and bolted out the other door, but there might be more attackers and Smythe would just chase her down, wasting precious time he could be using to help her mother. Shaking, fighting back frightened tears, she lay sideways on the leather bench seat and closed her eyes, listening, praying…

Please, God. Please don't take my mother from me. I can't bear it. Not that.

She prayed it over and over, her lips moving, teeth chattering at the sudden blast of ice freezing her insides. She wasn't sure how long she lay like that.

Minutes. Hours. Then sirens screamed in the distance, getting nearer.

Oceane sat up, stared through the windshield toward the backyard. The gate was open but there was no sign of Smythe, and no one else was around.

Heart pounding, she climbed into the front seat because the rear doors couldn't be unlocked from the inside, opened it and slid out. Her knees almost gave way when her feet hit the grass.

On wobbly legs she hurried to the gate, kept her back to it as she darted a glance into the yard. Smythe was on his knees beside her mother, who was sprawled out on her back, head lolling to the side, facing Oceane. He'd stripped off his jacket and shirt, using them to try and staunch the bleeding from the knife wounds.

Her mother's pain-filled dark eyes focused on her, a flare of relief flashing through them. "Oceane..." she managed weakly.

Smythe jerked his head up, let out a snarled curse when he saw her standing there. "Get back into the vehicle, *now.*"

Ignoring him, not caring what he did to her, she rushed to her mother's side and dropped to her knees to grip the limp hand in hers. "*Mami,*" she choked out. God, there was so much blood. Angry slashes at her throat, chest and belly. Her breasts lacerated. And there was more between her thighs...

Oceane swallowed, fought the wave of nausea that clenched her belly. They had raped and cut her. "Who did this?" she demanded, rage flooding her system.

Her mother seemed to struggle to keep her eyes

open, focused on Oceane briefly before rolling toward the house. "Ar…Arturo."

The shattered remnants of Oceane's heart plummeted into the pit of her roiling stomach. No. No, it couldn't be.

"Where's Arturo?" Smythe demanded in Spanish, leaning over her mother, his voice urgent. "Is he still here?"

"In…side. Run, baby," her mother said to her weakly, her eyes sliding shut.

A deep, burning rage took over, obliterating fear, wiping out all thoughts except for one: Arutro would die for this.

Oceane was up and running toward the house before she even realized what she was doing. Smythe's shout to stop barely registered, the need for vengeance so strong she didn't care what happened to her.

Her gaze caught on the pistol in the fallen marshal's outstretched hand. She bent down to scoop it up on her way past, barely breaking stride, and plunged into the back door of the house.

"Arturo!" she bellowed, weapon firmly in her grip as she burst into the kitchen.

The scent of her mother's famous enchilada sauce hung heavy in the air, the pots and pans still simmering on the stove. It looked like a horror movie set. Blood spattered the floor, smears of it going up the walls, the cabinets. Bloody footprints led toward the back door, and away toward the living room beyond it.

Her muscles were tight as steel cables, her gaze scanning restlessly for a target. A shadow moved in the living room, just beyond the kitchen.

Blood trailed along the hardwood floor, over toward the powder room. Someone had tried to wipe it up but hadn't done a good job in their haste. Whoever it was, she hoped they were in as much pain as her mother.

The shadow detached itself from the wall and a man's silhouette filled the darkened hallway. Oceane's nape prickled, her heart slamming against her chest wall.

Arturo.

The sight of him pierced her. He had a hand pressed to the front of his ribs. Blood glistened on his fingers and his breathing was quick and shallow. He held a pistol in his other hand.

Hands surprisingly steady, she raised her weapon, felt no fear as she stared down the barrel of the pistol. He had taught her to shoot. Had turned her into an expert shot, all in case she ever needed to defend herself and her mother.

She had never dreamed she would need to use it against him.

"Oceane, put the gun down," he said in Spanish in a low voice, so familiar that pain lanced through her.

A sheen of tears blurred her eyes as she stared back at him, the betrayal so acute it shredded her. "How could you?" she choked out, barely able to speak. How had he found them?

"You don't understand. Put the gun down and come with me. I don't want to hurt you."

She shook her head, a wave of nausea mixing with rage and despair. He'd betrayed them. "Liar. You fucking *liar!*" She pulled the trigger. The shot exploded in the silent hallway. Arturo grunted and dropped to his knees, his gun hand falling to his side.

"Wait," he gasped, reaching for the wall to steady himself, his face a mask of pain.

You cut my mother.

She fired again, hit him in the chest this time. Her whole body was shaking, tears pouring down her face. He'd betrayed them. The man she had trusted more than any other, and had risked so much to ensure her safety.

"Why?" she demanded, stepping closer, sickened by what she'd had to do. "*Why*, dammit?"

In the dimness his dark, glassy eyes rolled toward her. Blood bubbled out of his mouth, his nose. He choked, coughed. "Your father..."

She went even colder inside, the pain unbearable.

"Wants you...back. Had...to—" He broke off, choking.

Oceane turned her back on him, leaving him to die in the hall and swept the rest of the house for more threats. She found a man in a dark hoodie sprawled out on the master bedroom floor, his pants down around his ankles. Bile rushed into her throat at the thought of this pig violating her mother. She hoped her mother had killed him.

In a daze she went back outside, the dying sun too bright against her eyes. Marshal Smythe was slumped on his side now, barely having the strength to raise his head to look at her.

"They're all dead," she said woodenly in English, setting the pistol on the grass before kneeling next to her mother. Oceane took one chilled hand in her own and pressed it to her cheek, letting the tears track down her face. The sirens were in the driveway now.

Help coming too late. Too late.

"We're safe now, *Mami*," she whispered in Spanish. "Everything's going to be all right."

Her mother didn't answer, her chest barely moving with her too-shallow breaths, and deep down, Oceane knew that nothing would ever be all right again.

****

Mal turned up the radio in his truck and tapped along to the rhythm of a favorite pop song on the steering wheel as he steered out of the FAST headquarters near the Pentagon.

"God, how can you stand this crap?" Lockhart asked from the passenger seat, tugging the brim of his ball cap lower on his forehead. "Why can't you like country or rock, like normal people do?"

"Don't like my tunes? Should have thought of that sooner and brought your own wheels to work, then," Mal answered with a smirk.

"Trust me, I won't make that mistake again," Lockhart muttered with his trademark sarcasm. The guy was quiet, but funny as hell with his zingers. You had to pay attention, though. He and Granger together were something else, though Lockhart didn't crave the spotlight the way Granger or Maka did. "You wanna grab a bite or something before you drop me off?"

"Can't. Got plans."

Lockhart glanced over, the corner of his mouth pulling up. "Okay," was all he said, knowing damn well Mal planned to see Rowan. Most other guys on the team would have talked shit or grilled him for details, but not Lockhart. It was why Mal liked hanging around the former sniper so much. Lockhart knew when to keep his mouth shut. Unlike Maka, for instance, he thought with a smirk.

It had been another long but strangely satisfying day, having transferred Oceane and Anya into the custody of the U.S. Marshals before going to HQ to rejoin his teammates. They'd trained in the gym for a while before hitting the range together, and attended a meeting about the latest on Ruiz and Nieto.

Now he was free for the night, and he planned to run home and grab a quick shower before bringing Rowan some dinner. The woman never fed herself when she was busy working, and he would use any excuse just to see her again. Since he had the right security clearance and was on her short list of approved visitors, he could make it happen.

A familiar ring tone filled the truck cab on Mal's Bluetooth system. Surprised that Taggart would be calling when they'd only just left HQ a couple minutes ago, he answered. "Commander. What can we do for you?"

"The satellite WITSEC safehouse was just attacked."

What the fuck? "When?" Mal demanded.

"Fifteen minutes ago. They need a new temporary detail for Oceane. How soon can you guys get over there?"

But not Anya? "We'll head there now," Mal said, stunned but secretly glad it wasn't Rowan.

Taggart gave them the address. "I'll meet you there," he said, and hung up.

Malcolm pulled a U-turn in the middle of the street and raced off in the opposite direction.

"How the hell did the perps find them, let alone manage to attack fucking U.S. Marshals?" Lockhart said.

"No damn idea," Mal replied, driving faster.

When they arrived at the house ten minutes later, the road was choked with emergency vehicles. He and Lockhart jumped out, showed their ID and were allowed access to the backyard.

Paramedics were working on a marshal off to one side of the lawn, and they were rushing Anya toward the gate on a stretcher. She appeared unconscious. Her torso was covered with a bloodstained sheet, her brown skin an ungodly shade of gray and an oxygen mask placed over her mouth and nose.

Jesus Christ...

"Out of the way," one of the medics yelled, the urgency on his and his partner's faces making it clear that Anya was in dire danger.

Mal and Lockhart stepped well to the side, allowing them to pass. And when they turned around, he spotted Oceane in between two cops. They appeared to be holding her up as she watched with a tortured expression while her mother was hauled away. Her haunted gaze landed on them and the little composure she had left crumbled.

Her face twisted and she wrenched free of the cops' supporting arms to lurch straight to Lockhart. Mal caught the flare of surprise on his teammate's face an instant before she flung her arms around his neck and buried her face in his shoulder. Lockhart didn't say anything, just held onto her.

"They won't let me g-go with her," she sobbed, the pain in her voice so raw that Mal winced inside. "I need to go with her."

"They need to transport her as fast as possible and get her stabilized," Lockhart said, his voice low, calm, but not unfeeling. "As soon as we get everything dealt with here, we'll take you to the hospital to see her."

Oceane lifted her head to stare up at him. "P-promise?"

"I promise." He set her away from him gently, grasping her shoulders. "Now tell us what happened."

It took a few tries for her to get it out. Mal listened in shock as she described the scene she'd arrived to, ending with her finding and shooting her former bodyguard in the house. His brain hummed as he tried to put the pieces together. WITSEC was the best protection program in the country for a reason. There was no way anyone should have been able to locate the women, let alone within hours of moving them here. And to be able to get the jump on so many highly trained federal agents and kill or wound them all? What the hell?

He glanced over at the sagging back door as forensics techs emerged from the house. It would take a while for them to sort out all the evidence. He hoped they would be able to ID the other attackers and get a lead from them or the bodyguard. They needed a damn break in this case if they were going to crack it open.

Two FBI agents came to take Oceane in for questioning. She balked, protested again about needing to see her mother.

Lockhart intervened. "I'll go with you," he told her. "And I'll take you to her as soon as possible, okay?"

She looked up at him with swollen blue-gray eyes, and nodded. "Thank you."

The special agent in charge of the investigation came through the open back gate, spotted them and headed their way. His eyes fastened on Oceane, who'd gone still. He stopped in front of her, his expression sympathetic, and Mal knew what was coming.

Ah, shit... Even with all he'd seen and all his training, it was always hard to watch someone he knew suffer.

"Miss Nieto, I'm so sorry to tell you—"

"No!" she cried, her face paling even more, eyes dilating with shock. "No, she can't be gone!"

"I'm so sorry, she passed on the way to the hospital," the SAIC continued.

Oceane made a high-pitched sound of distress and clapped her hands to her face as her knees buckled. Lockhart caught her just before she hit the ground.

Chapter Nineteen

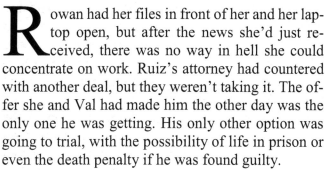

Rowan had her files in front of her and her laptop open, but after the news she'd just received, there was no way in hell she could concentrate on work. Ruiz's attorney had countered with another deal, but they weren't taking it. The offer she and Val had made him the other day was the only one he was getting. His only other option was going to trial, with the possibility of life in prison or even the death penalty if he was found guilty.

And he was *going* to be found guilty.

Her phone rang, and when she saw Malcolm's number her heart kicked hard. "Hey," she answered with a sigh, leaning back in her chair to stretch her back. "You heard what happened?" She was still shaken by it.

"Yeah. I wondered if you had." He sounded tired.

"They called my team right away. They're checking the building right now and putting another marshal outside for surveillance. God, I just can't believe what happened."

"Yeah. It was bad."

"Where is Oceane now?"

"The FBI wanted to interview her, but under the circumstances they've allowed her to go see her mother."

Rowan blew out a breath and rested her forehead in her palm, stunned. "She was incredibly loyal to and protective of her bodyguard. She trusted him." With her life. With her mother's life. God, how awful.

"I know."

Rowan had been furious when she'd thought Oceane or her mother might be involved with the bombing, but now she felt terrible for them both. To have to kill someone you cared about so much, and then lose your mother right after, and in such a horrifically violent way? Rowan didn't even know what she would do in Oceane's shoes.

"The *Veneno* cartel members are all animals," she said, her voice taut. Making Ruiz die in prison was a step. A small step, but an important one. It showed that even the top cartel hierarchy were vulnerable, and could be extradited to the United States.

"Not arguing."

"WITSEC is supposed to be completely secure," she said, getting angry now that the initial shock was wearing off.

"I know. It shouldn't have happened at all."

"And how did they find them so fast?"

"Exactly. That's what investigators are trying to find out."

"I asked my detail about Victoria but they haven't told me anything yet. Is she safe?"

"Yes."

"Are they going to move her now, in case everything's been compromised?"

"No. The orientation center is on lockdown and they're checking to make sure it's still secure. I don't think the location's been compromised. Taggart's sending Hamilton over to see her at a secret location now."

Rowan sat up and leaned back in the chair. "Good." She was an important source of insider info on the cartel. Names, faces she'd seen or heard during her research as a journalist and then her subsequent captivity. Not only that, but the woman had already endured far too much suffering. Rowan couldn't stomach the thought of anything more happening to her.

With Victoria on the stand, they could bury Ruiz. She had a powerful presence about her. They had all her statements recorded and transposed, but hearing her testimony in her own words would be twice as powerful. And Rowan wanted Victoria to have the opportunity to look at the piece of shit responsible for her suffering and know she was helping put him away forever. Maybe it would even help her heal a little.

"You hungry?" he asked, abruptly changing the subject. "I know you haven't eaten yet."

She sighed, pushing aside the stab of guilt for thinking of something so trivial as food when Oceane was hurting so much. "I'm starving."

"I'm gonna run home and shower, then I'll grab something and bring it over. Be there around eight or so. That okay?"

"That's perfect." She needed to see him.

Burying herself back into her work helped the time fly by. The next thing she knew, he was at the door. One of the marshals assigned to her checked the door before letting him in, and Rowan's heart swelled at the sight of him.

He gave her a smile, those dimples appearing in his freshly-shaved cheeks, his arms full of brown paper takeout bags. "Hope you guys are hungry. I brought Mexican."

It was a nice touch that he'd thought to buy dinner for the FBI agents too. He was so mouthwatering standing there in his dark jeans and button-down shirt.

She wanted to walk right over there, throw her arms around him and kiss him senseless, but that would be hella awkward given their audience, so instead she took two of the bags from him with a thanks and started putting everything onto the kitchen table.

Her security detail thanked Malcolm for the food, filled their plates and made themselves scarce in another room. Rowan sipped at the wine he'd brought, drinking in the sight of him over the rim of her glass. What she wouldn't give to be alone with him right now. All she could think about was what he'd done to her this morning, the way he'd pinned her beneath him. The feel of his hands, his mouth, the way he'd filled her...

He looked up and met her gaze, his brown eyes

darkening at the look she was giving him. Then his mouth twitched. "So, you make any headway with work today?"

She was thankful one of them was able to play it cool. Her body was on edge, needy as hell, and it was damn hard to sit here and pretend otherwise. Still, she wasn't up for an audience the next time she got sexy with him. "Some. Spoke to Val a few times, and my parents. My last update from Nick was that Kevin was awake and talking. He seems alert and like his normal self, so they've cut back the pain meds so he's not all drugged up. Nick said he'd call back tonight if Kev's up to it so I can talk to him."

"And your parents?"

"They're both at the hospital."

"How's your dad handling that, with Nick there?"

"Surprisingly well, according to Nick," she said with a small smile. "A bit stiff at first, but he's loosened up some since. He's making progress."

"About goddamn time."

Rowan cocked her head slightly, smiling at him. "I love that you're so accepting of Kev." From what he'd told her he'd been raised in a strict, religious home. Sometimes that made people judgmental about things like sexual orientation.

Malcolm shrugged the broad shoulders she wished were naked and she was stroking her hands over right now. "He's a good guy. Deserves to be happy."

That put a knot in her throat. "Yeah, he sure does." Setting down her fork, she reached across the table for his hand, grasped it and lowered her voice. "And so do we."

A slow smile curved his lips, making those crazy sexy dimples appear again. They were so much more evident without all the stubble on his face. "I'm glad you see it that way." He squeezed her fingers, his eyes promising untold pleasure the next time they got naked together.

"Kev somehow knew the way I still felt about you. The night he was injured, up in my office he warned me that we don't get any do-overs in this life. He'd had the courage to go after his own happiness. I finally found mine too."

Malcolm raised their joined hands to his mouth, turned them to press a slow, lingering kiss to the back of hers. "Then I guess I owe him a thank you next time I see him." He lowered their hands to the table.

"Can I ask you something?"

"Yeah, of course."

"Why did you leave the Navy? You told me once that you loved being a SEAL."

"I did love it. It was the hardest, most punishing yet most rewarding thing I'd ever done." He sat back, thought about it for a moment. "I was starting to get numb. I saw it happen to other guys, and I wanted to get out before I didn't feel anything anymore."

God, she couldn't imagine him being like that. "I'm glad you got out."

"It was the right decision for me. And it gave me a solid background to try out for FAST selection."

Suddenly the uncertainty of the days stretching out before her seemed like an eternity. An eternity of not having Malcolm. "So you'll be back with the rest of your team now?"

He nodded. "Rodriguez is flying back tonight. His

mom's been real sick, but she's on the upswing now so we've got the whole team together again as of tomorrow morning, and it'll be good to have him back. He's been on the team almost as long as me."

It was obvious how much he loved his teammates from the way he talked about them. But her mind was trying to work out the logistics of where this new transition left her and Malcolm. "You're going to wait for me, right?"

He eyed her in amusement, eyebrows raised. "You seriously worried I might not, after I waited this long?"

She shrugged. "Just looking for some reassurance."

He lowered his eyebrows, leaned closer and dropped his voice. "I might wait for you, if you promise to make it worth my while."

The sensual purr slid over her skin like the stroke of velvet, making her shiver. "I will."

Another grin, and it was all she could do not to climb up onto the table and grab his face between her hands so she could kiss that delectable mouth. "Then you've got nothing to worry about, sweetness."

Sweetness. She loved that so much. Until that moment she hadn't realized how much she'd missed it.

Releasing his hand, she reached for her wine because her throat was suddenly dry. "So. How long until I can get out of here, do you think?"

"No idea. But however long it is, it's too long for my liking."

Hers, too.

They spent the rest of the leisurely meal enjoying each other's company, talking about various things, laughing at each other's jokes. But there was so much that they didn't say. Things that would have to wait until they were alone.

He helped her clear the table and tidy the kitchen afterward. When he shut the dishwasher door they stood facing each other a few feet apart in the kitchen, pent up sexual tension crackling between them, and no way to relieve it. "Well," he said softly, hands braced behind him on the countertop, the pose emphasizing the powerful muscles in his shoulders and chest. "I should get going. I bet you've got a ton of work to catch up on."

Ugh. Work. She sighed. "Yeah." She had to talk to Val about the Ruiz counteroffer, then review the evidence they'd gathered so far and get it ready with the victim impact statements they'd gathered. If Ruiz rejected the offer they'd made to drop a few charges in exchange for a reduced sentence, then they would be going to trial soon.

"Gimme one second," he said, and headed to the next room. She picked up the low murmur of his voice as he spoke to her security detail, then he emerged a moment later. "Walk me to the door?" he asked, a gleam in his eye.

She followed, understanding why he'd asked that when she realized no one could see them at the door from the next room. At least they'd been given some measure of privacy to say goodbye. She'd take it, because it was better than nothing.

He stopped at the door, waiting for her. As soon as she got close, he grasped her hips in his big hands and turned them so that his back was to the room. Shielding her, even from the possibility of prying eyes.

"We've got two minutes until they come to follow protocol and lock me out," he said. "So I'm not wasting a single second." Sliding one hand up her back to plunge into her hair, he brought his mouth down on hers.

His dominant possession sizzled through her like a lightning bolt. He wasn't like Carter at all, didn't want to control her anywhere but in the bedroom, and that was more than fine with her. Desire streaked through her, so intense it made her dizzy. She grabbed hold of his shoulders for balance, flattening her body along his.

The hard ridge of his erection pressed into her belly, maddening her with the promise of what she couldn't have. His tongue teased hers, a slow, sensual caress that revved her arousal even higher. Rowan squirmed to get closer, standing on tiptoe to rub the seam of her jeans against his erection.

The hand in her hair tightened, squeezing as his other reached down to cup her ass and lift her higher, aligning their bodies until she got what she was looking for. God, she remembered what he had felt like inside her, how thick and hard he'd been, the way he'd shifted his hips so that he stroked just the right spot inside her while his thumb on her clit made her mindless. The friction now was torture, yet she didn't want it to end.

But of course it did.

All too soon he slowed the kiss, gentled his grip and lowered her back down until the soles of her feet were flat on the floor again. Rowan stroked her hands over the back of his head, feeling the slightly rough texture of his short hair. Down his neck to those gorgeous shoulders and across his back. Tracing the muscles, loathing the moment when she had to let him go and face an unknown length of separation from him.

Malcolm ran a soothing hand up her back, his fingers tracing the length of her spine as he kissed the corner of her mouth, paused to suck at her lower lip. Nip it.

"The next time I get you naked, I'm gonna take my time and kiss you everywhere," he whispered against the corner of her mouth. "Especially here," he added, rocking the hard ridge of his erection between her open thighs. "Until you melt all over my tongue."

Rowan barely managed to stifle a whimper, her whole body clenching with need. She'd imagined it countless times; it was her favorite masturbation fantasy. But she had a feeling that reality was going to blow her mind. "I'm going to hold you to that."

He raised his head, met her stare, his pupils all but swallowing the chocolate rim of his irises. "Good. I want you to hold my head between your thighs while I lick you until you scream and come on my tongue."

A torrent of molten desire pooled low in her belly, between her legs, her clit throbbing at the thought of his mouth on her. Oh, Jesus, the things he said in that deep, wicked voice... "That was dirty," she accused, aching and knowing she would have only herself to take the edge off with later.

"Oh, sweetness, that wasn't even close to the way I do dirty, I promise you."

A discreet clearing of a throat behind them made

her want to growl at the man. Malcolm chuckled softly, pressed a kiss to her forehead and stepped back. "Good night. Sleep tight. I'll be in touch."

She nodded, forced herself to let go and behave like an in-control adult. But she was suddenly cold without his arms around her. She wrapped hers around her waist, watched as the marshal went through the ritual of taking him out, locking the door behind them.

Hand pressed against the closed door, the sting of tears in her throat told her he'd just taken her heart with him.

Chapter Twenty

———◇◇◇◇◇———

Victoria Gomez walked out into the psychologist's waiting room expecting to find one of the two U.S. Marshals assigned to her personal security detail there, but stopped short when she saw Supervisory Special Agent Brock Hamilton instead.

He rose from his chair, a smile on his chiseled, masculine face as he set aside the magazine he'd been reading. His brown hair was short and neat after a recent cut. "Hi."

"Hi. This is a surprise." Except for the few hours she'd spent with him at the shooting range, the only time she left the WITSEC orientation center was to meet with lawyers or investigators, or for her twice-weekly appointments here. She was the government's key witness in the upcoming Ruiz trial, so they didn't take any chances with her safety.

He put his hands into his jeans pockets, made no move to come toward her, as though he knew it made her uneasy to be close to a man, especially when they were alone. Except he couldn't know that he was the one man she felt most at ease with. "The guys said it would be all right for me to come in, so I could talk to you."

She tilted her head, sensing something was wrong. Of course he wouldn't just show up to say hi. "About what?"

Those steel gray eyes never wavered from hers, and the sheer masculine authority of his presence would have been frightening if she didn't already trust him on such a deep level. He was a tall, physically powerful man in prime condition, and he had been trained to do violent things that, after what she'd endured, should have made her afraid to be alone in the same room with him.

Yet standing here alone with him, there was no fear. In fact, if anything, being this close to him made her feel safer. She would never forget what he'd done for her that night when she'd finally escaped the hellhole Ruiz's men had chained her up in. The way he'd wrapped her up in that blanket and carried her out of the forest. He'd sat next to her, holding her hand as the ambulance transported her to the hospital. Even there, he'd stayed at her bedside, a stranger acting as a sentinel, watching over her.

"We're not sure how it happened yet, but Oceane and her mother were just attacked at their safehouse."

Shock and dread coiled like a rattlesnake in the pit of her stomach. "Are they all right?" She might not like either of them, but in a way they were both victims too, caught up in the intricate web Nieto had woven for them.

"No. Anya's dead, but Oceane's all right. The men who attacked Anya..." He stopped, cleared his throat and broke eye contact as he debated whether or not to continue.

"They what?" Although Victoria was almost certain she knew what he had been about to say.

"The attackers sexually assaulted her."

Her whole body tensed, an instinctive reaction as memories she wished she could bury flashed through her mind. Images of her while held captive, naked and helpless. Of the things those animals masquerading as humans had done to her. The things she'd done, been forced to do, in order to survive.

She swallowed, forced back the wave of horror and panic trying to take over. With time and therapy she was slowly learning to shut off that fight or flight response when flashbacks hit her, but it wasn't easy and she still had a long way to go before she won that fight. But win it she would. Eventually. She had to. "And then they shot her."

"No. They used knives. And they didn't kill her outright."

Revulsion swept through her as his meaning registered. They'd been playing with Anya. Enjoying her suffering. Wanting to prolong it. "Evil, filthy pigs." She could just imagine how they'd laughed, probably gotten harder the more Anya had screamed and fought, the sight and smell of her fear, the blood, fueling their depraved lust.

Hamilton nodded, met her eyes once more.

"Oceane arrived in the middle of it. Her former bodyguard was there, hiding in the house, wounded. She shot him and he died on scene."

The news surprised her, and she paused a moment before answering. "Good for her." Maybe she'd been too harsh in her opinion of Oceane. God knew Victoria had wanted to hate her right from the moment they met, because of who her father was and the cartel he was part of. "Who were the attackers?"

"We don't have identities yet, but they're connected to the *Veneno* cartel. The FBI would like you to look at their pictures, in the hopes that you could maybe identify them."

She nodded. "Of course." Her captors hadn't expected her to escape before they shipped her off to a buyer in Asia with some other captive women, therefore they hadn't taken the precaution of blindfolding her or covering their faces during her time as a hostage.

A fatal error on their part that Victoria was doing her damndest to exploit. If she could bring even a percentage of those bastards to justice for what they'd done, it might help her sleep at night. "

"Who ordered the attack?" she asked.

"No hard evidence on that yet either. And nobody knows how they found the women."

Victoria frowned, a tiny, cold shiver working its way up her spine. "If the bodyguard was involved, then it stands to reason that Nieto ordered it." But it didn't explain how he'd found the safehouse.

"They're looking at all the possibilities."

"Where is Oceane?" They had more in common now than Victoria would ever have guessed possible.

And as much as she'd wanted to hate the girl, she couldn't. Not after this.

"At the hospital."

"Was she hurt?"

"Not physically."

She sighed. "I was wrong about her."

"What do you mean?"

"I thought she must be cut from the same cloth as her father. But it sounds like she's as much a victim as I was." And no one knew better than her what Oceane was going through right now, having watched her mother dying right in front of her.

"*Was*," he stressed.

She looked at him questioningly, the vehemence of his tone striking a chord deep inside her.

His gaze was steady on her. And his eyes held a hint of something that sent a wave of warmth through her. Admiration. "Not anymore."

"No," she agreed, the hint of a smile on her lips. For some reason his opinion of her mattered. She didn't want him to think of her as the broken woman he'd carried from the woods that night. She wanted him to see her for the woman she was trying to become. A warrior set on a quest for vengeance—even if it was only in the legal system.

"Especially now, since you could put a bullet in his heart from fifty feet away," he added, a teasing note in his voice.

She grinned. It felt strange, her face stiff as though her muscles were unused to the movement, but it also felt good. "I could, couldn't I?"

"You absolutely could."

Because of him.

She let her gaze flit over his face once more, pausing a fraction of a second on his lips. Her libido was as dead as her former life and she wasn't sure if she'd ever regain that part of herself again, and yet...there was something about this man that drew her powerfully, and she couldn't deny that she found him attractive. Not just physically, either. He intrigued her on all levels.

She pushed away the wayward thought, focused on the here and now. "What about my situation? Is there any threat against me?"

"Nothing credible that anyone's told me about. That's actually why they sent me down here, to make sure you know you're safe. They're doubling up security at the WITSEC facility right now and adding a backup team to your security detail for the ride back. Just to play it safe they're going to keep you there until they find out what happened today and figure out how the attackers found Oceane and Anya."

Victoria nodded. "That all makes sense." She paused. "I'm surprised they sent you to relay the intel, but I'm glad, too."

He shrugged his broad, muscled shoulders. "I wanted to be the one to tell you."

So he'd volunteered, then. Victoria studied him for a moment, trying to figure him out. He was FAST Bravo's team leader. He had countless other more important responsibilities and things to take care of than looking out for her. "Why?" She would hate it if he felt sorry for her.

His expression gave nothing away. "Because I did."

She hid a smile at his stubborn non-answer, wondering about his motivation. It was nice to know he cared about her well-being, but she couldn't let herself depend on or get attached to him. And he was the kind of man who made that idea far too tantalizing for someone recovering from an ordeal like the one she'd survived.

In the end, that was Ruiz's biggest mistake. He'd let her live. And now she would end his reign of terror, bring it all crashing down on him.

"Is my security detail outside in the hall? I'd like to go see Oceane right now," she said, changing the subject to steer her thoughts away from dangerous and useless territory.

He frowned a little at that. "Why?"

"Because I've been where she is. And she shouldn't have to face this alone."

****

"Lockhart. She in there?"

Special Agent Gabe Lockhart looked up from his phone where he'd been scrolling through his sports feed outside the door to the hospital morgue. The FBI SAIC he'd met back at the safehouse was striding down the empty hall toward him, a group of folders tucked under one arm. "Yeah."

"I need to talk to her."

Was he freaking serious? "Now?"

The SAIC nodded. "Sooner the better."

"She's saying goodbye to her mother," Gabe pointed out, attempting to make his tone respectful but unsure whether he pulled it off. Didn't care whether he had. *You know, the one she just watched bleed out from multiple stab wounds less than three hours ago?* "Only been in there twenty minutes with her."

"I'm sorry for that, but this investigation is moving faster than we initially anticipated. As she's still a primary witness, I need to update her on a few things, and then bring her in for more questioning."

Gabe wanted to argue with him, but it wasn't his place so he forced himself to be more diplomatic. "Can't we give her ten more minutes?"

"Five."

Fine. "Five," he agreed, mentally shaking his head. Oceane wasn't his official responsibility anymore and he barely knew her, but fuck, she should at least be allowed to take as much time as she needed to say goodbye to the woman who had not only been her mother, but her best friend as well. She was only twenty-four, but she seemed younger than that sometimes, and older at others.

What had gone down back at that safehouse would make a seasoned federal agent's blood curdle, but for someone like Oceane? Who had until recently been completely sheltered from the cold reality of the outside world? Come on. She was fucking devastated and barely coping.

The SAIC kept glancing at his watch, practically counting down the seconds as they waited. At the five-minute mark, he spoke. "You want to go in there and get her, or should I?"

"I'll go," Gabe muttered, getting to his feet. At least he was a familiar face to her. Maybe she didn't like or trust him, but better than a stranger right now.

God, this day sucked.

The outer room was an office for the medical examiner and the pathologists working for her. She was at her desk working on her computer when Gabe walked in. "I need to escort Miss Nieto out now," he said.

"Of course. Just through there," she said, indicating a locked door with a keycode box beside it. She led the way, covered the keycode with one hand so he couldn't see as she entered the combination, twisted the knob and stepped back. "Go ahead," she whispered. "I'll give you some privacy. She was pretty upset."

Yeah, well, no shit. "Thank you."

A wave of cold air surrounded him as he stepped into the refrigerated room. Oceane sat with her back to him on a stool beside the table where her mother's body had been placed, on her back with a sheet pulled up to her neck. She was holding her mother's hand, Anya's medium-brown skin a few shades paler in death, nearly the same now as Oceane's.

Hating to interrupt such a private thing but having no choice, Gabe quietly closed the distance and stopped a couple of feet behind her. Anya's face was calm in death, beautiful. The sick fuckers who had attacked her had left her face alone, and the sheet hid all the wounds. At least Oceane hadn't had to sit here looking at them.

After carefully choosing his words, he opened his mouth to speak but she beat him to it. "If we hadn't been caught in traffic on the way back, I might have gotten there in time to save her." Her accented voice was so quiet, heartbroken.

Christ, he didn't know what to say to that, stood there awkwardly, trying to pick his moment to deliver the news.

"She was my best friend. And I trusted Arturo."

"I'm so sorry," was all he could manage. His heart went out to her. No one should see what she had today. He thought of his own mother who had raised him as a single parent, tried to imagine what he would feel like if he'd had to watch happen to her what Oceane had today. He'd be in pieces.

Oceane twisted the stool around to face him. Her eyes were a pretty blue-gray, like the lake back home in Bend, Oregon. Her chocolate curls were looser than her mother's. And the utter devastation in her face was so raw it sliced at his insides. "I can't believe she's gone."

The shock of loss was something that never got easier. Not ever. So there was nothing he could do or say to make this part any easier.

"She's always been there for me," she continued in that same empty tone. "Even through all of this, even though I was angry with her and felt betrayed by her hiding the truth from me my whole life... I loved her more than anything. I thought we could build a new life together. I thought...I thought we'd have more time together." She pressed her lips together, sucked in a ragged breath.

"You should have had more time together," he said quietly, bringing her gaze up to his. "I'm so sorry for your loss."

She stared up at him for a long moment, then nodded. "Thank you." Shifting, she glanced down at the hand curled around her mother's, then back up at him. "I guess you're here to say I have to leave?"

He nodded. "The special agent in charge needs to speak to you. He's outside."

The distress on her face made him feel like dog shit on the bottom of someone's shoe. "I don't...don't know if I can leave her like this, I..."

Gabe reached out and put a hand on her shoulder. Even through the top she wore, he could feel how chilled her skin was. She shuddered, inhaled shakily.

"You're freezing. Come out into the hall and talk to the agent. You can come back and see her later if you want." He'd drive her here personally if he had to. This whole thing was bullshit.

Torment in her eyes, she turned to face her mother once more. Stared down into her still face for endless seconds. "*Vaya con Dios, Mami. Te amo,*" she choked out, then bent to kiss her mother's cold, pale forehead, released her hand and stood. "Hurry," she begged him, reaching for his hand as she took a step away from the table. "Before I lose my nerve."

She looked so lost and alone that Gabe couldn't help but wrap an arm around her shoulders and tug her close to his side as he hustled her to the door. God, she was a tiny little thing, the top of her head barely reaching his chin, her slender shoulders much too frail to bear this kind of burden. When she leaned into him, seeking either warmth or simple human comfort, even his battle-hardened heart squeezed in sympathy.

Out in the hall, the SAIC met them. "I have news on the investigation," he told Oceane, who hadn't moved away from Gabe. He stood there awkwardly with his arm around her, half supporting her, half protecting her. "Forensics shows that your former bodyguard killed one of the attackers."

Oh, hell.

She sucked in a breath and went rigid. "What do you mean?"

"Right now we think that he arrived after the attack commenced. He likely engaged and killed one of the attackers."

"He was…" She swallowed and continued, a quaver in her voice, and Gabe tightened his hold on her, a little afraid she might collapse again like she had back at the house. "He was trying to save my mother?"

"We can't speak to his motivation, but the initial forensics support the theory that he shot the attacker found in the bedroom."

"*No.*" She pushed away from Gabe, shaking her head, a hand over her mouth.

Even the SAIC didn't seem to know what to say. "The ballistics report will take a while, so we can't say for sure what happened. In the meantime, I can't speculate on why he was there except to say that chatter suggests that he was possibly there to collect you and your mother, at your father's request, and return you to him."

That lined up exactly with what Oceane had told them about her exchange with her former bodyguard.

"What we need to figure out is how he and the others found you in the first place," he continued.

"I don't know," she cried, tears shining in her eyes, her face drawn. "I don't know how they found us, who the others were, or who sent them. I don't *know.*"

The SAIC shared a look with Gabe before speaking to her. "I realize this is all very difficult for you."

"Difficult," she echoed, her mouth twisting into a humorless smile. "Yes, it certainly is."

"We'll need to question you further, once you finish here. One of my agents will bring you down to—"

"I'll escort her," Gabe said, understanding that business had to be seen to, but disgusted by the timing and delivery. The man had basically just told her she'd needlessly killed the man she'd trusted with her life for more than a decade, and now he was dragging her away from her mother's fucking body before she'd even had a chance to say a real goodbye. "But not until she's ready to leave here."

The SAIC nodded once. "Fair enough."

He walked away, and Gabe breathed a little easier. Oceane had composed herself, but now she just looked shut down, arms wrapped around her ribs. "Did you want to…" He gestured behind them at the morgue door, where her mother was.

She shook her head. "I can't right now. I can't deal with any more."

That he totally understood. At this point he considered it a miracle that she wasn't a hysterical, sobbing mess right now. "You want to go to the cafeteria? Get some coffee or something?"

She blinked at him, almost whispered her response. "I don't have any money."

Shit, of course she didn't. She was in witness protection and had just come from the scene of her mother's murder. "I'll buy."

Another shake of her head, her chocolate curls

bouncing around her shoulders. "I just need to sit and be quiet for a while." She moved to one of the chairs lined up along the wall and sank into it.

Unsure what to do, he took the second seat away and simply waited, giving her the quiet she'd asked for while hopefully making her feel less alone. And safe, hopefully.

"I can't even bury her," she murmured a few minutes later, almost to herself.

That was another blow on top of everything else, some salt to go into the gaping wound of her loss.

"She used to visit her parents' grave every week near where we lived in Veracruz. She bought a plot for us beside them. I guess I can't even give her her final wish and see her laid to rest there."

Gabe was pretty sure that once Nieto got wind of this—and that would be soon—he would pull strings from behind the scenes and have someone within his organization take care of everything. He didn't say it to Oceane, though, and he was never so glad for a distraction in his life than when his phone buzzed with a text from one of the marshals standing guard outside. Hamilton was here with Victoria Gomez, and requesting to see them. What did she and Cap want?

"My team leader's outside with Miss Gomez," he told Oceane. With the threat level and recent breach of security, the marshals and FBI agents standing guard wouldn't let anyone but agency personnel back here without his knowledge and permission. "They want to see us."

Oceane frowned. "About what?"

"Not sure."

She sighed. "All right."

He texted back that it was okay. The door at the far end of the hall opened a minute later and Hamilton walked in with Victoria Gomez. "Cap," Gabe said as he stood, still surprised. "What are you guys doing here?"

"We heard what happened. Miss Gomez wanted to come down and see if there was anything she could do."

At that, Gabe and Oceane both looked at Victoria, who stood watching Oceane with an unreadable expression. She wore jeans and a long-sleeve shirt with a high neck on it, even though it was still over seventy-five degrees outside. To cover the scars Ruiz and his men had inflicted.

"You...came here for me?" Oceane asked, sounding puzzled.

Victoria nodded once, shadows in her eyes. Oceane might be years younger than her, but that look in their eyes was the same age. Ancient way before their time from all they'd seen. Lockhart had seen it in some of the guys he'd served with in the military. "I heard what happened. I'm so sorry for your loss."

Oceane lowered her gaze to the floor. "Thank you."

"They want to move you into the orientation center tonight."

Oceane looked up, frowning. "Is that safe? After what's just happened?"

"It's the most secure facility they have," Hamilton answered. "No one but the Marshal's Service knows where it is. You'll be blindfolded anytime you come or go from the building, the same as me."

Oceane didn't answer, staring at Victoria for a long moment, then nodded once. "I have no one now," she whispered brokenly.

Victoria's carefully blank face filled with sympathy. With two quick strides she closed the distance between them and reached for Oceane, drawing her close into an almost protective hug, one hand cradling the back of her curly head. "I know what you're going through," she said while Gabe and Hamilton looked on, "and I know what it feels like to lose everything and everyone you ever cared about. But you haven't lost everything."

Oceane shook her head. "Yes, I have."

"No. You're still here. And you're not alone, not even now, because I'm here," Victoria said fiercely, this new connection between the two women instant and undeniable. "The two of us are not only going to get through this, together we're going to figure out how to survive. And while we do that, we're going to bring down the *Veneno* cartel and make every last one of them pay for all they've taken from us."

Chapter Twenty-One

The blood funneled out of Manny's face when he got the news.

His fingers slackened around the wine glass. It crashed to the glazed Mexican-tile floor and shattered, sending up a spray of ruby liquid and tiny glass shards. Like blood and crystal teardrops.

"What?" he whispered, stricken, reaching forward to grasp the edge of the table to steady himself. Praying he'd heard wrong. Or at least misunderstood.

David, his trusted head of security, shifted his stance nervously and cleared his throat. "Anya finally died of her injuries on the way to the hospital."

Finally? "What do you mean?"

He glanced away, as though unable to look Manny in the eye.

Manny's heart tripped, then sped into double time. "What did they do to her?" he snapped.

"Montoya's men. They sliced her up."

His knees gave out. They were vicious, he knew that. Yet even he had mistakenly believed they wouldn't dare touch anyone connected so intimately to him.

His ass hit the woven cane seat, his entire body wooden as he absorbed the blow. He shook his head, barely comprehending but there was something else in his bodyguard's expression. A kind of dread mixed with pity that warned Manny there was more. Much more. "What," he demanded. "Tell me. Is it Oceane?" Dear God, if anything had happened to—

"No, she wasn't hurt, from what I understand. But Anya. They uh…"

His patience fractured. "Say it, goddamn it."

"They raped her, boss."

Nausea rippled in his belly, mixed with a toxic, blinding rage so strong that for a moment he couldn't see. Couldn't breathe. He imagined Anya, with her dark Caribbean skin and those inky spiral curls, her hazel-green eyes laughing up at him with such joy and trust and worshipfulness.

Fuck. No, this was too horrible. It was supposed to be a clean hit. Humane, without any fear or suffering on her part. He'd ordered Arturo to take care of it personally instead of Montoya and his men, for that very reason. Manny had ordered him to find out Anya and Oceane's location from Montoya once he got it, then infiltrate and kill Anya with a single bullet to the back of the skull when she wasn't looking. One shot, without her ever knowing he was there.

Instead, she'd been raped and butchered…

He swallowed back the bile that rushed up his throat, hot and acidic like the guilt now burning a hole in the center his chest. Anya. Sweet, beautiful Anya. "Montoya," he ground out as the red haze of rage receded slightly. "I'll kill him. I'll fucking *kill* him."

"He wasn't there, boss."

Manny's gaze snapped back to his bodyguard, temporarily forcing back the blinding anger. "What?"

"He found the safehouse and alerted Arturo, but then Montoya left. He was trying to track down Oceane and wasn't there when his men attacked. He'd ordered them to stand down, wait for Arturo. But they didn't listen."

His jaw worked, his hands flexing restlessly. They hadn't listened because they were like a pack of jackals, hungry for the kill. "They're dead men."

"They were killed at the house. Along with Arturo. I heard Oceane shot him."

When the gravity of that sank in, of what it must have cost her to shoot someone she loved so much, Manny lowered his gaze to the tablecloth. His favorite meal was spread out before him but the sight of it turned his stomach. "My God," he whispered, frantic and sick inside. "My God, how is she ever going to forgive me now?"

****

Juan Montoya slumped down in the passenger seat of the unmarked van parked in the underground lot and checked his watch one final time. Six-fifty-one a.m. Seven minutes until the meeting that was supposedly going to take place between Oceane and the lawyers from the U.S. Attorney's office.

"You see any of them yet?" one of the guys asked from the back.

Juan checked the video feed on his phone that showed all the approaches to the building. He had four guys with him for this part of the op, including the driver, who was to remain at the wheel throughout this whole operation so they could make a speedy getaway. Another van was parked across the street, with five more of his men in it. All but two of them former Mexican Special Forces who had been lured to the dark side by a guaranteed salary of four times what they made in the military.

Yeah, Juan had the best *sicarios* money could buy.

"No," he answered, scanning the feeds.

Maybe they'd gotten bad intel. Or maybe they'd received a bogus tip about the meeting time and location. Even though his contact had worked his magic at the U.S. Attorney's office yesterday, charming the young receptionist in charge of booking appointments so she didn't suspect anything was wrong, it didn't guarantee she had been telling the truth.

"Even with the cameras down here disabled, I don't like doing this in plain sight, man," the guy in the back continued.

"I don't care if you like it or not, *cabrón*. This is the job and you'll damn well do as I tell you." After yesterday's botched hit, Juan had half expected to wake up in his motel room bed to find Manny holding a knife to his throat. His boss didn't like violence, and Juan knew damn well how enraged he would be right now after what had happened to Anya.

Juan hadn't had the guts to call Manny last night to explain what had happened, knowing word about the botched op would get back to him soon enough through the cartel network. Even though they hadn't had much of a relationship over the past few years, Manny had still loved Anya in his own way. Enough that he'd ordered Arturo to make the hit instead of Juan.

It had irked him to be rejected on that kind of high-level op, but he'd let it go and focused on the prize that would give him the most reward—Oceane. She was Manny's number one priority, and if Juan could bring her back unharmed to him then all might still be forgiven. While he'd been searching for her, his men had disobeyed orders and gotten...carried away and gone after Anya. All dead now. One less problem for Juan to deal with.

The office building they waited beneath wasn't marked, with no visible signage on it except for the address. Apparently the U.S. Marshals had chosen it to keep the meeting a secret and maintain security for Oceane and the lawyers.

Next to him, the driver yawned and folded his arms, leaning his head against the window. Juan punched him in the chest. "Hey. Wake the fuck up. This isn't the military, but I expect you to stay alert. All of you, get ready. When they show we're gonna have seconds to get this done. Seconds, understand? This is a one-shot deal. We screw up, we either die or go to jail here. Got me?" He had no intention of dying or going to jail today, or anytime soon. He was having way too much fun.

A grumbled chorus of *yeahs* sounded from the back.

On camera, a deep blue SUV rolled up and turned into the street that led behind the building, its windows tinted. "Hey," Juan snapped, watching closely as he alerted the other van with a button on his radio. They would take care of any backup that arrived, and assist with the main assault if Juan and his crew needed a hand.

Not that he expected to. A handful of federal agents armed with pistols and maybe a pump-action shotgun or two were no match for Juan's men and automatic rifles.

"Get ready," he ordered. This could be it.

The SUV turned and took the ramp into the underground parking garage. Juan sunk down farther in his seat, making sure he wasn't visible through the windows.

The SUV's front passenger door opened and a guy wearing jeans and a collared shirt popped out. He was a big guy with a military bearing and he turned his head this way and that, scanning the garage. Juan tensed when that alert gaze seemed to stop on the van. But then it moved away and the man reached for the back passenger door.

A woman's legs appeared, ending in a pair of high heels. Nice legs. Too pale to be Oceane's. A trim body climbed out wearing a snug skirt suit. She had long black hair.

Turn around, sweetheart, Juan silently urged her, needing to see her face for confirmation.

His hand gripped the door handle as he watched the camera feed, the other ready to tug down the black balaclava already on his head. His rifle rested in his lap, a full magazine ready to go. He could be up and out of the vehicle and ready to fire within a second.

The woman stood fully and turned to face the building's rear entrance, finally giving him a view of her profile.

Gotcha. He tugged the mask down over his face and alerted the other team with the push of a button, adrenaline pulsing through his veins in a dizzying high he'd never get enough of. "It's the lawyer. *Go.*"

"What about Oceane?" one of the guys blurted as he opened the back door. "Shouldn't we wait for her?"

They couldn't wait. "We get the lawyer, we'll get Oceane." Rowan Stewart would know where she was. And he would make her talk. "*Go.*" He threw open the door and brought his weapon up, ready to have some fun.

Chapter Twenty-Two

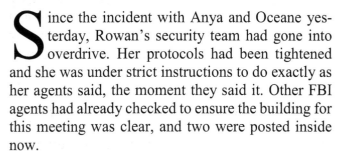

Since the incident with Anya and Oceane yesterday, Rowan's security team had gone into overdrive. Her protocols had been tightened and she was under strict instructions to do exactly as her agents said, the moment they said it. Other FBI agents had already checked to ensure the building for this meeting was clear, and two were posted inside now.

Rowan had been scheduled to arrive first, then Oceane a few minutes later, followed finally by Val. All in separate vehicles with their individual security details. Once the meeting about the financial information Anya had given investigators was over, Oceane would leave first, since she was at greatest risk. After that, Rowan and her boss would be driven to a different location to meet with Victoria Gomez, who would be waiting for them with her security team.

Rowan waited in the backseat of the SUV now, watching the FBI agent standing outside her door. The windows were darkly tinted but she could easily see him and hear what he was saying to Oceane's team via his earpiece, since they were still en route from the WITSEC orientation center.

"Be advised, there's an unmarked van across the street," the agent said. "Two males in the front. Unknown number in the back. There's another down here, not sure if it's occupied. Suggest you reroute and wait until we're in the building before approaching."

Rowan automatically swiveled around to look behind them. Sure enough, there was the van, parked over in the far corner. It was early, but not too early for service or construction workers to be here, and her team was simply doing its due diligence to play it safe. Still, in light of the horrible tragedy yesterday, she was a little on edge as she waited for the agent to open her door.

The agent knocked once on the window, signaling for her to get ready. She gripped her briefcase tight in her left hand and prepared to make the short run to the entrance as instructed.

The moment the door opened, she shot through it and jogged straight for the door to the elevator where another agent waited, holding it open for her. Halfway there, she vaguely picked up the sound of a vehicle's doors opening behind her.

"Get her inside, now!" her guard snapped.

Rowan wrenched her head around in time to see masked men burst from the van, holding rifles. Fear ripped through her. She swung her gaze front once more to find the guard at the door reaching for her, his weapon raised and his expression set. Urgent.

The staccato pop of semi-automatic gunfire shattered the silence. A scream locked in her throat as the guard at the door grabbed hold of her shoulder, yanking her inside the building.

Bullets slammed into the windows and door, spraying bits of glass down on them. The agent dragged her to the floor and landed on top of her, shielding her with his own body. The shooting got louder, more ferocious as the FBI agents returned fire. Bursts of shots came one on top of the other until it sounded like continual gunfire.

Then, suddenly everything got quiet. Over the ringing in her ears, the agent on top of her let out a vicious curse and scrambled off to drag her to her feet. "This way," he commanded, seizing her by the upper arm. "Run and don't stop until I say."

Heart in her throat, Rowan rushed after him, her high heels sliding on the bits of glass. Her shins and the front of her thighs stung in places but she barely noticed, racing to keep up with the man, who raised his weapon as he wrenched open another door and pushed her up the stairs in front of him.

As she turned the corner of the staircase and began to run to the second floor, she glanced back and glimpsed the two FBI agents beside the SUV down. And the masked men bearing down on the entrance with their weapons up.

Terror rocketed up her spine. She kicked off her stupid shoes and fled up the stairs, her heart racing. She bit back a scream when the man at the base of the stairs fired his weapon.

A volley of rifle fire answered him. Rowan didn't dare look back, didn't dare slow down, racing for the upper hallway.

Another agent appeared on the landing, weapon drawn. "In here," he shouted to her. Rowan ran for him, had almost reached the doorway he was in, holding out his hand to her, when an accented male voice called out from behind her.

"There's nowhere to hide from us, bitch." Then male laughter.

God, how many of them were there? More gunfire shattered the stillness. High-pitched pops amongst the staccato fire of the rifles.

Gasping for breath, her heart was about to explode, Rowan latched onto this new agent's hand. He was talking to someone via his earpiece, demanding backup as he dragged her inside, quickly locked the door, and herded her away toward the far side of the room to another door.

He shoved her inside it. "Lock it. Don't open it until I tell you to."

Her hand shook as she turned the bolt home, then retreated to the opposite side of the storage closet and stood there with her back pressed to the wall, her breathing shallow as she stared at the door.

This was it. Her last refuge. If the agent on the other side couldn't take down the attackers, then she was dead.

She squeezed her eyes shut, took a shuddering breath. She thought of Malcolm. Kevin. Her parents. *I don't want to die!*

The thought had barely formed before gunshots ripped through the room. She swallowed a cry and forced her knees to hold her upright, her chest so tight she could barely draw a breath.

The shooting stopped. The resounding silence reverberated against her eardrums, mixing with the terrified thud of her heart. There was no way the FBI agent had survived that. She had no weapon. Nothing to defend herself with.

Rapid Spanish filtered through the door. Her heart sank, fear giving way to denial. *Oh my God, you're about to die and there's nothing you can do to stop it.*

The door handle rattled. She shifted her stance, balled her hands into fists, ready to fight if she could.

More Spanish, and an oily male snicker that made her skin crawl. A single gunshot hit the door. She flinched and pressed her lips together, refusing to give them the satisfaction of hearing her scream.

A moment later the ruined door swung open. Before she'd even taken a single step, fist raised, hands reached in and plunged a hood over her head.

She fought it, grabbed at the fabric and tried to wrench it off but cruel fingers wrapped around her wrists and yanked them behind her, squeezing until her bones hurt. Something wound around them, imprisoning her hands.

"Don't bother fighting, *puta*," one of the men sneered, dragging her out of the closet.

"Or, go ahead and fight," another argued. "We love it when women have some fight left in them."

The smug male laughter infuriated her. Rowan yelled and kicked but it did no good. Two sets of hands had her now, immobilizing her as they hustled her out of the room.

Where were they taking her? Why hadn't they just shot her? If they were planning to do to her what they'd done to Anya or Victoria, she'd rather have died here and now.

She twisted and bucked, got nowhere. The hood was stifling, the total lack of light completely disorienting. It felt like there was no air. Like she was slowly suffocating.

The sound of the men's running footsteps changed as they hit the tiled hallway, then she bounced a little as they rushed down the stairs. They were going to take her out of the building. To what? That van?

Must. Get. Free.

Gritting her teeth, she wrenched up against the restraining hands. Her strength was waning, her muscles already weakening, but she couldn't give up.

"Better save your strength," the first man said with a chuckle. "You're gonna need it, *linda*."

The change in temperature told her they were outside now. She kicked her feet, hoping to smash the man holding her legs in the face. "Let me *go*," she roared.

They tossed her into the air. She had only enough time to suck in a breath and brace for impact before she landed with a bone-jarring thud on something hard and metallic. Pain radiated throughout her ribs and hip, the side of her head where it had hit whatever they'd thrown her onto.

Doors slammed shut and she started moving. A vehicle. Maybe the van. God, where were they taking her?

She struggled to her knees. Something slammed into her temple. Pain shot through her skull as her head snapped to the side. She crumpled onto the floor of the vehicle.

"Stay down there where you belong, *puta*," a hard voice warned, "or you'll get more."

Gasping, disoriented, Rowan curled onto her un-injured side and bit her lip to keep from crying. She had to be smart. Strong. Figure out how to survive whatever they had planned for her. Killing federal agents would rain hell down upon her captors. The FBI would be sending backup right now. A task force would be set up to find her.

Commander Taggart would be alerted. Malcolm would find out soon after that. He would do every-thing humanly possible to find her before it was too late.

Except she knew in vivid detail what these ani-mals had done to Anya and Victoria. Ice congealed in her gut, terror snaking through her body. How could she endure that? How could she survive it?

Even though she couldn't see through the impen-etrable black fabric of the hood, Rowan squeezed her eyes shut and sent up a silent prayer.

Malcolm, help me. Please help me...

****

"Good to be back?"

Mal looked up from gathering his gear at Khan, the team medic, who was watching him from over at his locker with a knowing grin. They were kitting up for a training exercise to work on their urban combat skills, followed by a trip to the range for some long gun work.

"You have no idea." He missed being with Rowan, but since that wasn't a possibility, the only other place he wanted to be was with his team. Here he had a purpose and it felt good to be back in the fold again, with guys he knew and respected.

From over by the door, someone let out a shrill whistle. Everyone stopped what they were doing and looked over to where Commander Taggart stood in the doorway. "Listen up," he said, closing the door behind him as he addressed the team. "We've got a major kidnapping situation unfolding right now."

When that aqua gaze landed on Mal, a warning prickle started at his nape. *Not Rowan. Jesus, not Rowan.*

"Armed attackers assaulted Miss Stewart's security team twenty-minutes ago."

Mal shot to his feet, his heart rocketing into his throat. *Fucking Christ.* Next to him, Maka put a steadying hand on his shoulder. Mal barely refrained from wrenching away from it.

"HRT Commander DeLuca is aware of the situation and his boys are on standby. But the way things are going, both our units might be needed if the call comes in." He paused a moment, his gaze lingering on Mal for a second, a kind of silent acknowledgment that he was aware of how Mal was feeling. "So everybody head to the briefing room. We'll be getting updates and new intel in real time, so I want us up to speed and ready to go at a moment's notice if they need us."

Mal was the first one out the door behind Taggart, his body pulsing with helpless fury. Where was she? Was she injured? If those assholes had killed more federal agents, then she might have been shot too. Was it Ruiz, looking to stall his upcoming trial? Or Nieto, looking to make a statement?

"Freeman, wait."

Mal stopped, realizing only then that he had barged outside instead of heading to the briefing room. Fighting to get control over his emotions, he slowly turned to face Hamilton and Prentiss.

Prentiss stopped a few paces from him, searched his eyes a moment. "I'm sorry, man. I know how much she means to you. And I know exactly what you're feeling right now. I was out of my mind when they took Autumn."

His little daughter, who they'd thankfully found and rescued in time. Mal didn't bother denying that Rowan meant something to him, because it was an understatement and it felt like his fucking heart was being put through a shredder right now.

"Come inside," Hamilton said quietly. "If we get the call, all of us need to be ready, so we can do what it takes to get her back."

He was right, of course. "I just... I need a minute." Mal's voice was hoarse.

"I get it. But when you're ready, come to the briefing room so we can get to work." Then he pointed at the building behind him, his expression earnest. "Every last guy in there is here for you. For her. We'll get her back."

If someone finds her and we even get the call.

Mal pushed the awful thought away and nodded, because what the hell else could he do, and his team leader was just trying to give him hope. When Prentiss and Hamilton turned to walk away, Mal couldn't help saying, "You know what they did to Victoria. To Anya." Hamilton had spent more time with Victoria than anyone else on the team. He'd seen in grim detail the damage they'd done to her. And Prentiss had been the one to find her in the woods that night.

His team leader turned to face him. His demeanor was calm and steady as ever. But those steel gray eyes glowed with deep, burning rage. "I know. But none of that's gonna happen to Rowan. They've already got teams out looking for her, and a net set up. Roadblocks into and out of the city are in place and they're analyzing CCTV footage now. She's going to be okay."

The fierce way Hamilton said it, Mal almost believed him. They *would* find Rowan. But there was another part, deep down inside where his most secret fears lay buried, that was fucking terrified they wouldn't find her in time.

Chapter Twenty-Three

Rowan couldn't stem the fear surging through her. Couldn't stop her mind from spinning out of control as she lay on the floor of the van while it bumped over the pavement.

They'd been driving for what seemed like a while, maybe around an hour, she wasn't sure. There were so many places they could be by now, and so far no one had tried to pull them over. Did the van have plates on it? Surely one of the FBI agents had reported it if anyone was still alive.

A shudder sped through her. She hadn't tried to fight anymore, not after the shot to the side of the face where her cheekbone still throbbed like it had its own heartbeat.

She rolled a little as the van made a left-hand turn. This time the driver went slower. They were no longer on the highway. The road here was bumpier. It had either some stoplights or stop signs, judging by the slowing and acceleration pattern. Were they getting close to their destination? They'd taken her alive for a reason. What were they going to do to her once they got there?

Horror curdled in the pit of her stomach. Details of what they had done to Victoria filled her mind. *No, stay strong*, she reminded herself. But when the van finally stopped and at least some of the men exited the vehicle, panic slammed into her like a wrecking ball.

Rough hands grabbed her by the arms and hauled her upright. She held herself rigid as they dragged her out the back. The moment she felt the breeze on her bare arms and legs, she struggled, survival instinct taking over.

"Help!" she cried, twisting, kicking. "Somebody help me!" She kicked out behind her, hope surging when the man holding her grunted. If she could get free, maybe she could run—

Pain sliced through her ribs as a fist slammed into her right side. She doubled over, the air knocked from her lungs. Growling male voices echoed around her but she couldn't understand them, too overcome with the fight for breath to focus on anything else.

Slowly the swimming sensation faded, a clammy film of sweat coating her skin. There was no escaping the cruel, iron hold on her arms and legs, the men's fingers biting deep with bruising force. They lifted her. Carried her quickly.

Their footsteps shuffled along pavement, then a door squeaked open. The man holding her legs let go. She stumbled, her knees slamming into the hard, unforgiving floor. Then the man holding her arms yanked her upright, shoved her backward and down. Her rear hit something hard, the unexpected impact jolting up her spine, making her teeth clack together.

A man muttered something in Spanish. The door opened again, then shut. A cold bead of sweat trickled down her ribs, her heart slamming against her breastbone.

Someone grasped the hood and roughly jerked it from her head. Rowan flinched and squeezed her eyes shut against the sudden brightness, but fear forced them back open, her entire body on red alert as she took in her surroundings.

She was in some kind of a small hut with no windows. A single bulb surrounded by a wire cage suspended from the middle of the ceiling.

Movement to her right made her snap her head toward it. A man stepped in front of her. Late twenties or early thirties, with bronze-colored skin and a dark moustache and goatee. His eyes were dark brown, almost black, and the evil gleam in them made her skin fucking crawl.

"Miss Stewart," he said in a thick Spanish accent. "So good to finally meet you at last."

Through her terror, it took a moment to place him. But when her brain at last snapped into gear, the chill inside her turned into an arctic blast.

Juan Montoya. Manuel Nieto's chief enforcer. One of the most feared and notorious criminals within the entire *Veneno* cartel. Vicious even by cartel standards.

Even though she was shaking inside, she met that awful stare and raised her chin, refusing to give him the satisfaction of allowing him to see how terrified she was. He needed something from her. Otherwise he wouldn't have gone to the trouble of kidnapping her.

One side of his mouth tipped up in an amused smirk. "I've gone to a lot of trouble to retrieve you, *puta*," he said softly. So softly the tiny hairs on Rowan's nape prickled in warning. "You'd best not disappoint me after all this."

Her spine was rigid as a steel rod, her muscles locked tight as she stared up at him. It was almost worse that he was a good looking man, his attractive exterior at complete odds with the evil that lurked underneath. But it showed in those dark, gleaming eyes that made her want to recoil. Only by sheer force of will did she hold her position.

He took a step closer. She braced herself for a blow, for him to grab her by the throat, but he merely placed his hands on his jean-clad thighs and leaned forward at the waist slightly, bringing his face closer to hers. "Where is Oceane?"

She'd expected this. Still, her mouth went dry. He wasn't going to like her answer. "I don't know." Her voice was faint but surprisingly steady.

His face tightened. The evil beneath the polished façade rippling just under the surface. "Don't lie to me, *puta*," he spat. "Where is she?"

There was no harm in telling him what she did know. It wouldn't put Oceane in any more danger than she already was. "I don't know. She was supposed to meet with me this morning at the building, but her security team must have diverted when mine saw your van and got suspicious."

He searched her eyes. "And?" he prompted.

"And when y-you attacked—" Damn, her voice was shaking a bit now. "Her team would have taken her back to the WITSEC facility."

His eyes narrowed. "Where is it?"

"I don't know."

He bared his teeth, his patience slipping, and seized a handful of her hair, wrenching her head back painfully. "Tell me where it is."

"I don't know!"

Releasing her hair with a rough yank, he reached behind him to withdraw something from his pocket and crouched in front of her, that frightening gaze freezing her in place. A quiet snick sounded as a bright silver blade sprang free from the switchblade he held in his hand.

The blood drained from her face, her entire body shrinking away from it.

"Do you know what my men did to Anya yesterday?" he asked silkily.

God, yes. She couldn't control the shudder that ripped through her.

"Ah, you heard. And who do you think taught them what to do, hmm? How to inflict that kind of damage without killing the victim outright?"

The monster poised in front of her.

"You don't want to find out firsthand what that felt like for her, do you? Such a waste, to have all this pretty white skin sliced up. " He eased the lethally sharp point of it toward her neck.

Rowan lurched back in her chair, cowering from that blade, but he merely set its tip to the notch between her collarbones. Her throat moved in a convulsive wave as she swallowed hard, her heart about to explode, the tiny prick of the blade nothing compared to what she feared was coming.

Then he jerked his wrist, narrowly avoiding her skin as the blade sliced through the fabric of her blouse like a laser through paper, exposing her cleavage to his roving gaze.

Slowly, so slowly it was agony, he eased the blade away from her skin, toying with it in his fingers as he dragged his gaze from her breasts up to hers once more. "Very nice. Classy, even. I'd prefer not to have to cut you, Miss Stewart," he continued in that scary as hell tone, "but that will depend on whether or not you tell me what I want to know." His features tightened. "So start talking."

Her heart pounded so hard she felt dizzy. There didn't seem to be enough air. She was gasping. Tiny, shallow breaths that came too fast. Too fast.

She couldn't slow it down. Couldn't tell him what he wanted, and if she lied he'd just kill her anyway when he found out. The truth was the only thing that might save her.

Or it might hasten her death when he decided she was no longer of use to him.

"I don't know where it is. No one does," she blurted, "not even the witnesses themselves. They're blindfolded each time they come and go from the facility. Only the Marshals Service knows the location. That's why WITSEC is so successful."

He stared at her for a long, agonizing moment while she held her breath, waiting. She exhaled in a relieved rush when he lowered the blade, only to cry out when he seized a handful of her hair again and dragged her from the chair. She stumbled after him;

it was either that or have a huge chunk of her hair ripped out of her scalp.

He yelled for someone named Javier. Two steps from the door, he yanked the hood back over her head, plunging her back into darkness.

The door opened and he rammed a solid palm into the middle of her back, pitching her forward. Without her hands to catch herself, she hit the ground hard.

A fresh wave of pain shot through her and she tasted blood in her mouth. Dazed, she struggled to lift her head. Could barely stand when someone hauled her upright. The world spun, worsened because she couldn't see anything.

Montoya said something else in rapid Spanish, his tone curt, annoyed. Whoever had her flung her up and over his shoulder and began carrying her off.

Exhausted, trembling all over, Rowan hung there limply in her prison of darkness and clamped her teeth together to keep a helpless sob from escaping.

"Hey, what are you doing?" someone called out in English, sounding far away.

Montoya let out a savage curse and Rowan jerked when gunshots sounded a moment later. Someone had seen her! Had Montoya shot him? Please no, whoever it was might be her only chance. If he was unhurt, maybe he was calling for help right now.

"*Undele*," he barked, and the man carrying her broke into a jog.

She bounced up and down, his shoulder slamming into her tender ribs and stomach with every step. She tensed her muscles to minimize it, but it didn't do much good.

Just when the pain got so bad that she had to grit her teeth to keep from crying out, she was dumped onto something softer. A seat of some sort. Then a door slammed and an engine started up and the car sped away, its tires squealing. Not the van. It smelled different. Cleaner.

This time the drive didn't take long, only a few minutes. She was thrown once more over that thick shoulder and carried somewhere else. The man was climbing now. Winded. Where were they? Had the man who'd spotted them called for help?

Montoya's voice snapped out a command. Metallic doors squealed as they opened and she was dumped inside. Even through her hood the smell hit her. Stale air. Unwashed bodies. Sweat.

Fear.

The doors squealed shut and someone ripped the hood off her. She winced against the bright beam of a flashlight aimed into her face. It lowered, and as she blinked her vision began to clear, filling in the details of where she was.

Her heart lurched when she saw Montoya towering over her...and the frightened faces of the handful of naked young women all cowering against the far end of what appeared to be a shipping container.

"Meet your new traveling companions," Montoya said to her, the satisfaction in his voice unmistakable. "You're going to be part of my next shipment—if I decide to let you live that long." His boot caught her square in the chest, knocked her backward hard enough that her back slammed into the metal floor. Her skull bounced off it, and a cry escaped her tight throat.

Montoya planted the sole of his boot against her sternum, pinning her in place as he stared down at her with pitiless black eyes. "Now are you going to give me any worthwhile information that I can actually put to use to find Oceane? Or will I have to use my powers of persuasion after all?"

Instead of pulling out the switchblade, this time he drew a pistol from the back of his pants and chambered a round, the deadly sound echoing throughout the container.

****

Too much time had passed.

Mal sat silent at the back of the briefing room, alone, his eyes on the analog clock on the far wall. Too much damn time had passed between when Rowan was taken and now, yet to him it felt like they were still sitting here on their asses while every other law enforcement agency in the city was mobilized, conducting grid searches, roadblocks, monitoring CCTV or satellite footage, red light cameras.

His commander and teammates were all in the room speaking in hushed murmurs, giving him a wide berth so he could have a little privacy as he struggled to compose himself. He bounced his knee up and down in a rapid rhythm, the movement uncontrollable. While inside, he was slowly coming unglued.

The cops and the FBI had sightings on the van using various cameras throughout the city, but they didn't have a current location yet. By now the kidnappers would undoubtedly have ditched the vehicle.

And they'd also had more than enough time to do...other things.

He swallowed past the baseball-sized lump in his throat, dragged a hand over his mouth and chin. The waiting, the inaction, was killing him. It sliced him up inside to think of Rowan frightened and alone, facing those fucking animals and the things they had repeatedly proven they enjoyed doing to female captives.

Fuck. He lowered his head into his hands, closed his eyes and struggled to clear his mind. In place of all the horrific things he feared Rowan was facing right then, images of them together replaced them. Her smiling up at him. The soft look on her face after he'd made love to her. The trust and hope in her eyes.

"Hey, man." A hand landed gently on his shoulder. Mal looked up at Lockhart, who lowered himself into the chair beside him. "You hanging in there?"

He nodded. "Yeah." *Barely. I don't know how the fuck to handle this.* Exhaustion, sleep-deprivation, hunger and pain, he could handle. But not this. He couldn't accept that there was nothing he could do to help Rowan. Nothing to study or get ready. Everything was done. All he and the others could do now...was wait.

Lockhart didn't say anything else, just leaned his head back against the wall and maintained that solid, silent presence Mal was so used to but hadn't fully appreciated until that moment. He couldn't have handled being around the others right now. They all meant well, were all good, solid operators and he liked them all a lot as people.

But if someone like Maka or Granger came over

and tried to lighten the mood with some lame attempt at humor in an effort to lighten the moment, Mal was afraid he'd punch them out. He was that keyed up. So having Lockhart sit beside him quietly while his mind screamed in the silence was actually a relief of sorts.

"We should have heard something by now," he finally said, feeling the need to say something. Someone had to at least know the van's current location. That would be a start.

"Taggart's holding the updates until we get something solid. He and Hamilton are monitoring all the channels."

Mal glanced first around the room, then at Lockhart, and realization hit. Taggart and Hamilton were missing. Running interference on the investigation from another room, probably Taggart's office, hoping to make it easier on him.

Mal exhaled hard, appreciative of their efforts and annoyed at the same time. "They don't need to do that." He was point man and a former SEAL. He didn't need to be shielded or sheltered from any of this. "But Christ, I want to be out there searching for her, not sitting here doing jack."

"We need to be here so we can deploy as soon as we get a solid lead. When that call comes, every minute's gonna count, so we need to be ready. And we are. Hamilton and Taggart are both on top of it. Let them do their jobs, wait until they have something concrete to give us."

He opened his mouth to respond but the briefing room door suddenly burst open and Hamilton came in, Taggart a few paces behind him, speaking on his cell phone. "Okay, boys, listen up," Hamilton began, his gaze halting on Mal. "We just got confirmation from a witness that someone matching Juan Montoya's description was seen carrying a female hostage from a warehouse district near the Port of Baltimore. At the time of the sighting, she was very much alive."

Mal's heart leapt, his attention riveted on his team leader. *Thank you, God.*

"Montoya shot at the witness, then took off in another vehicle and headed northeast, toward the port itself. Witness got a partial plate. FBI has confirmed the vehicle's location via CCTV footage. They're moving in on the port right now, with two of its SWAT teams. HRT is on standby, but because of Montoya, we've got precedence."

Yes, Jesus, just let them get moving—

"Helo crew is readying two aircraft for us right now," Taggart added, lowering his phone. "Let's get moving. I'll brief you with any updates on the way."

Mal grabbed his gear and ran for the door, desperate to find Rowan in time to free her from Montoya's clutches and a fate worse than death.

Chapter Twenty-Four

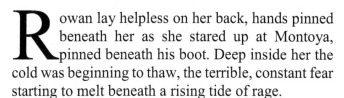

Rowan lay helpless on her back, hands pinned beneath her as she stared up at Montoya, pinned beneath his boot. Deep inside her the cold was beginning to thaw, the terrible, constant fear starting to melt beneath a rising tide of rage.

This piece of shit currently towering above her was a fucking coward, terrorizing her and all these women, keeping them bound and toying with them before he either killed them or sold them into a life of sexual slavery. All to get rich and make himself feel powerful.

Fuck. You.

She didn't dare say it aloud, because she wasn't stupid. But she let her eyes tell him exactly what she thought of him.

"What did Oceane and Anya tell you?" he pressed.

"About the attack in Mexico." Her voice was

rough, almost strangled.

His mouth tightened and he pressed down harder with his boot, compressing her ribcage. "About the *business*."

She searched her memory, her brain working slower under the bombardment of fear. "Some off-shore bank accounts. Assets."

"What else?" His voice was hard, implacable.

Jesus, she didn't know. What did he want her to say? "My case is against Ruiz. Not them."

"I don't care about Ruiz," he snarled. "I care about what Oceane and Anya told you."

Rowan shook her head, heart thudding. "I only know what they told me, about the finances and the attack. I'm not privy to whatever else they told the federal agents. I don't know anything else." How could she convince him that she was telling the truth?

He stared down at her for a tense moment, his face eerily blank. Then he removed his foot and lunged over to grab one of the women by the hair.

The prisoner cried out, her legs flailing as he dragged her along the floor of the container. Rowan cringed and scrambled into a sitting position. Montoya jerked the poor woman to a halt a few feet away from Rowan and wrenched her head back, exposing the line of her throat. Rowan's stomach contracted, fearing he was about to take out his switchblade and slash her throat.

"What's your name," he demanded of the girl in English, the beam of his flashlight illuminating her young face.

Frightened brown eyes settled on Rowan, the buried shame in them making her heart twist. "Gabriela," she whispered, her naked body shaking.

"And if you could have one wish granted right now, Gabriela, what would it be?"

She bit her lower lip, her shoulders hunching as tears clogged her voice. "I want to go home to my family."

Rowan's throat tightened to the point of choking her. This girl was barely out of her teens and she'd been ripped away from her home, her family, then abused and terrorized for however long by this bastard and his men. Now he intended to sell her off as a sex slave. God, she wished she had a gun so she could shoot him right in his disgusting face.

"Tell you what, Gabriela," Montoya went on in a silky voice, stroking the muzzle of the pistol over her hair. Gabriela shuddered, made a distressed sound. "If Miss Stewart tells me what I need to know, I'll let you go."

Both Gabriela and Rowan jerked their gazes up to him in shock. He was lying. But Gabriela was clearly now clinging to that desperate thread of hope because she turned heart wrenching, hopeful eyes on Rowan. "Please," she begged. "Please tell him. I want to go *home*."

"Yes, Rowan," he echoed, the gleam in his eyes making her ache to kill him. "Tell me."

Helplessness flooded her. "I don't know anything else," she insisted.

"No?"

"I already told you everything I know," she snapped, frantic to think of a way to—

He put the pistol to Gabriela's temple and pulled

the trigger.

Rowan jerked back, a scream locked in her throat as the opposite side of the girl's head exploded into a red mist. The other captives screamed too, started crying.

With that cold, evil stare drilling into Rowan, Montoya flung Gabriela's shattered head away from him. Her body toppled over and hit the floor with a sickening thud.

Rowan stared at the crumpled heap in horror. Christ. *Christ*, she was going to throw up. She gagged, was shaking so hard her bones hurt.

"Do I need to do that again to get you to talk?" Montoya asked, his tone almost bored.

Rowan struggled to find her voice. "I t-told you, I—"

He turned away, stalked toward the remaining women.

"*No!*" Rowan was on her knees now, shoving to her feet even though her legs wobbled. She wouldn't let him hurt anyone else. She would body slam him, kick and bite. Do whatever she could to stop this.

The chirp of a radio made everything go still, even Montoya. Facing Rowan, he pulled it from his belt and answered. Whatever the man on the other end said made the women in the back gasp.

The beam of the flashlight was lowered, but Rowan could still see Montoya's face. And the rage that contorted it.

He advanced on her slowly. She lost her bravado for a second, then braced herself and stood her ground. He was going to kill her now. She had to do whatever she could to fight for her life.

Maybe he saw the determination in her eyes, because he gave her a cold, almost admiring smile. "A bullet is too kind a death for a *puta* like you," he sneered.

He shot out the hand holding the flashlight. Rowan ducked, the blow hitting her on the shoulder rather than the side of the head as he'd intended. But she lost her balance and fell, landing hard on her hip. By the time she'd scrambled into a sitting position, he was at the far end of the container.

"*Adiós, chicas,*" he said, then exited the container and slammed the heavy doors shut with a bang.

Rowan sat gasping, her heart hammering in her ears. What was happening?

His muffled voice came from beyond the closed doors, then she thought she heard his footsteps moving away. She swiveled to look at the others. Did any of them speak English? She didn't know much Spanish, but she knew a few phrases. "*¿Qué pasa?*" she asked. "What's happening?"

"*No sé,*" one of them answered in a frightened whisper.

But she got her answer soon enough, when she got up and tried to shove the doors open with her shoulder. She lurched hard to the left, slamming into the side wall when the container suddenly began moving.

What the hell? They seemed to be going upward.

And then it hit her.

A crane. Someone was lifting the container with a crane. Packing them onto the ship with the rest of the cargo.

****

Cradling his rifle in his arms, Mal leaned forward to get a better look through the Blackhawk's open door as they neared the port. Another Hawk carrying the rest of the team was circling from the other direction, providing recon for the taskforce from the air. FBI and DEA agents were already on the ground, in the process of establishing a perimeter and hunting for Montoya and his crew, along with Rowan.

CCTV footage had backed up witnesses' reports of the getaway vehicle there, and someone had seen a bound woman being carried toward one of the ships. Four huge cargo ships were currently berthed in the port. One of the enormous port cranes stationed on shore was hoisting a shipping container high above the second ship's deck.

Mal scanned them as they circled overhead. Everything was in flux down there, crewmembers and port workers being evacuated from the area, making it impossible to spot Montoya. But with agents posted at all exits, every person was being checked.

To Mal's left, Hamilton waved his arm to get everyone's attention and spoke into his mic over the team frequency. "Fresh intel just came in. Montoya might have a shipment leaving from port. A human one."

A deep, burning rage built inside Mal. *Motherfucker*. "Any word on Rowan?"

"Not officially. But it sounds like he might try to hide her with the others."

Jesus fucking *Christ*. Montoya thought he could ship her off as part of his skin trade? He snapped his head back around, searching below them frantically. One clue. Something to give away her location. Anything. *Where are you, Rowan?*

His searching gaze snagged back on the suspended shipping container. It stuck out because it was the only one not stacked neatly on board the waiting ships. None of the other cranes were active. Could Rowan...? "What's the story on that container?" Mal asked.

Hamilton craned his head to get a better look, switched frequencies to speak to the pilots before responding to Mal. "They're taking us in lower for a good look."

Maka got up and moved next to Mal, crouching to inspect the container. "Someone's in the crane cab," he said. Khan and Hamilton moved closer to see as well.

A man sat high up in the cab, hands appearing to be on the controls. He shouldn't still be in there, not with the FBI and DEA clearing everyone else out. Leaving a container dangling like that was obviously unsafe. Was he just putting the container into position on top of the rest before he could shut down the crane?

Hamilton was back on the radio. Mal caught the moment when those gray eyes lifted and found his. Hamilton gave a shake of his head. "That crane's not supposed to be operating," he said grimly.

God dammit! Was Rowan in there?

Mal focused back on the container, his heart slamming. He had to fight to keep the sudden leap of emotion in check. "Get us down there." If Rowan and the other women rumored to be held by Montoya were in there…

Hamilton nodded, was already talking to the pilots. The helo descended, coming in closer to the crane cab. The operator was still at the controls. Uniformed FBI agents were converging on the crane, but it was a hell of a long way up to the cab.

As Mal watched, the crane swung the container out further, moving it away from the ship. His muscles bunched, his whole body tensing. *No.* "Jesus, tell me he's not gonna—"

The jaws of the clamp opened and dropped the container, sending Mal's heart plunging into the water with it.

Chapter Twenty-Five

Trapped in the blackness of the container, Rowan looked up toward the ceiling at the sound of helicopters flying nearby and her heart beat faster. Did someone know they were in here? Was someone coming to rescue them?

The container stopped rising. Then it seemed to be moving sideways for a few seconds, but maybe it was her imagination. They stopped moving again. The noise of the helicopters was louder now.

Please, please, she begged silently, praying it was someone coming to save them.

Then, just as hope began to expand inside her, she gasped and stumbled, unable to catch her balance as the container suddenly plunged downward at an alarming speed.

It didn't stop. She screamed, the shrill sound drowned out beneath the combined terror of the other girls.

They hit the ground, tossing them all into the air for a moment before they all crashed into the floor. A sharp pain bit into her wrists as whatever bound them snapped.

Rowan shoved up on her hands and knees, looking around in the darkness. A faint ray of light was coming in from the end where Montoya had left minutes before. The impact must have broken the locking mechanism. She rushed for the gap, her body stiff and sore, desperate to escape.

Two steps from the doors, cold water flooded around her ankles, the flow strong enough to almost knock her off her feet.

Sheer terror bolted through her as she realized what had happened. "They dumped us in the water," she cried, fighting to keep her balance as she slogged toward the doors. They had to get out before it sank.

The other women cried out and converged around her, all of them fighting to get to the only exit. But the flow of water was too strong. As the container filled with water and slipped beneath the surface, it swept them all off their feet and sent them crashing against the far end. Rowan bounced off someone. She sucked in a ragged gasp as icy cold water rushed around her thighs, her hips, climbing every second.

I'm not going to drown. I'm not going to drown. The words beat through her mind over and over.

Frantic, she tried to swim her way forward through the torrent. Couldn't.

Desperate hands grabbed at her. Tried to use her to propel themselves past her.

Panic took over. She kicked free of the restraining hands. She treaded water for a moment, raised her hand above her to gauge how much air they had left. Her hand hit the unforgiving metal roof now less than two feet above her head.

"Shit," she breathed, so scared she could barely think. She kept struggling through the water to the open door, watched helplessly while the water came in faster and faster, the light fading as they sank deeper. How far down were they? She had to be right next to the open gap when the water closed over her head, or she'd never get out.

The cold water was up to her chin now, and her muscles were tiring. All around her, frightened screams and crying surrounded her. She choked back a sob, flung an arm off her when it hooked around her neck, all her focus on getting close to the doors, trying to time her last breath...

Her head hit the ceiling. She wrenched her head back to steal those last few precious seconds. Water swirled around her jaw, dark and cold as a grave, waiting to drown her.

Mindless terror gripped her. She gulped in one big, ragged breath and ducked beneath the water, propelling herself toward where the doors should be.

A flailing foot caught her in the stomach, forcing precious air from her lungs. Rowan held her breath and kept swimming, her heart slamming so hard against her ribs she feared it would burst.

Her shoulder hit something hard and metallic. She reached in front of her, blindly shot her hand out and pushed. The metal door swung open.

Grasping the edge of it, she hauled herself through the opening and kicked upward with all her strength, her eyes straining to discern some light above her.

She didn't know how long she swam, the pressure of the water on her eardrums muting everything but the slam of her heart, her limbs freezing, lungs burning.

Up, up she struggled. *Oh God, please... I can't hold it anymore. Need air.*

Just when the burning in her chest became agony, when she couldn't hold her breath for another second, the water began to lighten.

With one final desperate burst of strength, she aimed for the surface and kicked for all she was worth.

****

Christ, the container was in the water and sinking fast.

"Get us down there," Mal snarled, staring in horror as the rust-red container slipped beneath the surface. He didn't know how deep the water was here, but if it was deep enough to allow container ships in and out, then anyone locked inside that metal box didn't have a chance.

The helo dove lower, each second that ticked past its own separate eternity. Mal chucked his gear aside and kept his eyes locked on that container until he lost sight of it. He stood in the open doorway, scanning the surface. Praying that Rowan would make it out—if she was even in there.

Maka moved into place beside him, his huge shoulders filling the rest of the doorway. "We gotta get those doors open," he shouted over the pulse of the rotors.

Mal nodded, his stomach in knots. He and Maka

were totally at home in the water, but they didn't have tanks or goggles, and every second they lost meant another second without air for the women inside that container.

"We'll cover you guys from the air until the zodiacs I've called for show up," Hamilton shouted as he appeared next to Mal. "As soon as we're aboard we'll pick you up."

"Roger that," Maka answered.

Mal stared at the surface as they descended, the rotor wash casting patterns on the water. *Come on, come on...*

Finally the crew chief gave them the signal.

Crossing his arms and feet, Mal jumped out feet first. He hit the water and surfaced immediately, turned to give a thumbs-up to the crew. Desperation made his heart pound. The container was already under too deep. They had literally less than a minute to get the women out in time.

Maka hit the water, surfaced and signaled the crew, then turned and swam with Mal toward where the container had gone down. Salt water sprayed their faces as the helo engines increased power and lifted. Mal kept swimming, gauging the current. The tide was going out, the water trying to pull him away from shore and out to sea.

Taking a deep breath, he bobbed up and then dove straight down, slicing through the water as he searched for the container. It was murky as hell, viz next to zero when he got a half-dozen meters down. He couldn't see shit, let alone the container or any survivors.

He kept swimming, surfacing over two minutes

later when the burn in his lungs turned critical. After another breath he dove down again, searching frantically, praying that he'd spot something.

He thought he caught a flash of movement to his three o'clock but couldn't be sure. Surfacing, he saw Maka's head break the surface a dozen yards away. "See anything?" he yelled.

"Got something over here." He dove back under. Mal swam over as fast as he could and followed his teammate. Then, out of the corner of his eye, he spotted something moving beneath him.

He dove deeper, using big strokes to cut through the water. Someone was thrashing their way to the surface. Mal put on a burst of speed and grabbed for the person, hooking an arm around the waist before shooting upward.

They broke the surface a few seconds later. But the woman in his arms wasn't Rowan. She was naked, sucked in a desperate breath and started choking, her limbs thrashing weakly.

"I've got you," Mal said, turning her onto her back and hooking an arm around her torso in a rescue hold. He glanced around. Maka had resurfaced with another woman, but from the way her head lolled limply, it was already too late.

Fuck. Mal turned in the water, started towing the woman toward shore, searching around him. *Rowan, Christ, please don't be in that container...*

A deafening bang from on shore made him snap his head around in time to see a plume of smoke come from the base of one of the gigantic cranes. Then the sound of rending metal screeched through the air, a long, metallic groan and another, louder thud shook the air. A tall plume of dust rose up, and the crane began to topple forward.

Mal bit back a curse and started swimming away as the huge metal skeleton came crashing down into the water, sending a huge wave of water rushing at him.

He turned the woman. "Hang on and hold your breath," he warned, and ducked under the surface with her. He watched as the wave crashed overhead, the force buffeting them like leaves in a hurricane. The woman fought his grip, panicked. Mal kept his eye on the surface, waited until it was safe before kicking them back up.

The woman dragged in a desperate breath and started crying. Mal looked around.

One Blackhawk still circled overhead, but he wasn't sure whether it was Hamilton's or not. Where were the damn zodiacs?

A boat's engine sounded behind him in the distance.

He spun around as a black zodiac sped toward them. With steady strokes he kept swimming toward it. Something surfaced off to his eleven o'clock. A body, floating facedown. His heart seized for a moment before he saw the blond hair fanning out in the water.

Not Rowan. It was selfish as hell for him to be relieved, but he was so fucking afraid of finding her body here to care.

The zodiacs drew closer. Rodriguez was at the helm of the first one, Hamilton and Khan leaning over the bow as it drew alongside Mal. The other took off toward Maka.

Mal towed the woman in his arms toward the boat. Hamilton and Khan both reached over and hauled her into it, immediately wrapping a blanket around her. Then Hamilton turned back to Mal and reached a hand down. Mal grasped it, propelled himself up and over the rubber gunwale.

"Any others?" Hamilton asked him as Mal got to his knees.

"Over there," he said, panting as he pointed toward where he'd seen the blonde.

Rodriguez whipped them around and took off toward the woman. They hauled her body in, covered her with a blanket. There were more bodies in the water now. All naked, their hands bound.

Mal swallowed, ready to puke. If he had to find Rowan dead and pull her body from the water knowing he'd been so close when she'd died and unable to save her…

A crushing pressure filled his chest, like a vise was closing on his ribs.

"There!" Khan shouted.

Mal jerked his head around to look where his teammate was pointing. Sure enough, a brown head was bobbing up and down on the surface. Heart in his throat, he stared at it as Rodriguez sped them over, but his heart sank when he saw it wasn't Rowan.

They pulled her out, wrapped her up, and Rodriguez set his hands on her shoulders, speaking to her in Spanish. Mal caught the name Rowan, guessed Rodriguez had given a description of her.

Teeth chattering, body shaking uncontrollably, the woman nodded. "S-si," she answered, and said something else.

Rodriguez looked up at him with sympathetic amber eyes. "She was in there with them."

Mal swallowed back the rush of tears and looked away, scanning the water. Refusing to give up, but not seeing how she could possibly have survived. Hamilton was on the radio to the other boat. Colebrook's voice came back loud and clear that they had only found three victims so far, none of them Rowan.

Grief welled up, sharp as a razor blade. Slashing Mal's heart to pieces. He felt like he was slowly dying inside, bleeding to death from a million cuts. He didn't know how he would bear this.

Hamilton set a hand on his shoulder.

Mal didn't bother shaking it off. "I'm gonna find her," he said roughly. "I'm gonna find her and take care of her."

"We're not leaving without her," Hamilton promised, and stepped back to give him room.

He couldn't answer, his whole world imploding around him.

Then Khan suddenly shot to his feet and turned toward the stern, as if he'd spotted something. "Freeman, look!"

Mal whipped around, heart pounding, hope a painful pressure under his ribs. He shoved past Hamilton to get a better look as Rodriguez spun the boat around.

And then he saw what Khan had spotted. A lone woman with inky dark hair swimming toward the wreckage of the fallen crane just above the water line. His throat closed up, a raw sound of gratitude that came from the bottom of his soul.

Rowan.

"It's her," he grated out, fighting the urge to dive back in the water to get to her. "*Go.*"

"We're going," Rodriguez answered, and opened up the throttle.

Chapter Twenty-Six

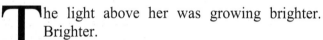

The light above her was growing brighter. Brighter.

Rowan was out of air, her lungs on fire, and the surface was so heart-breakingly close but she couldn't reach it…

Then, just when her limbs were about to give up, just when she couldn't take it another second and her body was about to take over and suck in a breath of water, her head broke the surface.

She hauled in a ragged, life-saving gasp of air, almost a sob, and kept moving her limbs weakly. Her head swam, the shock hitting her like a truck. Over and over she dragged air into her starving lungs, her body so cold, numb.

I'm alive.

It didn't seem possible. She couldn't feel her arms or legs. Could barely move at all. But she was breathing. Somehow she'd made it.

Moving weakly, she searched for the shore. The port was to her left, but it seemed an impossible distance and the current was dragging her farther and farther away from shore every moment.

Her frantic gaze snagged on something in the water not too far away. Something bright red. She swam toward it, her exhausted body threatening to shut down.

When she got close she threw out an arm. Her hand was too numb to grasp the metal frame of whatever it was. It slipped and fell into the water, as if her arm weighed a ton.

No! She hadn't survived everything else to quit now.

With a low growl of determination she threw her arm out again, managed to hook her forearm around the metal as the water tried to push her past it. The force pinned her against the metal for a moment. She struggled to hook her legs through it and hung on, shaking so hard it hurt, her body going limp.

Her eyes slid closed. Shock and horror swamped her. Tears burned her eyes. A sob tore loose, shuddered through her. In all her life she'd never felt so small and helpless, so alone.

Come on, Rowan. Fight. You've made it this far.

She choked back her tears. She couldn't think about what had just happened. But when she summoned the strength to raise her head, she wanted to cry again. The shore seemed so far away right now. She had to get off this thing and get to shore, but she was too tired and no one seemed to have noticed her, not even the helicopter circling the port. She'd never make it.

The metal frame she clung to gave an ominous shudder. Rowan stopped breathing, automatically tightened her hold. Whatever it was started to tip sideways.

She cried out in alarm as she began rising, foot by foot, higher and higher out of the water. Oh God, if she slipped and fell from this height, she'd drown. She didn't have the strength to swim anymore. And if it fell and turned over into the water, it would take her down with it.

Her heart shot into her throat, stayed there as the metal frame jerked to a sudden halt, the metal arm vibrating. She slipped, swallowed a scream and hung on, her exhausted muscles failing bit by bit. She looked down at the freezing water beneath her, knew instinctively that she couldn't survive it if she fell in.

Over the roar of the blood in her ears, the sound of a loud motor registered. Searching for the source, she spotted a sleek, small black boat approaching her. Men were in it.

She didn't dare let go with one arm to try and wave them down. Clinging to the metal, she locked her eyes on it, urging them to see her. Save her.

Then a voice called out over the noise as the boat began to slow. "Rowan!"

Her focus sharpened, a flare of hope igniting. Malcolm?

"Rowan!" He was at the bow now. She could see him waving his arms at her.

A rush of tears blinded her. "Malcolm..."

"Hold on. Just keep holding on," he shouted.

She nodded, barely able to make her head move. It was like her body was shutting down, the surge of relief sapping what little strength she had left.

The boat slowed and maneuvered into place directly beneath her. A few of Malcolm's teammates were with him but she didn't look at anyone but him. Couldn't. "I c-can't get down," she called down. "C-can't hang on much l-longer…"

He was standing at the very point of the bow, his gaze locked on her, the sight of him so incredible she wanted to cry. "It's too risky for me to climb up to you, the crane could shift at any moment and throw you off."

A crane? That's what she was on?

"I don't want to bring in the helo, because the downdraft might make you slip." His expression was concerned, yet calm. "You're gonna have to jump."

Jump? Rowan measured the distance between her and the boat. It was too far. "I c-can't."

"Yes you can. We're right underneath you. Unwrap your legs one at a time. I'm gonna get in the water. Then you're gonna jump and I'll grab you. It's the only way."

She shook her head, the motion involuntary.

"Rowan, look at me."

She did, stared down at him through a blur of tears. "I…"

His eyes stayed locked on hers. "Rowan, you can do this. I'm going to grab you as soon as you hit the water. I swear it, baby." With that he climbed onto the front of the boat and jumped in, never breaking eye contact while he treaded water beneath her. "Jump, Ro. I'll catch you, I swear."

She believed him. Trusted his word and his ability to do as he said. But she was still so afraid. *You have to.* Have *to.*

It took everything she had to unwind her uncooperative legs from the bars she'd been clinging to.

"That's right," Malcolm coaxed, looking up at her. "Now let go and jump to me."

She swallowed once, unhooked her left arm. Let her right slide slowly around the metal she could no longer feel.

Taking a deep breath and holding it, she forced herself to let go.

A scream echoed in her ears as she plummeted down and plunged beneath the surface. The icy embrace of the water engulfed her, dark and terrifying.

Before she could even try to kick to the surface, hard, powerful arms locked around her upper body and shot her upward. Her head broke the surface inches from Malcolm's. And he smiled as he pulled her into him. "I've got you, sweetness," he choked out.

She turned toward him, her leaden arms coming around his neck as she clung to him. A minute later she was being hauled out of the water.

Someone set her down inside the boat and whipped a blanket around her. Then Malcolm was beside her, water sluicing off him as he hauled her into his lap with a deep groan and crushed her to him.

Rowan shuddered, buried her face in his neck. "Don't let go," she whispered brokenly, her body shaking apart.

"I won't," he promised against her ear, his voice as fierce as his embrace. "I won't let you go."

MAL'S THROAT WAS thick with tears as he held

Rowan in his arms while Rodriguez raced them back to shore. She was freezing and in shock and might have serious injuries, but hell, she was alive. *Thank you, God*, he said silently, his body wrapped around her for warmth.

"When we reach shore you stay with her," Hamilton said to him over the roar of the engine.

Mal nodded, relieved, because there was no way in hell he was leaving her side until she was ready and he knew for certain she was okay.

Medics were waiting for them as soon as Rodriguez pulled up to the dock. Khan and Colebrook carried the other female survivors off. Mal cradled the back of Rowan's wet head, kept her face firmly tucked into his shoulder so she wouldn't see the blanket-covered body they passed. He carried her directly over to a waiting ambulance and climbed inside with her, sitting down on the gurney to settle her in his lap.

"Ro, are you hurt anywhere?" he asked, rubbing a hand up and down her spine.

Her teeth were chattering so loud he could hear it. "N-not bad," she managed, burrowing closer.

They'd see about that.

A paramedic climbed aboard and shut the doors to give them privacy. Mal got her soaked clothes off her, checked her over for bleeding and broken bones while the paramedic did his own exam.

Not finding any, he allowed himself another measure of relief and laid her back on the gurney. She had bruises on her back and sides, down her arms and legs. But nothing seemed to be broken and she didn't show signs of significant head or internal injury.

Another relief.

Wrapping her up with a couple of blankets, he leaned over her to brush back the strands of wet hair that clung to her pale, blue-tinged face. "We're gonna get you warmed up," he promised, running his hands gently over the blanket, trying to get her circulation going.

Her gorgeous, deep blue eyes gazed up at him, clear and alert despite borderline hypothermia and the horrors she'd just survived. God, he loved her. Couldn't imagine his life without her. "You caught m-me," she whispered.

His heart turned over. As long as he lived he'd never forget the moment he'd thought he'd lost her forever, and the moment when she'd trusted him enough to take that literal leap of faith when he'd asked her to. "I'll always catch you, sweetness."

Her lips quivered. She drew in a shaky breath and reached for him. Mal groaned and reached his arms all the way around her, gathering her close. He couldn't shield her from the trauma she'd just been through. But he could be there for her through whatever came next.

As soon as he got her settled, he wanted to know how the fuck this had happened in the first place. Starting with how that bastard Montoya had found her this morning.

****

Oceane's head spun as she struggled to take everything in. When Rowan's detail had been attacked this morning, her own detail had whisked her straight back to the WITSEC facility. Now she sat with Victoria Gomez in a private room while various agents came and went. Some peppering her with questions.

How did Montoya find you again? Have you been communicating with him somehow? How do you know him? When did you last see him?

She didn't know anything, was as confused and stunned as everyone else was, though no one seemed to believe her.

"They think I'm lying," she murmured in Spanish to Victoria, who held her hand.

"They don't like not being able to figure out what happened," she said, squeezing Oceane's hand in support. Things had shifted between them yesterday at the hospital. It helped to know someone cared about her. To have someone else who understood what it was like to have your life shattered in an instant.

"I don't know how else to tell them that I can't help them."

"Then don't. You've made your position clear, and you've been watched constantly for the past few days, so they have to know there's no way you were involved with any of this. You're not the problem. Maybe the leak is somewhere inside WITSEC," she finished in a hard tone.

Oceane sighed and leaned her head back against the wall. "I've been thinking the same thing." Her eyes hurt. In the privacy of her room here at the orientation center, she'd cried herself to sleep, soaking her pillow as she thought of her mother lying so cold in the hospital morgue. Her whole body ached and she felt…empty inside. Almost as though she didn't care what happened to her anymore.

They could interrogate her all they wanted. Throw her in a dark cell and toss away the key. She didn't care. Everything and everyone she'd ever loved had been taken from her. There was nothing left now but the hunger for justice.

A soft knock came at the door. Commander Taggart stepped inside with a couple of FBI agents and Special Agent Hamilton, a device about the size of a cell phone in his hand. "Found a couple of these on Montoya's men at the port," he said, crossing toward Oceane.

Hamilton moved to one side of the door and crossed his arms, giving Oceane a wink that helped ease her anxiety. She must not be in trouble.

"What is it?" she asked Taggart.

"Homing device. Military grade, although pretty outdated now. Extremely expensive."

Oceane didn't see what that had to do with her.

"Montoya's men," Victoria said, interrupting her thoughts. "Did you capture them alive?"

"One. The other two thought they could make a getaway in a semi loaded down with a full cargo container on it. They crashed into one of the huge forklifts instead, and both vehicles slammed into the base of one of the shipping cranes. Snapped it in two, sent it crashing into the water. The counterweight came off and crushed the cab of the semi."

Victoria's hand tightened on hers. "Good. Just too bad it was a quick death for them."

Taggart's eyes gleamed in agreement, then sobered. "Montoya's gone."

Oceane sucked in a breath. She didn't understand

what her godfather's goal had been, but she was pretty sure it was to find her and bring her back to her father. Oceane never wanted to see either of them ever again.

"Gone?" Victoria asked.

Taggart nodded. "Video footage at the port shows someone resembling him walking away dressed in a cop uniform. He was right near the base of the crane when the crane crashed. If it was him, he couldn't have lucked out more in terms of a diversion, because he slipped through the perimeter without any trouble in the confusion."

"You have to find him," Oceane said harshly.

The DEA commander nodded. "We will."

She wasn't sure if she believed him. If Montoya and her father had hidden everything from her all her life, if they had both evaded authorities this long, then who was to say they couldn't evade them for-ever?

"And now, if you'll humor me..." He stepped closer to her, hit a button on the device he held. A high-pitched beeping sounded immediately, stayed steady as he moved it through the air, following the line of her body from head to toe. The FBI agents stepped forward to check the screen along with Tag-gart, then all three of them looked at her.

Oceane frowned. "What?" Whatever that thing was, whatever it was picking up, the signal couldn't be coming from her. They'd checked her again for electronic bugs right after the phone incident the other day and hadn't found anything.

Taggart glanced at the device, hit another button and did another sweep, this time beginning at her feet. The high-pitched beeping was still there but muted, in the background almost. Nothing else happened as he raised it higher, up her legs, her torso. But when he reached her head, a rapid clicking sound started.

Oceane blinked, surprised, and the men all looked at each other. She reached up to touch her earlobes. "I'm not even wearing any earrings," she protested, thoroughly annoyed. They'd let her keep her mother's favorite diamond earrings and necklace, but they were currently being analyzed in some lab somewhere and she wasn't sure when or if she'd get them back.

One of the FBI agents moved even closer, peering at Oceane's face intently. "You have any dental work done recently?"

What? She scowled at him. "I don't have braces or a retainer, if that's what you mean."

"What about fillings?"

"Well, yeah, I've got a few fillings."

"When was the most recent one?"

She had to think about that. "A couple years ago." She put a hand to the left side of her jaw, concerned.

Taggart moved the device from her left to right, and back again. The clicking sound was way faster on the left.

Her eyes widened in disbelief. "You think there's a tracking device in my *filling*?" she cried, unable to believe it.

"It would explain how Montoya found the safehouse yesterday."

No. She'd been seeing that dentist forever, since she was a child. Her mother was a longtime patient of his too, and her father as well whenever he—

She sucked in a breath, the blood draining from her face.

Taggart lowered his hand, switched off the device. "What?"

"My father," she whispered, shock detonating inside her. Could this be real? "He saw my dentist that one time when he came to stay with us a couple years ago. My appointment was two hours after his…" She trailed off, too horrified to say the rest aloud. What if her father had paid the man to implant a tracking device in her filling without her ever realizing?

The taller FBI agent looked at the shorter one and snapped, "Get a dental x-ray set up for her *now*."

If it was the last thing she did, Oceane would make sure Montoya and her father both rotted in hell.

Chapter Twenty-Seven

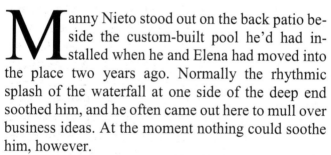

Manny Nieto stood out on the back patio beside the custom-built pool he'd had installed when he and Elena had moved into the place two years ago. Normally the rhythmic splash of the waterfall at one side of the deep end soothed him, and he often came out here to mull over business ideas. At the moment nothing could soothe him, however.

He dialed Montoya's encrypted phone again for the fifth time. Once again, the fucking little weasel didn't answer. That had better mean he was dead, because if Montoya was just too chicken shit to face Manny after everything that had happened, then he would be dead soon enough anyway.

Manny had no time for cowardly shit like that, and now Anya had not only been brutally murdered and raped—something he was still enraged about—Oceane was in the wind once more and Montoya had botched yet another opportunity to find her by targeting the female Assistant U.S. Attorney instead. He knew the whole story. How Montoya had wanted to take a page out of Ruiz's playbook and make money on the side in the flesh trade.

Manny had to immediately distance himself and deal with Montoya personally, before *El Escorpion* came after *him*.

He spun around to find his head of security standing a few yards away beneath the shade of some palm trees. "You sure he's not dead?"

David snorted and gave a nod. "I'm sure."

Manny set his jaw. "*Madre de Dios*," he muttered, scrubbing a hand over his face. "Find him and bring him to me. He has to answer for all of this."

Manny had to reassert his power now. There were too many signs of weakness going on, and in this business that could prove deadly. Montoya had to face the consequences for his actions—and repeated failures. Retrieving Oceane now was next to impossible. The Americans would bolster security even more. Dammit, he needed to see his daughter. Explain everything. Maybe she could find it in her heart to forgive him one day. But he doubted it now.

Brimming with impotent rage, he stalked back into the house. He had work waiting for him in his office. Tax issues and forms from his accountants to be signed. New bank accounts to be authorized, assets to be sold. To stay ahead of the authorities both here in Mexico and in the States, Manny had to be fluid, ready to change directions at a moment's notice. Threatening or paying off people down here would only go so far.

Pausing at the wet bar outside the butler's pantry, he caught sight of his reflection in the antique mirror above it and froze in the act of reaching for the crystal decanter of scotch he kept there. He looked like shit, all haggard with dark shadows beneath his eyes. He hadn't slept much this past week and it was catching up with him. He couldn't remember when he'd last eaten a full meal.

This thing with Oceane was corroding him from the inside out. Until he had her back safe and sound, until he could explain everything and make her understand it all, he couldn't rest.

At first he'd assumed Ruiz was behind the attack that had caused them to flee, but none of his contacts had been able to turn up any evidence to support the theory. But who else? Who the hell else would have the balls to do something like this?

The door leading to the attached garage opened on the other side of the hall. Elena breezed in, more shopping bags in her hands. She stopped when she saw him, gave him a disapproving frown. "A little early for your nightcap, isn't it?"

"Yes," he answered, a testy edge to his voice. This was his damn house. He was under a lot of stress, not that she seemed to notice or care, and would drink anytime he damn well pleased.

She shrugged and headed into the kitchen. "I'm starving. Is dinner ready yet?"

Manny lowered the decanter, something about her lighthearted tone grating on him. He walked to the kitchen entrance, stood watching her as she took her new clothes from the bags, humming as she laid everything out on the marble-topped island in the center of the room and began cutting off the tags. Not a care in the world, secure in her life of luxury. Not a single consideration for his distress, and there was no way she hadn't noticed it.

His drinking alone at three in the afternoon wasn't the only sign that something was wrong. She'd been his wife for more than twenty-five years. She knew damn well he hadn't been sleeping, had barely been eating lately. Yet she didn't seem to care, beyond admonishing him that he ate less than she did.

It wasn't like her. The total lack of wifely concern was strange. As was her sudden improved mood over the past week or so.

He rounded the island, placed his hands on it as she worked. He hadn't told her what was bothering him, because he couldn't. But normally she wanted to know everything, be involved in his life in whatever way he would allow it. Something was...off.

Elena stopped to look up at him. "Something wrong?"

"Yes."

Surprise flashed in her eyes and she set the scissors down to give him her full attention. "What is it?"

He chose his words carefully, a niggling suspicion taking root that he could no longer ignore. "There have been complications with several operations this week."

"Concerning what?"

"Juan Montoya."

Her face stiffened ever so slightly, the change subtle enough that he would have missed it completely had he not been watching so carefully. "Is that so?" She reached for the scissors again. "What has he done this time? Or not done, I should say."

"He was supposed to take care of two very important things for me."

"What things?"

"Taking care of a certain problem. And then finding something important for me."

She looked down at the clothing. Avoiding his gaze. "And he failed, I take it?"

The tiny thread of suspicion in his gut expanded, even as his brain refused to connect the dots his subconscious laid out for him. It was impossible. She didn't even know about Oceane. He was so run down and sleep deprived, he was becoming paranoid. "Yes." Holy hell, his heart was thudding, an awful tension forming in his chest.

"Well, I'm sure it will all work out." She looked up at him through her lashes, flashed him a smile that seemed a little forced. "It always does." She set the scissors back down and gathered her clothes before turning and walking away.

Manny stared at her retreating back with hot, unblinking eyes. "Elena."

She stopped, cast him a weary look over her shoulder. Or was it wary? "What?"

His hands curled around the edge of the countertop. "Tell you don't know what I'm talking about."

She gave a frustrated sigh. "Manny, it's been a long day and I'm in no mood for cryptic riddles. I'm going upstairs."

Oh no you're not. He stepped around the island, stopped to face her without a barrier between them. "Do you know what's happened?" he demanded, testing his suspicion, unable to control the anger bubbling beneath the surface.

For a long moment she didn't answer him. Then something shifted. Almost as if she'd been waiting for him to ask it. She lifted her chin and raised a dark, perfectly-groomed eyebrow. "And if I did?"

It felt like someone had kicked him in the diaphragm.

For a second he couldn't answer, the shock and pain sucking all the air from his lungs. "Did you do it?" he whispered in horror, unable to accept the truth that was staring him right in the face. "Did you?"

The haughty edge to her expression melted away. Her face twisted into a mask of pain and hatred, the look in her eyes sending a cold chill racing down his spine. "Yes," she hissed, eyes shooting sparks at him.

His eyes bulged. "You ordered the attack?" How? How was that even possible?

"You're damn right I did," she shouted, indignant as she threw her new clothes onto the tile floor and spun to face him, thrusting an accusing finger at him. "You think you could humiliate me like that and get away with it? Keep your whore and your precious bastard tucked away for twenty-four years in a luxury estate paid for with *our* money? You didn't think I'd find out someday? Well I did, you lying piece of shit. And so I did what any woman in my position would do. I took care of it."

Manny didn't think. He reacted. Before he knew what he was doing, he had his wife by the throat, pinning her to the kitchen wall, his entire body vibrating with fury. "You bitch," he snarled, his breathing choppy. He was out of control, unable to rein the rage in.

Elena choked and stared up at him, her dark eyes wide with fear…and loathing. "You betrayed me," she shrieked in his face, clawing at his hands. "You betrayed everything we have together, everything! Why? All because she could give you a child and I couldn't?" Her eyes filled with tears as he squeezed harder.

"*Manuel*."

David's sharp rebuke from behind him jerked him out of his rage-fueled haze.

He shook himself, yanked his hands off Elena's throat as if she'd burned him and took a stumbling step backward. His wife drew in a gasping breath and clutched her neck, the red marks from his fingers livid against her skin. They stood mere yards apart and stared at one another in the awful, suffocating silence of the room.

Something cold and hard and bitter formed inside him. Encasing his heart in an icy, impenetrable shell. "Get out of my sight," he rasped out, afraid he might actually kill her if he touched her again.

Throwing him a look of mingled devastation and contempt, Elena spun around and fled from the room, her running footsteps growing muffled as she raced up the carpeted stairs. A moment later a door slammed shut overhead. She was smart enough to know to bolt it shut against him.

Slowly, Manny turned to face his head of security. David was watching him with a deep frown creasing his forehead. "What the hell, boss?"

He sucked in an unsteady breath, fought to get control of himself. "She ordered the attack on

Oceane and Anya," he said, shaken, queasy.

"Are you sure?" He sounded as shocked as Manny felt.

"Yes," he snapped, reaching behind him to grasp the countertop for support. What the hell was he supposed to do now?

"What do you want me to do?"

"Find my daughter," he rasped out, unsure whether he was going to puke or break down like a child. Jesus, his own wife had done this to him.

"What about Elena? Should I take her to a hotel, or…?"

"No. I'll leave." He couldn't stay another minute in this house, under the same roof with her, afraid of what he might do.

He strode to the foyer, stared hard at the keys to his new Jag where they lay on the entry table. His mouth twisted as the truth hit home. Guilt. That's why she'd bought it for him. He should have known. God, how had he missed the signs?

He reached for the keys to his Porsche instead, spoke over his shoulder without looking back. No more looking back now. Only forward. "Find my daughter, David, and bring her back to me. That's all I want you to do."

He stalked out the door, his life and heart in ashes. Oceane was the only good part of him left. She was his blood, his sole heir. The only way he could live on after he left this world was to pass the empire he'd built to her one day, free of the cartel.

He *had* to get his daughter back, whatever it took.

Chapter Twenty-Eight

Now that she'd had a few minutes' peace and relative quiet after the whirlwind of everything that had happened in the aftermath of being pulled from the water, exhaustion hit Rowan hard. Lying on the hospital Emergency room bed, she shut her eyes and tried to make her mind go blank.

The flurry of agency and other law enforcement personnel had finished interviewing and questioning her. The nurse had just left, the doctors were done with their tests and exams. Now she was just waiting for clearance so they would release her.

The pale blue curtain acting as a privacy screen around her bed parted. She looked up as her parents stepped through it. Her mother appeared on the verge of tears and her father's face was pale, his deep blue eyes haunted.

"Oh, sweetheart," her mother said, and grabbed Rowan in a fierce hug.

"Ow," she whispered, pushing her mom away a little when she squeezed the bruises on Rowan's ribs.

"Sorry." Her mom eased the pressure but didn't let go, her cheek pressed to Rowan's hair. "Oh my God, we were so scared."

"They wouldn't tell us anything," her father added, coming around the other side of the bed to take Rowan's hand, as though he needed the contact with her. "You were already at the hospital by the time we got any more news."

"I'm okay," Rowan said, patting her mom's back and squeezing her father's hand. "Just a little banged up." *And traumatized. Let's not forget that part.* "All my tests came back fine, so they're sending me home."

Her mom leaned back to search her face, a worried frown puckering her brow. "Are you sure? You're so pale, and…"

"Physically I'm fine. I just want out of here." She looked between her parents. "How's Kevin?"

"He's worried sick," her mother answered.

"Does he know I'm okay?" Of course he didn't. Rowan sighed. "Mom, you'd better go up there right now and tell him I'm fine before he makes Nick put him in a wheelchair and bring him down here." When her mother hesitated, Rowan raised her eyebrows. "You know he'll do it."

"Yes. You're right." Her mom kissed the top of her head and got up. "I'll be back—without your brother."

"Tell him I'm fine and that I love him. I want to see him, but not right now. I'll call him once I get some sleep."

As her mother left, the curtain swishing shut behind her, Rowan's dad sank down on the edge of the bed, his fingers still locked around hers. "How are you, really?" he asked, the concern in his eyes filling her with warmth.

"I'm lucky to be alive."

He nodded once and glanced away, clamped his lips together as though he was fighting for control over his emotions. Except Aiden Stewart never displayed that sort of emotion.

And yet when he looked back at her a moment later, his eyes were wet with tears. "I couldn't stand that I couldn't do anything," he choked out, and Rowan's heart cracked open.

"Ah, Dad…" Leaning forward, she pulled him into a tight hug, not caring if it hurt her bruises. Although it was a little weird that she was the one comforting him after all she'd been through.

"I love you," he whispered fiercely into her hair. "So much."

She smiled, that piece inside her that would always be the little girl desperate for his approval blooming like a wilted flower denied water and sunlight for so long. "I love you too."

He held her close for a long moment, then squeezed her and took an unsteady breath, clearing his throat. "You must be tired."

"So tired," she agreed. "Have you seen Malcolm?" He'd been with her on the ride here in the ambulance, had stayed with her through some of the questioning before he'd been pulled away by his commander over an hour ago.

"He was out in the hall talking with some agency

people when we came down," he said.

"Could you go see if you can drag him away for me? As soon as I get the okay, I want out of here."

Her dad smiled at her, brushed his knuckles over her cheek. "Sure."

A few minutes later he reappeared through the curtains. "Look who I brought."

Malcolm stepped through, giving her a little smile as he ran an assessing gaze over her. "Just got the official word. You're free to go."

Thank God. She cast him a desperate look. "Get me out of here." All she wanted was to be alone with him.

He grinned. "Yes, ma'am."

Her father went and got a wheelchair. Over her protests, she consented to sitting in the thing and allowing her dad to push her out to the side entrance where Malcolm pulled his truck around.

Two armed agents stood guard as they transferred her into the front seat—they weren't taking any chances with Montoya still at large. God, she couldn't believe that he'd found Oceane with a tracker that Nieto had ordered implanted into her freaking filling. Rowan was never complaining about her father ever again.

With a wave at him and a promise to call her parents later on, she breathed a sigh of relief and leaned her head back against the headrest as Malcolm drove off. She couldn't remember ever being this tired.

"Do you want to go home?" he asked her as he turned out of the parking lot. "FBI's got a security team ready for you if you do."

"No." God, look how that had turned out last time.

The only person she felt truly safe with right now was Malcolm. "Your place, if you don't mind." Until Montoya was in custody, she wasn't going home. She needed time to start sorting through everything that had happened, and after a day or two of rest, she had a case to prepare for.

"My place it is." He sounded relieved. Reaching over, he took her hand and laced their fingers together. "You warm enough?" Stopping at a light, he reached over to adjust the dash vents so warm air blew directly on her.

"Getting there," Rowan answered, just glad to be alone with him finally. All she wanted now was to curl up in Malcolm's arms and sleep for about a week.

She must have dozed on the last part of the drive to his place because next thing she knew he was waking her gently. "We're here," he murmured.

She groaned and straightened in her seat, every ache and pain letting themselves be known. "I feel like I've been in another car accident," she muttered.

"No surprise," he said, and jumped out to come around and lift her from the truck.

"I can walk," she told him, even as she looped her arms around his neck.

"Don't care if you can run. I'm carrying you." Using his hip to slam the door shut, he strode for the elevators.

"Hey, good timing."

At the male voice Malcolm turned her around to find a truck pulling up next to them. Kai Maka slid out. "Hamilton said you guys just left the hospital.

Glad I caught you." The huge, good-looking Hawaiian leaned into the back of the cab and emerged with a big box in his arms. "Brought you guys some food."

Aww. Rowan offered him a smile. "That's so sweet of you."

He shrugged. "Wasn't just me. Colebrook brought over some stuff too. Piper's got some baking in here." He reached into the box to shift things around. "Looks like a fruit pie and some of her famous brownies." He frowned down at them. "She's never made *me* a pan of brownies."

"Piper?" Rowan asked.

"Colebrook's better half," Malcolm answered. "And Colebrook's sister is Rodriguez's better half." At her confused look, he laughed. "You'll meet everyone and get their names and connections sorted out soon enough." Then to Kai he said, "Thanks, man."

"No worries. I'll bring it up for you. Being that you've got your hands full right now." He winked at Rowan.

Rowan laid her head on Malcolm's shoulder and closed her eyes, enjoying the sense of security it brought her to have him take care of her this way. She'd been so much luckier than Anya or Victoria, and the other women in the container had been saved from fates worse than death.

Three *Veneno* thugs were dead. Even if Juan Montoya was still alive and at large, some positive things had happened today. And he couldn't evade justice forever. She and the others involved with this case would see to that. Right after she helped hand Ruiz a life sentence without the chance of parole.

They reached Malcolm's condo and he continued

to hold her as he fished the key from his pocket. "You really can put me down for a minute."

"Nope." He shifted her, stubbornly held her to him as he unlocked the door and walked inside.

Kai followed them in. "So, you guys hungry? I've got one of Abby's lasagnas in here. I can pop it in the oven for you."

Malcolm looked at her, raised his eyebrows. She shook her head slightly, hoping he understood. "Thanks, man, but I think we'll wait on dinner for now."

"Yeah, no worries, *brah*," Kai said. "I'll put everything in the fridge."

Malcolm carried her into the living room and set her on the couch, wrapped in the blanket. By then Kai was finished putting the last of the food away and Malcolm walked him to the door. "You guys just call if you need anything, yeah?" Kai said, his gaze shifting between Malcolm and her.

"We will. Thanks, brother." Malcolm held out a hand.

"Anytime." Kai looked down at the hand, gave Mal a *you're kidding me* look then gathered him up in a manly back-clapping hug instead, and left.

After locking the door, Malcolm turned back to her with a smile and sighed. "Alone at last."

"Yes."

He crossed back to her, put his hands on his hips. "What do you want right now?"

"A shower." Oh, God, she'd kill for one. "Then bed."

"Perfect." Without pause he scooped her up and headed straight for the master bedroom, carrying her into the en suite.

Setting her on the granite counter with the blanket still wrapped around her, he turned on the shower before coming back for her. He ran a hand over the top of her head, smoothed it down her hair, his warm, chocolate-brown eyes searching hers. "You know how much I love you, right?"

Startled, a smile broke over her face. "I was hoping you did."

One side of his mouth tipped up, that ridiculously charming dimple appearing in his cheek. "Well I do."

She put her hand on the side of his face. "I love you too."

He inhaled what seemed like a relieved breath, curled his fingers around the back of her neck. "Good," he muttered, and leaned in to kiss her.

Rowan sank into him, her breasts flattened against his chest, her free arm banding around his back. The kiss was deep but slow, almost reverent. As though he wanted to worship her, reassure himself she was here in front of him.

She barely noticed when he pulled the blanket from her shoulders and began taking her clothes off, too intent on maintaining the connection of their kiss. With a few twists of her spine and an arch of her hips, she was naked and reaching for the waistband of his tactical pants.

Malcolm reached behind him to fist the back of his shirt and peeled it over his head, revealing his sculpted chest and shoulders in all their naked glory. While she explored them with her mouth and hands, he shucked his pants and underwear and lifted her, bringing her legs around his waist as he stepped into the shower.

Rowan sighed at the feel of the hot water rushing over her skin, the sensation of being pressed to his hard, warm body, those strong arms cradling her so protectively it made her throat tighten. "I'm never letting anything bad happen to you ever again," he vowed against her temple, hugging her tight. "You're mine now, Rowan, and I protect and take care of what's mine."

His words melted her insides. She sought his mouth once more, got lost in the feel and taste of him, letting time drift while they stroked and caressed each other, gliding soap over sensitive skin, shivered when those strong fingers massaged shampoo into her hair and rubbed over her scalp.

By the time he'd cleaned her and set her down on the built-in bench along the back wall she felt drugged with arousal, a languid, syrupy warmth rather than the blazing fire of before, yet every bit as intense.

She flexed into his hold, rubbing her achy breasts along his slick chest, telling him without words that she needed more than tenderness right now. Malcolm's eyes darkened and he cupped both mounds in his large hands, bending to tease the hard centers with his lips and tongue.

Pleasure streaked through her, arching her spine, her hands holding his head close. Demanding more. Offering everything she was to him: heart, body and soul, nothing held back. She made a soft sound in the back of her throat, this level of vulnerability with another human being completely new, thrilling and frightening at the same time.

"I got you, sweetness," he murmured against her hot flesh, one hand sliding down to curl around her hip in a possessive grip. He tugged her forward a little, his palm pressing at the small of her back as he sank to his knees before her and used his other hand to ease her knees apart. "Remember what I said I would do to you next time?" he asked against her stomach.

The next time I get you naked, I'm gonna take my time and kiss you everywhere. Especially here, he'd said, rocking his erection between her thighs. *Until you melt all over my tongue.*

Her muscles tensed once, a quiver rippling through her, turning the melting heat between her thighs into a liquid pool of need. "I remember," she whispered back, running her hand over the back of his head, watching his every move as he made good on his vow.

His lips worshipped her naked skin, pressing hot, open-mouthed kisses to her face, neck, breasts. Her shoulders. Breasts again, then her ribs, belly, and the tops of her thighs. He kissed every mark and bruise, kissed every bit of her he could reach, ending with the soles of her feet before slowly working his way back up the inside of one leg.

Rowan bit her lip and waited, dying a little, the pulse of arousal between her thighs overtaking everything else.

Settling his hands on her inner thighs to keep them apart, he lowered his face and nuzzled the soft, flushed folds there. She tightened her hold on his head and moaned a little, arching her hips to press against his hot mouth.

His lips were so incredibly soft, the stroke of his tongue over her clit making her shudder. She widened her thighs and gasped out his name, her head falling back, each soft swirl of his tongue sending her closer to the edge.

He didn't rush her, took his time licking and caressing, building the pleasure before sinking into her core. Tasting the arousal he'd created before coming back to give her swollen clit more of that same loving attention.

"Malcolm," she groaned, shuddering. It didn't take long before she was panting, eyes closed, lost to the rising tide of sensation, craving the release that glowed just on the edge of the horizon.

Then he stopped.

Her eyes popped open in shock. "No, I'm—"

"Gonna make you come while I'm inside you," he said in a dark, possessive voice that shot another thrill through her, and hauled her upright, setting her on her feet before turning her to face the wall.

She planted her palms flat against the wet tile and looked over her shoulder at him, waiting. Water sluiced over his beautiful brown skin, his erection standing thick and proud from his body as he rolled a condom down his length.

Settling behind her, he pulled her hips back, arching her spine so he could ease his cock into position, a hot, heavy brand against her super-sensitive flesh. She moaned and dropped her forehead against the wall when he slid it along her folds, the slick caress against her clit sizzling along her nerve endings, and yet not nearly enough.

"I love the way you wrap around me when I slide

inside," he whispered against her neck as he did just that, pushing the thick, hard head of his cock into her.

Rowan hummed in her throat and pushed back to meet him, but he stilled her with a solid grip on her hip. Once she obeyed he slid that same hand up to cradle her breast, his thumb and forefinger playing with the nipple, and reached his other hand up and to the right.

A moment later a stream of warm sluiced over her thighs. It moved up her folds to stimulate her swollen nub.

Her whimper turned into a throaty moan as he hit just the right spot.

"Right there?" he whispered, nipping gently at her skin.

She could only nod and brace herself against the wall, unable to form a single coherent thought, much less a word.

"Oh, sweetness, you have no idea how goddamn good you feel," he ground out, and flexed his hips, burying his cock inside her.

Rowan mewled and fought to hold still, needing the stream of water exactly where it was but dying for more of the internal friction he gave her. "Oh God, just fuck me," she gasped out, unable to help herself.

Malcolm let out a low, erotic growl and eased back to thrust forward once more. Slow, steady strokes that hit her inner sweet spot while the warm water caressed her clit and he teased her sensitive nipple. Her body tightened, gathered in on itself, preparing for the coming explosion. She gave herself to it, crying out her pleasure, writhing in his arms.

He released her breast and put the shower head back in place, both muscled arms coming around her to cradle her to him, careful of her tender ribs, and thrust deeper. Rougher, his teeth scraping along the tender skin where her neck and shoulder joined.

Rowan reached one hand back to grasp the back of his head and braced herself with her free arm, reveling in his need for her. His arms held her fiercely, a strangled roar coming from him when he buried himself deep and started coming.

Slowly they both relaxed, Rowan leaning both forearms against the wall as their panting breaths mingled with the rush of the water.

With a soft kiss on her shoulder Malcolm withdrew gently and rinsed them both off. He even dried her off, spending extra time on her hair, dropping tender kisses all over her face. But the best part was when he gathered her close once more and carried her to his bed, where he drew her into his arms and pulled the covers over them both.

Boneless, utterly relaxed, she draped herself over him, her body all but melting into his. She yawned, head on his solid shoulder, his heart beating inches below her cheek. Today had been a nightmare in so many ways. She was so damn lucky it had ended this way.

"I knew you'd come for me," she whispered in the darkness, breathing in the scent of soap and the man she loved more than anything.

Even in the bleakest hour when all seemed lost, she'd known that whether she was alive or dead, Malcolm would find her. That he would take care of her, no matter what. It had given her courage, and also a measure of peace that had startled her.

His arms tightened around her and he kissed the top of her head. "Always, sweetness. I'll always be there for you."

She smiled against his skin, the vow reverberating deep inside her, like the pitch of an internal tuning fork. "I love you."

He made a gruff sound that might have been a groan of gratitude. "God, I love you too."

He was finally hers again. But the best part was, this time she was his in return.

All of her, body and soul.

EPILOGUE

———◇◇◇◇◇———

"Shall we say grace?"

At Pops's question that wasn't a question at all, but rather a command, Mal reached his left hand out to Gram, and his right to Rowan. Meeting her gaze, he gave her a little smile as they all joined hands around the old wooden table that had been in the house since before he'd come to live there, and bowed their heads.

"Heavenly father, thank you for the food before us, the family beside us, and the love between us," Pops said. "Amen."

"Amen," everyone chorused.

"Oh, I love that," Rowan murmured, smiling over first at Pops, then Mal.

She squeezed his hand before letting go and he slid his onto her knee, pushing the hem of her skirt a few inches up her bare thigh so he could sweep his thumb over her silky skin. She darted a warning look at him and grabbed his hand, but he kept it right where it was. Any excuse he got to touch her, he was taking it.

"One of my favorites," Pops said. "Short and sweet. So, Rowan," he said as he helped himself to the bowl of mashed potatoes. "I understand you've been through a tough time lately. How are you doing now?"

Mal mentally winced at Pops's blunt question and squeezed her thigh gently in silent apology. Pops had a big heart, except he wasn't always necessarily tactful in his delivery.

But he should have known Rowan would handle it with grace and poise. "That's one way to put it, yes," she answered evenly, not seeming at all offended. "I'm doing pretty well, I think. It's been an eventful and trying few weeks, but I was fortunate to have Malcolm there to stand by me through everything. I don't know what I would have done without him." She gave him a private smile, her heart shining in her eyes, and it filled his whole chest with warmth.

The eight days since the incident had been a whirlwind of interviews, appointments and meetings with various agency personnel and other investigators. Montoya and Nieto were both still in the wind, despite an ongoing manhunt.

Though Rowan had faced most of this past week alone while Mal was with his team, she'd done so bravely, facing it all head on. And at night, it was his privilege to hold her close in the darkness, be there for her through the bad dreams and the insomnia.

The Ruiz trial was scheduled to begin in another month, and Mal had managed to get the weekend off to bring her up here. He'd wanted to get her away from everything, but also to meet the people he loved the most, besides her and his teammates.

"Well we're just glad everything worked out and that Malcolm has brought you here to visit us," Gram said, shooting her husband a warning look and jabbing him in the ribs with a sharp elbow.

"What?" Pops said, all surprised innocence. "What are you jabbing me for, woman?"

"It's her first visit, John, and that's hardly dinner table conversation, let alone the kind of question to be asking her right now after all she's been through." Smoothing out her expression, Gram turned a warm smile on Rowan. "Sorry about that, dear. You just ignore him and talk with Malcolm and me."

Rowan hid a grin behind her napkin, covered a chuckle with a cough before lowering it back to her lap, clearly having figured out who really wore the pants around here. Pops liked to think he was head of the household, but only because Gram allowed him to believe it. "It's fine, really."

"Well why can't I ask her?" Pops argued, glaring at Gram now. He gestured at Malcolm. "He brings her home, that means it's serious, so I want to get to know her. How am I supposed to get to know her without asking real questions?"

Gram jabbed him again with her elbow, making Pops's eyebrows shoot up. "Pass the gravy, Malcolm dear. Rowan, try this meatloaf. It's Malcolm's favorite."

"It's the glaze. She makes it every time I come home," Mal said, and passed it over to Rowan.

"Maybe we can have that conversation later on to-night, Pops," he said to his grandpa, smothering his own grin. His grandparents were a trip. Almost fifty years together and they never lost their devotion to one another.

Pops scowled and stabbed a bite of meatloaf, shoving it into his mouth. "Didn't mean anything by it."

"Pops, Malcolm tells me you've preached for over forty years here in Detroit," Rowan said, tactfully changing the subject as she took two slices of meat-loaf.

Pops lost the scowl, his expression brightening. "That's right. Same two churches the whole time." He shook his fork at Malcolm, his expression full of pride. "Raised this boy right. Church every week, and Sunday school on top of that when he was little. Our Malcolm's a good Christian man."

"Yes, he is," Rowan agreed, her eyes laughing at Mal, who was back to stroking her inner thigh now.

After that, the conversation flowed easily around the table. They answered questions about how they met, Rowan talked about her family and her job.

"I think it's wonderful that God's brought you two back together again after all this time," Gram said, her expression delighted.

Pops nodded in agreement. "He works in mysteri-ous ways."

"That he does," Rowan said. "But I'm grateful for it."

With that, his grandpa was utterly and completely charmed. As the conversation progressed his expres-sion turned from curious and speculative to one of admiration and enthrallment. Then Rowan helped clear the table and insisted on serving dessert—homemade banana cream pie, Mal's favorite—winning Gram's heart forever.

After coffee he and Pops started on the dishes while Gram took Rowan into the living room to show her some photo albums of Mal when he was little. Pops shot him a look out of the corner of his eye as Mal washed a serving platter and handed it over. "Been a long time since you brought a lady friend to meet us," he said slyly.

Mal nodded, enjoying the game. "Long time."

"This one's as smart as she is beautiful."

"She is."

"Smart enough to make you buy the cow instead of giving the milk away for free."

Mal couldn't help but laugh as he turned to face the man who'd raised him. "The cow analogy, Pops? Really?" He already planned to ask Rowan to marry him. But it was fun watching Pops get all worked up, so he didn't tell him.

Pops's gray eyebrows snapped together. "I'm just saying, you don't wanna lose her, then do something about it. None of this modern living together crap before you decide to make an honest woman out of her. We raised you better than that."

"For heaven's sake, John, hush your mouth and leave the boy alone," Gram muttered, coming up behind them to get the magic bars she'd baked earlier. "Here, have this," she said, popping a little square of one into Mal's mouth, and patting his cheek. "It's so good to have you here, sweetheart. We've missed you."

Pops frowned at her. "Where's my bite?"

"In the pan, when you finish interrogating him and come into the living room where you're going to act like a civilized human being and watch what you say," she shot over her shoulder.

"Forty-eight years," Pops muttered, shaking his head at her. "Forty-eight years of devotion and fidelity to her, and that's what I get."

"Who're you trying to kid, you love her sass," Mal said.

Pops didn't answer as he went back to drying dishes, but a grin was tugging at his mouth.

They all visited for another couple of hours, Pops on his very best behavior. But Mal was anxious to get Rowan back to the hotel.

Wrapping his arm around her, he made their excuses and pulled her to her feet. She hugged his grandparents at the door, and Mal could tell by the gleam in his Gram's eyes that she knew Rowan was The One. She stopped him on the doorstep. He gestured for Rowan to go on to the car and faced his grandmother.

"I'm so happy for you, Malcolm," she said, her eyes shining with tears. "She's wonderful."

"Wonderful," Pops echoed, settling his arm around Gram's shoulders.

"I'm glad you both think so," Mal said, his heart overflowing with love for them all. "And I'll tell you what, though I hated every minute of it, she was worth the wait." He hugged them both, kissed Gram's papery cheek. "I'll call you in the morning. Rowan and I would like to take you both to dinner before we fly out."

"We'd love that," Gram said, leaning her head on Pops's shoulder, her smile dreamy.

Malcolm was halfway to the rental car when Pops called out to him. "Malcolm. Just remember, milk isn't free!"

"*John*," Gram admonished, and Mal didn't have to look back to know that she was delivering another jab to the old man's ribs. Grinning to himself, he raised a hand in farewell and kept walking to the driver side door.

"They're amazing people," Rowan said to him as he drove away, her fingers laced tightly through his.

"They are. I'm lucky to have them."

"Thanks for bringing me here." She leaned close to trail her fingertips down the side of his cheek, down his neck.

He met her gaze, his blood heating at the sensual promise and love in her eyes. "Thanks for coming with me."

It took way too long to get back to the hotel. Once there, he hurried her into the elevator and caged her in against the wall, his hands in her thick, glossy hair as he kissed her with all the hunger and need he'd been suppressing all day. By the time they reached their room, they were starving for one another.

Their clothes lay scattered hastily on the carpet as he took her down on the bed and covered her naked body with his own, then proceeded to make love to her until she was crying out his name and arching beneath him in climax. Only then did he allow himself to let go and lie panting for breath in her arms.

Groaning in utter contentment, Mal rolled over and pulled her into his arms, cradling the side of her face with one palm. "I'm gonna marry you," he whispered.

She stilled, then arched an inky brow, a slow smile curving her mouth. "Is that right?"

"Yes, ma'am."

She hummed and wiggled closer, sliding a sleek, bare thigh over his hip. "Well we'll see about that, won't we? First you'll need to talk to my father. Not that I want or need my father's permission or even care whether he approves or not, I just like the nostalgia of it."

"Already did."

She blinked at that. "You did? What did he say?"

"Something about wondering whether I could support you financially."

She huffed and rolled her eyes. "Of course he did." She slid her finger down the length of his nose. "But you still haven't asked me."

He'd intended to wait until tomorrow after dinner, where he'd planned to propose in a romantic spot he'd picked out in the park bordering the restaurant. But fuck it. He didn't want to wait another day to do this.

Rolling out of bed, he rummaged on the floor for his jeans, and pulled out the ring.

Turning back to her, he sank down on one knee, held up the ring and reached for her hand. He'd made up a little speech yesterday before flying up here, but damned if he could remember any of it with her staring at him with that kind of love in her deep blue eyes, so here went nothing.

This strong, smart, unbelievably brave and beautiful woman owned him. She filled all the empty spaces in his heart, in his life. Going through it without her was unimaginable.

He took a breath, and spoke from his heart. "Rowan, I love you for the incredible woman you are, but also for the man I become when I'm with you. I want to build a life together, have a family with you. Will you marry me?"

She smiled so wide her teeth gleamed in the half-light, then she launched herself at him, throwing her arms around his neck and hugging tight. "Yes. Yes, I will."

He groaned and squeezed her hard, burying his face in the curve of her neck. Mine. She was going to be his forever.

"I can't wait to see Pops tomorrow night and tell him to his face that you bought the cow," she murmured.

Mal's eyes sprang open in surprise. Then he burst out laughing. "Sweetness, I can't wait either." Taking her hand, he slid the ring onto her finger and tipped her face up for a slow, thorough kiss.

—The End—

*Coming soon: Victoria and Hamilton in *Fast Vengeance**

Dear reader,

Thank you for reading *Fast Justice*. I hope you enjoyed it. If you'd like to stay in touch with me and be the first to learn about new releases you can:

- Join my newsletter at: http://kayleacross.com/v2/newsletter/
- Find me on Facebook: https://www.facebook.com/KayleaCrossAuthor/
- Follow me on Twitter: https://twitter.com/kayleacross
- Follow me on Instagram: https://www.instagram.com/kaylea_cross_author/

Also, please consider leaving a review at your favorite online book retailer. It helps other readers discover new books.

Happy reading,
Kaylea

Excerpt from
Fast Vengeance
DEA FAST Series

By Kaylea Cross
Copyright © 2018 Kaylea Cross

Prologue

"*Tía* Victoria, do you want some more chicken?"

Seated in the last spot next to the kids' table, Victoria handed off the platter of sautéed green beans and turned her head to smile down at her six-year-old nephew. "No thanks, sweetie, my plate's so full I can't fit another thing on it."

He put the chicken platter down and went back to staring longingly at his own plate, knowing better than to so much as pick up his fork until they were all given the signal. Everyone knew the rules.

She leaned over to whisper to him. "Go ahead and sneak a bite. I'll cover for you."

He grinned and snatched up a bite of cucumber from his salad, doing his best to chew without drawing any notice.

Victoria smiled to herself. It had been a few months since she'd been able to come to Sunday dinner at her parents' house, and she'd missed it. The usual suspects were present: her siblings, grandparents, aunts, uncles, cousins and their children. Her father's side of the family, all living right here in Houston, filling the old dining room with life and noise in the way that only a big, extended family could. They always celebrated special occasions together. It was loud and chaotic, but she wouldn't have it any other way.

When all the dishes had been passed around the table and everyone had filled their plates, her father raised his wineglass for a toast to signal that the meal was about to commence. "To the cooks," he said, indicating him and Victoria's mother, his deep voice cutting through the room with ease.

Then he turned to his parents, seated as always side by side to his right. They'd been married for more than fifty years, had risked everything to leave Mexico as teenagers with only the clothes on their backs, and start a new life here in Houston. "And to my father, the patriarch of this family, on his eightieth birthday. This family exists and enjoys a wonderful life because of your bravery and sacrifice. I hope we're all gathered around in this same room in twenty years for your hundredth."

Smiling fondly at her grandfather, Victoria raised her glass in salute. "To *Abuelito*." With a hearty cheers and clinking of glasses all along the two tables set end to end, everyone sipped and then dug in. Conversation and laughter flowed freely along with the wine.

She'd finished her first helping and was reaching for another serving of roasted veggies when tires squealed on the driveway. Victoria and several others turned around to look out the tall windows that overlooked the front of the house. From her vantage point she could just make out the back bumper of a minivan had pulled up behind her grandparents' car.

"You expecting anyone?" she asked her father.

"No," he said, putting down his napkin and pushing his chair back. "I'll go see who it is. Back in a minute."

He was halfway to the front door when something slammed against it. He jerked to a halt and everyone else went silent, all of them staring at the door, wondering what the hell was going on.

Before anyone could move or say anything, it burst open. Victoria jumped and smothered a gasp as her father stumbled back and three masked men stormed in. They all carried military-style rifles.

A wave of terror broke over her. Cries of alarm rang out from around the table but she couldn't tear her eyes off the intruders. She instinctively grabbed her nephew and turned her body away from the men, shielding the boy while parents gathered up their frightened children and retreated to the rear of the room. She sat there staring at the men, frozen, her muscles rigid, heart hammering in her throat.

Her father hadn't moved from his spot. He had a gun safe, but it was down in the basement. And even if they used all the guns in it, they didn't have a prayer of fighting off three men armed with automatic rifles.

"Get the hell out of my house," her father snarled, bravely blocking their way.

The masked man in the lead stepped forward and shoved him so hard he crashed into the wall. Then he turned to face them and it seemed to Victoria that his gaze landed on her.

"Victoria Gomez," he said in a tone that sent chills racing down her spine. "My boss has been so looking forward to finally meeting you."

She blanched as realization hit home. Carlos Ruiz. He'd come for her.

Her sister-in-law wrenched Victoria's nephew from her arms and ran to her husband, her entire family now gathered against the far wall at the end of the dining room, the men standing in front of the women. They were trapped in here, the only way out past the armed intruders.

Victoria's entire body was numb as she woodenly pushed to her feet, fear flooding her entire body. But when one of the other men stalked over to grab her father and wrench him to his feet, the anger snapped the band of fear wrapped around her ribcage. "Let him go," she demanded, taking a step forward. They were here for her, for what she'd uncovered. Her family had nothing to do with it.

The man in front, clearly the one in charge, smiled. A cruel twist of his lips within the hole revealed by the mask. His black eyes glittered like a snake's. "Come here." He held his palm up, crooked his fingers at her. Like she was a dog he expected to come to heel when called.

One of her brothers grabbed her shoulder, tugged her backward. "Vic. Don't," he whispered, his voice tense.

She was afraid to move, but more terrified of what would happen if she didn't. "If I do, you'll let him go?" she said to the man, surprised her voice was working.

The man dropped his hand. Shrugged. "Sure."

Indecision warred inside her. But what choice did she have? She had to protect her family.

"Vic, no," her brother warned.

I have to.

Twisting away from her his restraining grip, she ignored the frightened cries behind her and forced her feet to carry her toward the man. Her belly was clamped tight, nausea churning in waves, each step a small eternity. Some of her siblings or their significant others would have their phones in their pockets. One of them would have dialed 911 already. Maybe the dispatcher would figure out something was wrong and send the cops.

They won't get here in time.

When she came within reach, the leader snaked out a hand and grabbed her by the hair. She stifled a cry and stiffened as he hauled her up against him, grabbing his wrist to try and pull free. It was no use. He was too strong. She shuddered at the unforgiving outline of his rifle digging into her right hip.

With a jerk on her hair he wrenched her around to face her family, all huddled around the children against the far wall behind the table, some of them crying, others staring at her with stricken expressions. Victoria stared back at them and met her mother's eyes, panic flooding her system.

The leader spoke to the one holding her father. "Let him go."

Her father immediately rushed over to gather Victoria's mother into his arms and stood with the others, trying to shield his wife. His parents cowered behind him, clinging to one another, their lined faces wet with tears.

Victoria swallowed hard and stood rooted to the spot, her hand wrapped around the powerful wrist holding her hair, not daring to move. Then the man who had been holding her father crossed over to grab her wrists, wrench them behind her and bind them with something tight and hard that bit into her skin. Zip tie.

"Don't hurt them," she blurted, her voice husky as she fought not to cry and beg. She'd spent more than three years tracking the rise of the *Veneno* cartel, and the past nine months using all her contacts to research Carlos Ruiz. She knew what he did to his enemies. And she also knew all the horrific things he did to his female captives.

"We've got to go now," the man said, his mouth right beside her ear, making her cringe. "Say goodbye, Victoria."

Mind working frantically, she swept her gaze over her beloved family. The sight of those frightened faces staring back at her broke her heart. There was nothing she could do to escape. This was the last time she would see them. Ruiz's men would take her to a hideout somewhere off the grid, torture her for days or maybe even weeks before killing her or selling her off, like they had with the other female captives.

Tears flooded her eyes. She couldn't control it. Couldn't stop it. "I love you all," she said hoarsely. "Goodbye."

"No. Victoria, *no!*" her mother cried, her face twisting with grief as she tried to push away from her husband.

Victoria expected the men to haul her away. Instead, the hand in her hair tightened, arching her neck back at a painful angle. Holding her fast there in front of her family. "Do it," he commanded.

The other two men stepped in front of him, raised their weapons, and opened fire.

"No! Oh my God, *no!*" Victoria's screams of horror were drowned out beneath the thunder of automatic gunfire as it ripped through the room. Her family fell like a field of hay to the sweep of a scythe.

She shut her eyes and tried to twist away but it didn't block out the screams and cries of agony above the noise, the thud of the bullets hitting home.

She kept screaming and fought her captor, trying to wrench free, to stop this somehow. She screamed until her throat was raw, was still screaming after the gunfire had stopped.

The silence finally registered over the roar of blood in her ears. And when she opened her eyes to face the carnage at last, her entire family lay dead or dying on the dining room floor. They lay on top of one another like cordwood stacked at the far end of the room, parents collapsed on top of their children, having desperately tried to shield them with their own bodies.

A high-pitched sound of grief tore from her. From beneath her brother's body protruded her nephew's little leg. It twitched in the rapidly spreading pool of blood staining the tile floor.

He was still alive, but not for long.

Soul-shattering grief slammed into her. She was shaking all over. The pain was unbearable. Searing her lungs, ripping her heart apart. She couldn't breathe. Couldn't bear the agony.

A hood plunged roughly over her head, hurtling her into darkness as the man holding her dragged her from the house. But even in the blackness, all she could see was that horrific tableau of her dead family burned into the backs of her eyelids.

It's my fault. They had been murdered because of her. For however long she had left on this earth, she would have to live with that.

Her captor shoved her onto a seat as an engine roared to life. Doors slammed shut and the tires squealed as the vehicle raced off.

And through the crushing pain of guilt and loss, she was well aware that her suffering had only begun.

About the Author

NY Times and USA Today Bestselling author Kaylea Cross writes edge-of-your-seat military romantic suspense. Her work has won many awards, including the Daphne du Maurier Award of Excellence, and has been nominated multiple times for the National Readers' Choice Awards. A Registered Massage Therapist by trade, Kaylea is also an avid gardener, artist, Civil War buff, Special Ops aficionado, belly dance enthusiast and former nationally-carded softball pitcher. She lives in Vancouver, BC with her husband and family.

You can visit Kaylea at www.kayleacross.com. If you would like to be notified of future releases, please join her newsletter. Direct link: http://kayleacross.com/v2/newsletter/

Complete Booklist

ROMANTIC SUSPENSE

DEA FAST Series
Falling Fast
Fast Kill
Stand Fast
Strike Fast
Fast Fury
Fast Justice

Colebrook Siblings Trilogy
Brody's Vow
Wyatt's Stand
Easton's Claim

Hostage Rescue Team Series
Marked
Targeted
Hunted
Disavowed
Avenged
Exposed
Seized
Wanted
Betrayed
Reclaimed
Shattered

Titanium Security Series
Ignited
Singed
Burned
Extinguished

Rekindled
Blindsided: A Titanium Christmas novella

Bagram Special Ops Series
Deadly Descent
Tactical Strike
Lethal Pursuit
Danger Close
Collateral Damage
Never Surrender (a MacKenzie Family novella)

Suspense Series
Out of Her League
Cover of Darkness
No Turning Back
Relentless
Absolution

PARANORMAL ROMANCE
Empowered Series
Darkest Caress

HISTORICAL ROMANCE
The Vacant Chair

EROTIC ROMANCE (writing as *Callie Croix*)
Deacon's Touch
Dillon's Claim
No Holds Barred
Touch Me
Let Me In
Covert Seduction

72203273R00214

Made in the USA
San Bernardino, CA
22 March 2018